About the

CODE: C000069663

Michael J Ritchie was born in 1988 after, using fiction as a means to escape ordinary life and responsibility ever since. The University of Roehampton enabled him further by awarding him a degree in Creative Writing in 2009. He started his book review blog, *Fell From Fiction*, in 2013, and has occasionally worked as a freelance journalist, as well as writing fiction. He tends to work best with a glass of wine to hand. *The Third Wheel* is his second novel.

He can be found on Twitter and Instagram at @fellfromfiction.

THE THIRD WHEEL

THE THIRD WHEEL

MICHAEL J. RITCHIE

Unbound Digital

This edition first published in 2018

Unbound

6th Floor Mutual House, 70 Conduit Street, London W1S 2GF

www.unbound.com

ISBN (eBook): 978-1-912618-59-0
ISBN (Paperback): 978-1-912618-58-3

Design by Mecob

Printed and bound in Great Britain by Clays Ltd, Elcograf S.p.A.

For Mum, Dad, Katie and my family.
You can't choose your family, but I would've picked you anyway.

Dear Reader,

The book you are holding came about in a rather different way to most others. It was funded directly by readers through a new website: Unbound.

Unbound is the creation of three writers. We started the company because we believed there had to be a better deal for both writers and readers. On the Unbound website, authors share the ideas for the books they want to write directly with readers. If enough of you support the book by pledging for it in advance, we produce a beautifully bound special subscribers' edition and distribute a regular edition and e-book wherever books are sold, in shops and online.

This new way of publishing is actually a very old idea (Samuel Johnson funded his dictionary this way). We're just using the internet to build each writer a network of patrons. Here, at the back of this book, you'll find the names of all the people who made it happen.

Publishing in this way means readers are no longer just passive consumers of the books they buy, and authors are free to write the books they really want. They get a much fairer return too – half the profits their books generate, rather than a tiny percentage of the cover price.

If you're not yet a subscriber, we hope that you'll want to join our publishing revolution and have your name listed in one of our books in the future. To get you started, here is a £5 discount on your first pledge. Just visit unbound.com, make your pledge and type DEXTER18 in the promo code box when you check out.

Thank you for your support,

Dan, Justin and John
Founders, Unbound

Super Patrons

Kirk Baillie
Rachel Baron Singer
Jackie Bates
Victoria Batley
Felix Blakeston
Amanda Brown
Jonny & Kristina Casto-Ardern
Christopher Cherng
GMark Cole
Richard Cooper
Pat Cornwell
Ed Cornwell
Paula Costello
Vicki Cox
Robert Cox
Mavis Creaney
Sarah D'alessio
Chris & April Dawson
Pauline Dellar
Suz & Lucy Diamond-Wall
Jenny Doughty
Keith Dunbar
Sarah Dunsworth
Nigel Dyer
Ellie Edwards
Graham Edwards
Amanda Egleton
Lucy Ellis
Rachel Ellis
Ember
Denise Emmerson
Brioney Euden

Lee Exelby
Dave Fisher
Abi Fraser
Susan Godfrey
Caroline Green
Sabrina Greenberg
Jenni Hardman
Vikki, Garry & Alfie Harnblow
Kevin Hawthorne
Brooke Hepburn
Merna Horthy
Sue Hunt
Lorraine Jarvis
Marilyn and Richard Jarvis
Lyn, Rob, Harry & George Jarvis
Thomas Jeram-West
Laura Johnstone
Suzanne Kalamar
Ella Kennedy
Ella Kennedy
Dan Kieran
Anwen Kya Hayward
Julie Lovell
Adam Lowe
Bill Lumley
Sam Mawson
Lois May-Miller
Amy Mayhill
Gary McQueen
Alice Meadows
Karen & Andy Meed
Christopher Melvin
George Mirabelli-Montan
John Mitchinson
Christopher Money
Emma Moore

Carlo Navato

Sue Nieland

Enrique Nieto

Christopher O'Dea-Giordano

David Pig Henshaw

Justin Pollard

Katherine Pontefract

Alex Ritchie

Katie Ritchie

Ian Ritchie

Helen Ritchie

Jenny Ritchie

Lindsey Roots

Barnaby Saltmarsh

Ste Sharp

Kristiane Sherry

Roxanne Smith

Phil Sparrow

Quentin Spender

Ross Strudwick

Greg Thompson

Mike Scott Thomson

Claire Toynton

Jacqui Trowsdale

David G Tubby

Aziz Twaijri

Kimberley Walter

Chris Wells

Jon-Paul Wheatley

Richard Williamson

Karen Williamson

Margaret Woodhead

Prologue

The room is perhaps eight feet square. It's rather grandiose to call it a room, really, so I'll call it what it is. It's a cell. It's a prison cell on an alien spaceship. I'm by myself here though, once again, and I assume the others have been separated too. We don't know what's going to happen to us.

I sit in the one of the corners of the plain room. The walls and floor are solid and uncomfortable, sheet metal so smooth and featureless that it's impossible to see where the door is. The cell is lit by a small orb of light – not a bulb, it hangs freely – in the corner opposite me. I hug my knees tight and wonder what's happened to the others. Have they been given the same treatment as me? Is it better? Worse?

I run a hand through my greasy hair and, with care, scratch an annoying itch on my broken nose. It's not so much bent out of shape as it is flattened, and I'm thankful that the walls aren't reflective. There's nothing to do and, in another lifetime, I'd be mesmerised by the fact that I'm hurtling through space – I can feel the quiet thrum of propulsion through the floor – but instead I'm overwhelmed by the notion of leaving everything I knew behind on that tiny blue dot that wasn't prepared for its sudden demise.

I chew at my nails, blood and grime on my tongue. I rip at the thumbnail with my teeth too hard and it starts to bleed. I don't do anything to try and stem the flow. There's no point any more.

My ears prick up at a new sound. There are footsteps nearby, but I can't work out which direction they're coming from. I tense a little, wondering if I'm going to be dragged out of here again, but they grow faint and disappear.

It's ironic that I'm sitting here by myself. A week ago, my biggest problem was that I was single, and all of my friends were – not intentionally, I assume – rubbing their coupledom in my face. But that was before the aliens landed and we lost the planet. I guess I'm getting ahead of myself, but with nothing else to distract me in here, I'm left alone with my thoughts. And my thoughts aren't pretty.

It started about a week ago.

One

The End of Term

By the time you reach your mid-twenties, if not before, you realise that the world is built for couples. Everything is designed with them in mind – tables for two, weekend breaks for two, competitions with two tickets to a gig or show or theme park as the prize – and that's just the way things are.

I am the only person I know who is currently single. My friends are coupled up, but I don't hold it against them. They have stopped being single entities and become Jay-and-Kay (married), Shell-and-Terry (dating), Iris-and-William (cohabiting), Peregrina-and-Pete (engaged), Lara-and-Steve (engaged, wedding imminent), Gavin-and-Frederik (cohabiting), Priti-and-Art (dating), Annie-and-Matt (newly dating), Ruby-and-Alex (cohabiting). And then there's me, Dexter, the third wheel.

Don't get me wrong; I'm not that bitter. I like being by myself, on the whole, and I don't often feel lonely. I'm too selfish to share my life with one other person, anyway. I like being a free agent. I don't buy into the societal ideal that we're not complete until we've got a partner, but sometimes it feels a bit crap to spend another evening at home with no one but Catsby for company, and no hand to hold. I still see most of my friends on a semi-regular basis, but it's not like it used to be. I can't call them up in the evening and drag them to the pub on a spur of the moment. They need warning and time to prepare, and often there's an assumption the invitation encompasses the partner too.

Mind you, I can't even pretend that unplanned evenings in the pub were a regular occurrence anyway, not since I started working at Fairmill Community College. I'm pretty good if I do say so myself, but I did sort of cheat to get the job. Ruby (one half of Ruby-and-Alex) had put my application to the top of the pile. People think English is a doddle to teach, but they're wrong. Ruby teaches history and between us we read hundreds of essays a week. Occasionally one will have a unique thought, but a quick Google search will find it in an earlier form on Wikipedia.

It's 3.25 on Friday afternoon and my Year 10 class have long since given up on pretending to pay any attention to me. Matt Hogan is texting under his desk, Perry Delaney is doodling on rather than filling in his worksheet and Kimberley Thornton is reapplying her make-up for the hundredth time, because she can't *possibly* be seen next to the bins outside Tesco Express after school without a face full of slap.

We had been reading *Dr Jekyll and Mr Hyde*, a book even I have difficulty pretending to enjoy, and while the kids had tolerated me so far, it was a mere five minutes before the start of the Easter holidays, so there was no way any of them were going to get anything else done.

'OK, you lot have obviously shut down for the holidays, so you can pack your stuff up and wait for the bell,' I say, turning off the electronic whiteboard. There's a scuffle and rattle of furniture as rucksacks and satchels are pulled up and stuffed with pencil cases and exercise books. A few of the boys have already taken their ties off. Kimberley Thornton is putting in dangly earrings that the school frowns upon. I don't have the energy to protest.

'Mr Scithers?' says a voice in the front row. It's Sharon Merton; she always calls me that rather than the 'Sir' favoured by the other children.

'Yes, Sharon?'

'Are you looking forward to the holidays?'

'Of course, I am,' I say. 'Not that it's much of a holiday – lesson plans and marking to do!'

'Aren't you doing anything fun, sir?' chimes in Perry Delaney.

'I'm going to a wedding tomorrow,' I offer. Some teachers never reveal a thing to their students about their private lives, but I always figure why the hell not? It shows I'm human, and I find that gets me a tiny bit more respect. I'd die before I added any of them on Facebook, and my Twitter account is private and doesn't include my name, but

I can throw them the odd bone. They're entitled to be curious – I was about my teachers.

'Whose wedding is it, sir?' says Farzana Chauhan, a look that suggests she thinks she might be pushing it a bit.

'Um, a friend of mine from school, way back when,' I say.

'Have you got a date for it, sir?' Perry Delaney says, snickering to himself. Little shit.

'Just me, but lots of friends going.' I give a forced smile. 'Good opportunity to catch up.'

'Don't you have a girlfriend, sir?' says Sharon Merton. Blast. I must've mentioned Georgina at some point. Hell, it's almost certain that I did, but I've no idea what I said. How come they can remember that I had a girlfriend, but can't remember what day their homework is due?

'No, I don't,' I say. 'Anyway, enough about my private life. Does everyone understand the homework?' They chorus a bored 'Yeeeessss' which melts into the sharp trill of the bell that jolts them into activity, and they scurry off to do whatever it is teenagers do these days. I'm twenty-six, still technically counted as 'young' by many, but it seems forever ago that that was me.

In the corridor, I hear 'Oi! No running! Yes, you Matthew!' which signals the arrival of my friend, colleague and fellow wedding attendee Ruby. Her finely textured blonde hair is up in a somehow-perfect ponytail, and she's got a large tote bag full of, presumably, textbooks and, probably, a bottle of wine.

'Alright?' she says, sitting on one of the tables in the front row. Her skirt is too short and tight, so it's an awkward perch.

'Mmm,' I say, non-committally. I fiddle about with my laptop, pulling out the cables and shutting it down. I'm tempted to leave it here for the Easter holidays so I can't do any lesson plans, but I'd only be screwing myself over. 'One of the kids asked about Georgina.'

'Little shit,' says Ruby. 'You didn't tell them you'd broken up, did you?'

'Not directly,' I say, shoving my laptop into my shoulder bag. 'The bell went before we could get too far into it. I'm not about to discuss my explosive break-ups with a bunch of fourteen-year-olds.' I get up and sling the laptop bag over one shoulder, and my rucksack full of exercise books from Years 7 and 11 over the other one. Teaching does wonders for your upper body strength.

As we leave, I turn the lights off and, unable to find my key and unwilling to unload myself to look, don't bother locking the door. No one but cleaners here over the holidays. Up the corridor, I can see other teachers still working away – Anita won't leave until gone seven – but nothing is going to stop me from getting out of there. In the car park, we pass Iris Burke (one half of Iris-and-William) getting into her car. She waves and says she'll see us tomorrow at the reception and drives off. Ruby and I walk in tired silence to the train station. Thankfully, most of the kids live locally so, by the time we get on the train, we've lost most vestiges of the work day.

Three stops: Blackpond, St Simon's and South Greenfield. That'll be me home, a cuddle with Catsby and a large glass of wine. I may even get a takeaway and find a film on Netflix. As if on the same wavelength as me, Ruby asks what I'm doing with my night. I tell her and ask the same back.

'Alex and I are celebrating our anniversary,' she says. I can hear the love heart dotting the 'i' in 'anniversary'.

'You got together in September though, didn't you?'

'Yes, but it's the anniversary of us moving in together,' she smiles. If this was a Jane Austen novel, she would be swooning at this point. I forget how many different anniversaries that people have when they're in extended relationships. The longest relationship I've ever had was way back in sixth form. I was happy to stay with her but she wanted to go and fuck people from a different county at Bournemouth University. I didn't get much say in the matter.

The train arrives and we get on, scoring an empty table. A few rowdy sixth formers get on after us and, although we've got our backs to them, it becomes apparent that they've invented a game that involves spraying each other with shaken-up fizzy drinks. Not our problem – we have no control over them outside the school gates. In fact, we have little control of them within the school gates.

As we pass through Blackpond, we discuss arrangements for Lara-and-Steve's wedding tomorrow. The train lurches through the uneven track at St Simon's and we talk about the stupid beard the headmaster is growing and how trendy he thinks it makes him look. At South Greenfield, we're so busy complaining about the upcoming changes to the curriculum that we almost forget to get off.

We arrive at the estate, entering as usual via the south entrance of Ottley Street by the municipal recycling bins. We part ways with an air kiss, Ruby back off to her boyfriend, me off to the cat. It's a nice estate, built in 1985, with streets named after British Olympic medal winners from the 1984 Los Angeles Olympic Games. Thankfully, we won a fair amount of medals that year, or else the estate would be tiny.

There's a few of my friends on this estate. Ruby-and-Alex live on Thompson Avenue, Shell (one half of Shell-and-Terry) lives on Budgett Close and there's also Peregrina-and-Pete up on Redgrave Street. I try not to read anything into the fact that their streets are named for gold medallists and mine, Eckersley Road, is named for someone who won bronze.

The second I step through the door of my modest house, Catsby – short for The Great Catsby – is in the hall, mewing. It might mean he's happy to see me, it might mean he's hungry. With cats, it's usually the same thing. He slinks around my feet like the little ginger tripping hazard he is as I move to the living room to take my boots off.

The evening progresses at a snail's pace as I make dinner and listen to a podcast about the Egyptian Pyramids, and by six-thirty I'm gunning to see someone. It's Friday night! I'm in my twenties! I should be out painting the town red, or at least a pale shade of mauve. I pick up my phone and scroll through the contacts list. I send Annie a message and ask if she's up for a drink. I pour myself a glass of Merlot and put on the TV while I wait for a reply. Twenty minutes later, she tells me that she's off to the cinema with Matt.

I call Gavin to see if he's free for a chat, but he's trying to put together a flatpack wardrobe and doesn't have time to talk. Iris told me at work that she'd see me tomorrow, so she's out, and I know that Jay-and-Kay are on a date night with another couple.

Among the names of contacts that I haven't spoken to since university, met on Tinder or see every day in the staff room, Lara is the next person I could call, which I consider for a second before remembering that she's getting married tomorrow and probably has other things to be doing. I message Peregrina, but she and Pete are already half an hour into a film at home and don't want to go out. Priti doesn't respond at all, and Ruby... no, she has anniversary plans. I call Shell but instead Terry answers her phone and informs me that she's in the shower and they're going out to meet some of his army friends.

Alone and out of options, I eat a Cornetto and fall asleep on the sofa with Catsby on my lap during an interview with a French police-woman about unidentified lights in the sky over France. Around midnight I wake up again, put the dregs of the wine back in the fridge and make my way to bed. My final thought, which happens in that fuzzy place in between awake and dreaming, is of Lara-and-Steve joking in their wedding speeches that 'at least they didn't end up alone like Dexter', and everyone laughing.

Like I said, generally I'm fine being alone, but some nights it's worse than others.

Two

Priti-and-Art

My friends. I wonder what happened to them. I know the final fate of some of them – I was there – but others I'll never know. That's the trouble with real life. In a story, you get all the answers. They tell you why Bertha was locked in the attic, or why Yossarian can't escape the army. You might not like the answers, they might not make sense, but they're there.

I try to think about what I do know, and what I remember. I think about my friends. They may have been moving on and pairing up, but I didn't love them any less. You can't begrudge your friends happiness. Things change, and sometimes it's a struggle to keep up, that's all.

With one exception, I originally knew each couple that I count among my friends as singletons. That is, I was friendly with one half before the second half came along. Truth be told, I get on well with the new halves as well, but it's never quite the same, is it?

My friends were – are – the most wonderful people and I've known a lot of them a very long time. Take Priti.

Priti Sengupta is my oldest friend, having held the position for about twenty years. We were in the same class from Year One upwards. It's funny but, with the friends I made later, the stories of how we came to be friends are more detailed, like a lot more effort went into those friendships. Priti and I have always been friends in the way that the Pyramids have always stood and the Rolling Stones have always been performing – it began so long ago, it's irrelevant exactly when or why.

There are three incidents, however, in the first year of our knowing each other that stand out for me, and the combination of them probably cemented a bond between us that has strained at times but never

9

snapped. They are, in order, the Rabbit Incident, the Scarf Incident and the Maze Incident.

The Rabbit Incident occurred when, early in Year One, a small petting zoo was established in the school playground one morning for us to see and study various small animals. There was a goat, some guinea pigs, a couple of ducks, a sheep and, most importantly, a rabbit. It was a large female, the colour of a foggy autumn morning, with long droopy ears.

Priti had won the jackpot in my five-year-old eyes, as she'd been allowed to hold the rabbit on her lap. I hadn't spoken to her much before this moment, although I was aware of her. She was one of the few non-white kids in the school and, in a small town like ours, that made you stick out. She was very quiet and had few close friends, preferring not to speak to anyone she hadn't already formed a bond with. However, she had a very nice rabbit on her lap, and I was desperate to stroke that rabbit. I *had* to speak to her, so I approached slowly while she tickled the rabbit between its ears.

I sat down next to her and pretended to have no interest in the rabbit, but once my inner excitement had become too much to contain, I burst out, 'Can I stroke her too?'

'She likes it on her head, here,' said Priti, not looking at me, keeping her eyes focused on the grey bundle in her lap. Taking Priti's lead, I moved my hand to where she'd been stroking the rabbit and put my fingers against the warm fur.

'She's really soft,' I said.

'I like her,' said Priti. She was very quiet, as if speaking above a certain level might be dangerous. Together we stroked the placid bunny for a few minutes, before she was handed on to someone else. Something about that moment, however, meant that we were able to talk when we saw each other in the playground or during class group work. Over the next few weeks, most of our conversation revolved around one of us saying, 'Hey, do you remember the big rabbit?' and the other declaring how much they loved it. At five, you can sustain a friendship with that.

The Scarf Incident occurred in late November, a couple of months after the Rabbit Incident. Priti and I were getting our things together off the pegs of the Year One cloakroom, when she squealed and tears pricked at her eyes.

'What is it?' I asked. She held up the end of her blue woolly scarf. It had been cut roughly and looked like a ferret had been at it. We both knew who was to blame: Tyler North and Thomas Townsend. Even at five, you knew they were eventually going to end up in prison. They delighted in the suffering of others and trading your tears for their laughs. They spent an inordinate amount of time being told off, but neither could be expelled as their mothers were both rich as hell and served on the board of governors.

Priti's scarf was ruined. Presumably they'd been at it with some scissors. We stared at it in horror and Priti whispered, 'Mummy is going to be really mad.' I looked at my own scarf. It was, aside from the damage, exactly the same as hers. I held it out to her and she looked at me, perhaps a little hurt and thinking I was rubbing in the fact that mine was fine.

'Take my one,' I said. 'We'll swap them. My mummy and daddy might be a bit cross, but they'll be OK. I'll ask for a new one for Christmas.'

'Are you sure?' Priti said, reaching up for the scarf with a tentative hand.

'Of course,' I said with a smile. 'You let me stroke the rabbit.'

The Maze Incident took place the following March and was the final thing that ensured Priti and I would be best friends for the rest of time. We were on a school trip to a Tudor castle. It was a crumbly old one surrounded by a green-watered moat, and after we'd explored it and been spoken to by a grey old man who looked old enough to have been an original inhabitant, the teachers let us off to discover the far more exciting adventure playground and hedge maze.

Despite what happened within that maze, I have always loved them, and I've always been good at them, even before discovering in my mid-teens that there is a blindingly simple way to get out of pretty much any maze.

I ran on ahead, laughing with a boy called Darren I was friends with at the time. Veering round a sharp left, we found ourselves at a dead end.

'There was another turn back there,' I said, and we set off giggling to find where it was. However, we didn't reach it, as we had been cornered in our dead end by three bigger boys. They wore blue jumpers, unlike our red ones, and were around eight or nine. They were much taller than us, like giants towering over frightened villagers, with faces contorted in evil grins that haunted my dreams for months afterwards. They were from another school, and that, by the logic of childhood, made them our enemies. It was the law of the playground.

'What's this?' said one of them, the biggest of the three. He had blonde hair shaved down to a few millimetres and was missing one of his incisors.

'Can we get past, please?' I said, possibly a little more bravely than I felt. I don't think I considered these people a serious threat. You don't at that age.

'What do you wanna do that for?' said the boy. His two friends, one either side of him, sniggered and looked at him with a pathetic awe.

'We're trying to find the middle of the maze,' said Darren, timidly. The boy tutted and stepped forward a pace. His cronies followed suit, like infant bodyguards.

'Make us move,' he said.

'Can we pass, please?' I tried again.

'No,' said the boy, reaching out a meaty hand and jabbing me in the shoulder.

'Leave them alone!' said a quiet voice. Our unfriendly acquaintances turned to see who had spoken, only to find the diminutive figure of Priti standing further down the run. She stood with hands on hips, legs askance, her long black hair in a ponytail resting on her shoulder. She was wearing my scarf.

It's hard to recall exactly what happened in the next couple of minutes because it happened so fast. I remember the boy threatening this new interloper, although saying that he didn't want to hit a girl, so she should go away. (He didn't actually use those words, though, thus leading to the first ever time I heard someone say the words 'fuck off'.)

Priti didn't take kindly to that and, like I say, there were some fast movements, a mere blur, and the boy had been unflanked. His companions had run off, and he was on the floor, dirt and mud up his black trousers. He'd lost another tooth as well. It stuck out pale yellow with a fleck of red among the hedge roots.

'Alright, I'll go,' he said, tears streaking down his face. He got up and, without even pausing to look back at me and Darren, he ran off, having learnt a valuable lesson about how you shouldn't judge things by their appearance, because even the smallest and most docile-looking girls might already have had a year's worth of karate lessons.

'Thank you so much,' I said, running at Priti and hugging her. It appeared to catch her off guard and she did an awkward half-squeeze back and pushed me off.

'It's OK,' she shrugged. 'It was my turn to help you.' She smiled, and I grinned back. Our friendship was sealed.

They say that the best friendships are forged during times of great stress or war, and while we didn't have a troll to fight like Harry Potter and Hermione Granger, or get put in detention for the day like the Breakfast Club, it seems that doing battle with three eight-year-olds will definitely have the same effect.

Priti met the unconventional and ever-so-wealthy Art Callaghan three years ago on the Greek island of Icaria, where she was on a long weekend break from work and he was staying in one of the villas owned by his father. It was nothing like love at first sight.

Priti was in the Kambos Museum, home of various archaeological antiquities, and looking at a particularly impressive and beautiful sarcophagus, marvelling at the engravings of fruit and garlands, when she became aware of someone standing next to her. The museum was very quiet, and she was irritated that the person who may well have been the only other visitor had decided to invade her space. She turned to move off when the figure spoke.

'Hi there,' he said. 'Were your parents Greek gods?' She turned to look at him, finding that he was about seven inches taller than her, with lapis lazuli eyes and a strange excuse for a beard on his chin. 'They must've been to make a goddess like you.'

'No,' she said, tonelessly. 'They're marketing consultants from Croydon.' That had thrown him. According to her story, she'd given him a withering look, as if daring him to come up with something better. Realising that he was beaten, he instead shrugged, held out a hand and said, 'I'm Art.'

'Priti,' she said. He confided in me much later that at this point he'd wanted to say 'Yes, you certainly are', but felt that it wouldn't have been well received, so instead settled for asking her out to dinner. Priti, not knowing anyone else on the island and having dined alone for the last two nights, figured that he didn't look like a rapist, so at worst he may turn out to be crass and boring; it would at least be some company and he might even foot the bill.

As it turned out, his family owned the restaurant and paying the bill was not even remotely an issue. They had a number of things in common, mostly tastes in music and deep passions for video games that sacrificed plot for big guns. Since he lived in Kensington, and South Greenfield isn't too far on the train from London, they decided that it was possible to begin and maintain a relationship.

Privately, I (and some of the others) have often wondered if Priti would be so interested in Art if it wasn't for the enormous piles of money that he and his family are sitting on. Although she does appear to love him in her own distant way, he idolises her in a way that isn't reciprocated as far as we can tell. I guess it's just one of those things that we're not allowed to see – you don't stay with someone for three years and put up with them if you don't actually like them, regardless of the money.

For what it's worth, too, Art is one of my favourite other halves and the two of us have met up for drinks without Priti on a few occasions, although we are often cross-examined later by Priti for anything either of us may have said that she doesn't approve of. Whether or not it's true love or he's hypnotised by her, they make a solid couple.

Then again, Yellowstone looks solid, but no one would be surprised if it exploded.

Three
The Wedding

The weather is perfect in the manner usually reserved for television weddings. Lara-and-Steve have exchanged vows and rings, kissed to seal the deal and are now being moved around by the photographer, who is trying to get as much of the old hotel they've chosen as a wedding venue into the background as possible. It's a gorgeous location and we gather on the lawns with glasses of champagne.

Everyone is coupled up and talking about white goods or whatever it is long-term couples talk about, so I focus on the alcohol and check my phone. Maybe I can get in a level of *Candy Crush* – I've been stuck on Level 433 for weeks.

'Come on, get that phone away,' I hear. I look up and find Jay-and-Kay approaching, beaming. He's tall, broad-shouldered, wearing dark glasses and a smart trilby. She's short, pale and pointy like an Arctic fox. On the occasions I do get bitter, they're probably the couple I have least bitterness about, as they were already married by the time I met them, so I've never had time to resent the idea of one of them being stolen from singlehood.

'Beautiful ceremony wasn't it?' smiles Kay. She's from Brooklyn, and it strikes me once again how much louder an American voice is on British soil.

'Lovely,' I grin back. 'Couldn't happen to a nicer couple.' I mean it too. Lara and Steve make a great couple. He's about three years older than her, and they've been together nearly ten years, since she was sixteen.

As Kay launches into a speech about the sudden prevalence of meteor showers that have been seen over Europe lately – I remember seeing headlines about it on Google News – I notice a face in the crowd. I've managed to avoid Georgina so far, but now she's seen me. Crap, crap, crap. I swivel my head back round with a speed that means

I risk whiplash to look at Kay, and laugh at the wrong point in her story. She gives me a weird look.

'OK, friends of the bride!' shouts the photographer, and I see Lara beckoning us over, smile so wide she's in danger of the top half of her head falling off like the Canadians from *South Park*. I stand behind the happy couple, with Ruby-and-Alex, Jay-and-Kay, Kerry-and-Mia and, yes, Georgina in there somewhere too.

As her name comes unhyphenated, it may appear that she's single but, nope, she has a new boyfriend. They started dating after the invites had been arranged and there was no extra plus-one to accommodate him. Plus, I don't think Lara likes him all that much. I don't either, but if you say it out loud you look like the bitter ex who can't move on.

Photos are taken, and we disperse as Steve's friends get into position. Jay, Kay and I retreat to a bench next to the hotel's back steps and look on. I can't see Georgina any more. Jay produces cigarettes and we light up. The smoke curls up in the still air and disperses in a thin cloud across our faces.

Eventually, either there are no possible permutations of photographs left to take or the photographer is getting bored, and we traipse back inside for the wedding breakfast. If someone invites me for breakfast, I expect there to be bacon at the very least, but hopefully also mushrooms, hash browns and fried eggs. In the backwards world of weddings, breakfast here means melon balls, roast beef and crème brûlée. I mean, fine, but it's no bacon sandwich.

I am the token single person on this table. I'm not left out of the conversation but every now and then the couples turn away to check in with one another and I'm left drinking too much wine to compensate. We're the only table to so far have asked the waiters for another bottle, and I'm a substantial part of the reason.

'Have you spoken to Georgina?' says Ruby, next to me. The question comes from so far out of the blue it's green.

'No. Has she said anything to you?' I'm trying to lower my voice even though Georgina is a good three tables away, but the fifth glass of wine has turned off the part of my brain that controls volume awareness.

'She said hello, but that's it,' Ruby shakes her head. 'Why don't you try and get back with her?' This is strange, as Ruby never much cared for Georgina. I think she feels embarrassment on my behalf for me being, as she assumes, lonely.

'Have you forgotten how it ended?' I chide, gesticulating with my glass. 'She threw my Kindle in a pond and I set fire to her dress, although in fairness it was accidental on my part.'

'Well, you could still say hello,' says Ruby, sipping her water. I shrug and turn to talk to Kerry-and-Mia about their new puppy.

The plates are cleared away, the speeches are made (my dream does not come true) and we toast the happy couple, before moving off to the gardens again while the tables are cleared away and the room becomes a dance floor. In the interim, Lara and I talk about her and Steve's upcoming honeymoon. She mentions the meteor showers in the news too, but neither of us knows much about them. The evening guests begin to arrive, including Iris and Annie (one half of Annie-and-Matt), both without partners due to Lara not really knowing either of them and guest space being at a premium.

We put our cigarettes out and are allowed back into the function room, which looks much bigger now it lacks tables. A few waiters are setting out a buffet, and while I don't know how anyone can even consider eating, Steve, Alex and Jay simultaneously make a move for it. I'm not your average man – most of the ones I know seem to have bottomless stomachs and an overriding love of sport. Some of the many reasons I've always been more comfortable being friends with women.

Once Steve is dragged away from the chicken legs he's gorging on, they cut the cake, have their first dance (Adele's 'Make You Feel My Love') and the rest of us, buoyed with alcohol, swarm onto the dance floor like ants honing in on a dropped toffee apple.

The music is what one has come to expect from weddings – the *Grease* soundtrack, Abba, Jackson Five – followed by hits from ten years ago that make us scream with recognition and excitement as the first notes play and we are taken back to being sixteen and seventeen, partying every weekend at someone's house, circulating around the town so that parents had time to replace everything that got broken before that house hosted another one.

I move on to gin and tonics and, soon enough, I find myself in a corner of the hotel's gardens under a bush shaped like a jumping stag, with Georgina.

Through the alcoholic fug, it's not clear who approached whom, but someone asked the other one for a light and we both stand there, the music thumping away back in the hotel – it sounds like 'Dancing Queen'.

'What a lovely evening,' she says, dragging deeply on her menthol cigarette. Her hair is dyed an emerald green, which at sixteen would've been experimental and cool, but now looks like someone struggling with the reality of adulthood.

'We should go back in,' I say, thinking I'd rather have root canal surgery than a conversation with Georgina.

'No, Dex, hang on a second, I want to say something,' she says, reaching out and stopping short of grabbing my wrist, a gesture we both know would be inadvisable. We've not seen much of one another since we split up, and certainly haven't been left alone. Any touch at all is by its nature intimate, and I think my boundaries are still more solidly guarded than hers. I decide to see what she wants to say.

'I'm sorry,' she doesn't say.

'We should get back together,' she doesn't add.

'Do you think we could try again?' she doesn't query.

Instead, she says, 'Why didn't you fight for me?'

It's typically selfish of her, a trait I allowed myself to notice in the last couple of weeks of our relationship. I let the words hang in the air with our smoke and hope that she sees how ridiculous they sound. She doesn't, though, so I have to answer.

'I didn't fight for you because I didn't want to be with you any more,' I say. 'You pissed off my friends, accused me of cheating on you, drowned my Kindle and were barely letting me have my own life. You were turning up every single night – I was so behind on my work because you couldn't take a hint.'

'Because I was in love with you and I wanted to see you! Besides, you set fire to my dress.'

'I didn't *mean* to,' I say, my voice rising. We're too far away for anyone else to hear. 'The thing is Georgina, up until that point, I had been pretty into you. But you didn't let it happen on its own; you were trying to force something that was never going to get any bigger.'

'So you'd rather be alone than with me?'

'Pretty much, yeah.' It sounds horrible as an excuse to break up, but she had gone psycho on me and sometimes it's better to back out than try and make something impossible work. Some would call it cowardice; I viewed it as bravery, pissing off a human firework.

She slaps me and I walk off but, after a couple more gin and tonics, a heated conversation on the hotel's main staircase, discussions with Ruby and Annie about what I'm going to do about her (Ruby says fuck her, and Annie says fuck her, but they mean entirely different things) and a long, mostly sleepless night, Georgina and I wake up together in my hotel room, stark naked and shagged out from some of the most acrobatic, contortionistic manoeuvres ever seen outside a circus.

I get up and go into the bathroom. My hair is flat on one side and sticking up with clumped wax on the other. Red scratches cover my chest and back, alongside smears of Georgina's plum lipstick. My eyes are bloodshot with dark rings circling them – I look like a panda that's traded in bamboo for a different kind of grass. Any more vigorous and she might have actually broken my nose.

'This has been a huge mistake,' says my reflection.

'Yeah, tell me something I don't know,' I growl back, my voice box coated in sharkskin sandpaper.

I pee, wrap one of the fluffy white towels around my waist and go back into the bedroom. She's still asleep, green hair billowing out around her on the pillow. The thick duvet covers most of her, but is bunched up at the end and one foot sticks out, an angry red mark and the beginning of a blister on the ankle. The sun is prising itself through a tiny gap in the curtains, so I pull the heavy fabric back and let it invade.

I find my boxers and put them back on, run a comb over my hair and rummage in my overnight bag for a clean shirt and chinos. My watch says nine-fifteen and I'm in desperate need of some genuine breakfast food. As I pull my shoes on, Georgina stirs and sits up, make-up smudged. She smiles the tired, lopsided smile of a romantic comedy heroine.

'I'm going to get some breakfast,' I say, throwing a grey striped shirt on, having to do up the buttons twice as my fingers are still drunk and falling over each other like D-list celebrities on the first week of *Strictly Come Dancing*.

'OK, sweetie,' she says and I raise a hand to stop her.

'No, no, none of that,' I say, a magma-tinged force in my voice that surprises her, as well as myself. 'Last night was a one-off. Bonus night, call it. You've got a boyfriend, remember? We're finished. If you want to be friends, we can begin working up to that again, but we're not getting back together.'

'Fine,' she says. She pulls the duvet from around her and I can tell she wants to storm out like someone in a film, except she's naked and first has to find and put on her knickers and bra (which don't match), before wriggling back into her dress. She doesn't ask me to do up the zip, just picks up her high heels and finally is able to go. I hold the door open for her and follow her out. She turns left and I turn right, down to the restaurant.

Jay-and-Kay are sitting at a table with Lara. They're laughing but as soon as they see me, they stop and their faces take on a concerned appearance. They indicate for me to sit down, but I need food first, so I go to the breakfast buffet and get bread, butter, jam, a few rashers of bacon and a scoop of scrambled egg.

'What happened to you?' says Jay. He looks refreshed, although is still wearing his dark glasses so he might be hiding his hangover behind them.

'Georgina,' I sigh, shovelling eggs into my mouth. I turn to Lara, 'Did we ruin your night?' She's got her long ginger hair up in a pony-tail which swishes side to side as she shakes her head.

'Nope, you didn't do anything! We sort of guessed the two of you might have gone off together. Ruby saw you talking earlier in the night, then you had a row in the hotel lobby, and you both vanished at the same time. We did wonder if she'd called Marcus and gone home.'

'You haven't got back with her, have you?' says Kay, spreading marmalade on half a slice of toast.

'No, don't worry,' I say. 'I mean, well… no. We slept together, but there wasn't anything you could pick out as romantic about it.' I pre-empt their next question. 'Before you ask, I couldn't tell you who initiated it, but there's no way we're getting back together.' I ran briefly over what I remembered of our conversation the night before, and my three friends nod and keep their opinions to themselves.

'Where's hubby?' I say to Lara, noticing Steve's absence for the first time.

'Still in bed,' Lara huffs. 'Sodding Jamie and him were downing shots by the bucket.' I laugh but she looks serious. 'No, I mean it, they found a bucket and filled it with champagne and all sorts of… god knows what. He needs to sober up; we need to be in Portsmouth by lunch time tomorrow.'

'I still can't believe you're going on a cruise,' I say with faux despair. 'Are you looking forward to spending your first ten days as a married couple surrounded by the living dead?'

'Look, if his grandparents want to give us a free holiday as a wedding present, I'm taking it,' says Lara. 'I'll put up with a lot of old age pensioners talking about rationing and leg pain for ten days in the Mediterranean with bottomless booze and good weather. Besides, given what Jay was saying this morning, it's a good job we didn't decide to go to France.'

'What do you mean?' I ask. I've not bothered checking my phone this morning yet, as most of the people who might have messaged me are here.

'It was on the news this morning that France has gone into techno-logical shutdown,' says Jay. 'You know, like when Egypt did during the Arab Spring riots? The news said they can't even get on Twitter. I didn't even know there was a political situation brewing there. The newsreaders were implying terrorism, as they do.'

'This is what I was saying yesterday,' says Lara, 'There was a huge meteor shower there this week. I saw something about shooting stars.'

'Yeah, loads of European places reported that,' says Kay. 'Nothing had been predicted so it kind of came out of nowhere. Maybe something landed last night and crushed the President or something.'

My mind has tuned to a channel playing nothing but white noise – I'm too tired and hungover for political discussion – and I focus instead on my breakfast.

We don't see Georgina come down for breakfast, but her room is definitely empty by the time Jay drives us home.

Four

Lara-and-Steve

As I think back on the events of the last week, they feel like they're a half-remembered history lesson. Something that happened to someone else, many years before. It seems unreal that just a week ago (I'm guessing at a week – how long I've been trapped in this cell is impossible to estimate) I was watching Lara-and-Steve say their vows.

I never did get to properly say goodbye, so instead I focus on the hello.

Lara Greedy – well, Hutchinson now, I suppose – appears to have come into my life to be the sole reason for my varied vices. She is the person who formally introduced me to cigarettes, alcohol and sex. Granted, I couldn't exactly be labelled an innocent in any of these subjects before her arrival at sixteen, but she definitely led to them being given a bigger place in my life than they had done before.

I hadn't known her before sixth form, at which point we shared English Literature classes and found ourselves seated next to one another. Our friendship developed naturally, the way two people bond when sitting at the same table three or four times a week for several months. By March, we had become close enough that she invited me to a party she was hosting that weekend. I was given directions and told to bring some friends before she departed with a battered copy of *Titus Andronicus* under her arm, lighting a cigarette before she'd even got out of the English department and into the school car park.

I rustled up Priti, Peregrina and Shell, as well as Shell's man of the moment Ashley, and we arrived at Lara's fashionably late with bottles of cider bought from the newsagents that didn't ask for ID. The door was open, teenagers pouring out into the front garden, so we went in and set ourselves up in an unoccupied nook in the dining room.

Lara eventually stumbled – the perfect word – upon us with a grin that would've freaked out the Joker, genuinely happy to see me, or at least drunk enough to suggest it. Her thick ginger hair was up in a complicated-looking bun and she was wearing a tight blue dress that showed off every last one of her curves. Her sea-green eyes shone with excitement and I was aware that this was the first time I had seen her in a situation that wasn't school based. She looked *hot*. Cigarettes were thrust into our hands; she snatched up a bottle opener from a nearby emo kid and cracked open our ciders.

I tried to speak to her, thank her for inviting us, but she was drunk and only nodded, her white-toothed grin getting bigger.

'Oh my god, I love this song!' she squawked, although I could have sworn that the song had already been playing a couple of minutes without any reaction from her. She danced off, leaving us feeling like potted ferns. We recognised a lot of the people at the party, but we didn't know any of them well enough to throw ourselves into a conversation. These people were too 'cool', a word so devoid of meaning that it's a wonder we still use it.

The evening was warm and the dining room full, so we moved out into the back garden to cool down where we all (except Peregrina) lit up cigarettes and began sussing out the other guests. We were probably the soberest people there, but once we'd drunk our ciders and taken swigs from the bottle of absinthe that had been passed around everybody as a dare – thinking on it, I dread to think how many people had backwashed into that – we had definitely caught up.

Shell and Ashley had retired upstairs for reasons that should be obvious, Peregrina had bumped into someone she knew from school that we didn't and was chatting to her about some concert or other, and Priti was swaying alone in the corner of the living room to the music, half a cigarette hanging from her mouth, ash perilously close to falling onto the carpet but somehow defying gravity.

Lara found me again but was once more useless for conversation. Realising that I was alone, however, she grabbed a nearby girl with raven hair and dragged her in front of me.

'This is my cousin, ———,' she screamed over the music. The gap is because I couldn't hear the name of this cousin. She shared Lara's pale complexion and was pretty, but her nose was red like she was recovering from a cold and she still wore braces.

We half-shouted a conversation but it was fruitless and eventually I suggested we go somewhere a bit quieter. I asked her name again, but still couldn't hear it. ——— and I made our way upstairs to the spare bedroom, finding it occupied by Shell and Ashley. The master bedroom was currently in use by another couple, so we settled on Lara's bedroom, a lilac and cream paradise, wall to wall with chick lit novels, romantic comedies and stuffed toys, most of them elephants.

It was there, on Lara's bed under the watchful glare of over thirty fabric pachyderms that I lost my virginity to ———. She was by no means the first girl I'd fooled around with, but to this day I don't know the name of the first girl I had sex with. I could never ask Lara as she mentioned a week later that her cousin ('Who you met at the party, remember?') had that week got engaged to her boyfriend of three years, and was moving to Seattle the following month with him for his work. Turns out that ——— was twenty-two. I never heard Lara mention her again, and I never discussed what happened at that party, although I did always feel a bit weird whenever I had cause to be in Lara's bedroom after that point.

That was the one secret I kept from Lara – she believes that I lost my virginity to my next girlfriend, Clare, and I'm happy to let her think so. Despite that, we've been solid friends since that time, the sort who can go a month or so without seeing one another and then pick up immediately where we left off. Most of our bonding takes places in bars over wine and cigarettes. Through her, I found Georgina for that short period, so I can happily blame Lara for any events involving *her*.

Not too long after Lara and I became closer friends, she met Steve Hutchinson. There aren't many relationships that form over someone having their stomach pumped, but I guess everyone has their story. Lara and I had gone up to the hospital from school one day to meet her mum, a nurse, who was going to give us a lift out to Ruby's place for a party.

If you're not there to visit someone, recover or work, hospitals are pretty dull places, although I'm aware they're also really boring if you are doing one of those things. Still, with Lara's mum held up with an emergency, we had some time to kill and so we took ourselves off sneaking around the hospital. We weren't stopped once, which seems remarkable. It's not like we were going into operating rooms or marching into A&E wards, but surely someone would've had something to say about two teenagers stomping around the place, sipping on bottles of Sprite that were actually gin and tonics.

On the third floor, we were sitting in an otherwise unoccupied waiting room drinking and talking about the upcoming evening, when the swinging doors were pushed open and a guy on a gurney was pushed in by a nurse who looked like she had already been at work for eleven hours and had another thirteen to go.

'Mr Hutchinson, I'm sorry for the mess up,' she said, running fingers through her flyaway hair. 'We'll try and find you another bed. You hold on here for a few minutes, I'll get the ward sister.' She bustled off, black shoes squeaking on the shiny floor.

'Not like I can fucking go anywhere!' Steve shouted after her, because this was indeed Steve on the gurney. Abandoned by the NHS, he lay his head back down and stared at the ceiling. Lara wasted no time in jumping up and going over to him. Slightly unstable on my feet – these were not our first drinks – I followed.

'What happened to you?' said Lara, leaning over this poor guy who was as pale as clotted cream, with tiny beads of sweat on his forehead which were partly due to his condition and partly due to the thermostat – as ever with a hospital – being stuck on the Floridian Mangrove setting. Like her, he was ginger, his hair cut short, something about it suggesting that it normally had product in it.

'Been in to have my stomach pumped,' he said, trying to make it sound like it was something all the cool kids were doing and the mark of a life being successfully lived. He attempted to prop himself up on his elbow, but something was causing him pain and so he gave up. 'They're keeping me in a bit longer. I'm Steve.'

'I'm Lara,' she said, beaming down at him as if she'd never seen someone so cool in her life. I thought he was a bit of an idiot, but in my experience the line between the two is very thin and very subjective. 'This is Dexter.' I waved my fingers at him. He looked at me in the same way you look at a disappointing smudge on the wallpaper of a hotel you thought was upmarket, and turned his attention back to Lara. I couldn't work out his age, but he was definitely older, and I wondered if he should be talking to her.

Then I remembered that she had started talking to him.

'Why haven't you been put in a room?' she asked, shoving her Sprite bottle into her coat pocket and resting her hands on the side of his trolley.

'They had me in one, then someone came in from surgery and they had to move me out and find me somewhere else.' He rolled his eyes. 'Not well enough to go home yet, according to the *experts*, but I feel fine.'

'You look alright,' said Lara. He gave a short smile.

'Maybe I'm dying and they've sent me an angel,' Steve winked and had I had anyone else with me, I would've made throwing-up gestures with them. Lara blushed and giggled and Steve, in a moment of clarity when he realised he'd better cover his own back, said, 'How old are you, Lara?'

'Sixteen,' she said, adding in her own attempt to make herself look better, 'but nearly seventeen!' Bored of being ignored, I slumped back over to the hard chairs to sit down and drink my gin and tonic. The two of them continued muttering to each other. I wasn't able to hear what they were saying so I texted Ruby to let her know that we were running late.

After a few more moments of Lara and Steve gazing into each other's eyes and pretending that the whole situation was romantic, Lara's mum burst into the room with her coat on and a battered-looking rucksack slung over her shoulder.

'*There* you are!' she snapped. 'I'd been waiting for you downstairs until Poppy came down to tell me you're swanning about up here like you've got free rein of the place! Hello, Dexter. Come on, if you want to go to this bloody party!' She swept out again and I saw Lara sneak her phone into her pocket. We followed at a safe distance while Mrs Greedy powered through the sterile corridors, nodding at people she knew. We followed her down the stairs and Lara showed me her phone as we went.

'He gave me his number,' she said, as if she'd been presented with a celebrity's autograph.

'Is that a good idea?' I asked. 'He's a guy you met in the hospital. I mean, it's a bit weird.'

'He's really nice though!' she protested. I didn't force the issue, and it was only when we were in the car and halfway to Ruby's place that the topic came up again, this time from the front seat.

'Why were you talking to that boy?' Mrs Greedy asked.

'He was in pain – I was seeing if he was alright,' Lara replied, a consummate liar to the end. Her mum, however, is not a pushover and wasn't content with that as an answer. She pursed her lips and murmured low like Marge Simpson.

'If I discover that you have anything else to do with that boy, you will be in serious trouble, young lady,' she said. 'He's too old and is nothing but trouble. That's not the first time we've had him in.'

Being sixteen, Lara naturally proceeded to ignore her mum and started dating him, but Steve never found himself back in the hospital for any self-inflicted or immature reasons; just once when he tripped over a child on an ice rink and cracked his head open. It's almost impossible to think that those were once Mrs Greedy's words when, about a decade later, she would be beaming proudly at her daughter's wedding to 'that boy', and counting him among her favourite people in the world.

Oh sure, Lara-and-Steve had their rocky patches, and neither of them has still entirely grown up, but they both realised that life was simply better when they were going through it together than when they were apart and so they fought for it, no matter what got in their way. Say what you like about hospitals, but never rule them out as a place to find happiness.

Five

Breaking News

It is Sunday lunchtime, a few hours after my return home from the wedding, and I am with Shell-and-Terry and Priti-and-Art having coffee and cake, hoping that further food will keep my hangover manageable.

None of the four are friends with Lara save through me, so I run over the events of the wedding. Shell and Priti are interested, asking lots of questions that I can't answer about the bridesmaids, the dress, the place settings, Lara's family and Steve's family, while Art and Terry discuss how to get a bigger gun in a violent video game with a hack one of them found online. I fill the girls in on what happened with Georgina.

Priti, the less forgiving of the two, thinks I'm idiotic and tells me so.

'You're idiotic,' she says, throwing her scrunched-up paper napkin at me. 'For a start, she has a boyfriend. For seconds, you have been doing well without her – you broke up with her, remember?'

'A shag's a shag, though,' shrugs Shell, fiddling with the many, many rings that cover her fingers. The only finger devoid of any glitz is the one reserved for a wedding ring. One day Terry might take the hint. 'At least you both know what to expect from one another, but yeah, it probably wasn't the smartest thing you've ever done.'

'I thought you were happy being single?' says Priti.

'I am,' I say, shredding the napkin in my fingers. 'I was. I don't know. It was a weak moment after a night of mixing my drinks. Plus it's hard being a single person at a wedding, no matter how happy you are. Yes, it was stupid, but I made it very clear the next morning that we weren't getting back together.'

'Did you though?'

'I think I used those exact words,' I nod. 'I said we could be friends

again, if she tones down the crazy, anyway, but that there was nothing else going on.' Priti makes a noise that suggests she isn't convinced. I become aware that the television on the far wall has had its
volume turned up.

'Hey, um, some real shit is going down,' says Art. With a small
furrowing of eyebrows, we turn our attentions to the television. The
screen shows footage from a helicopter of central Paris. It's difficult
to explain what we can see. It's a large, boxy shape, metallic but with
nodules and bumps up its flanks. Steam rises up from the base, as if
burning the grass it has landed on. It stands taller than the nearby
Eiffel Tower. The police have formed a perimeter of uniforms and
guns around it, but huge crowds of people have gathered to stare. The
footage is fairly distant, but you can tell that almost everyone present
is holding their phone up, filming the strange thing.

'What the hell?' whispers Terry.

'Jay said earlier that something was happening in France,' I say.
'Terrorist, he figured.'

'That's not terrorists,' says Art, jabbing a finger at the screen, even
though we're already looking. I turn my attention to the bold white
words on the red banner that scroll across the bottom of the screen.

–SED TO REMAIN CALM. MYSTERIOUS OBJECT HAS
APPEARED IN PARIS, FRANCE. BELIEVED TO BE
EXTRATERRESTRIAL IN ORIGIN. PEOPLE BELIEVED TO
HAVE BEEN CRUSHED. WORLD GOVERNMENTS HAVE
ENTERED EMERGENCY TALKS. POPULATION ADVISED
TO REMAIN CALM. MYSTERIOUS OBJECT HAS APPEARED
IN PAR–

You've got to be shitting me.

One of the waitresses switches through the channels – both BBC
One and Two, ITV, Channel 4, Five, all the same. Even Dave has
stopped showing *Top Gear* and has footage of the object playing on
a loop. Back on BBC One, the feed cuts to a terrified looking newsreader at a desk. His tie is askew and he's as white as a snowdrift.

'Breaking news, I guess,' he says, his attempt at a composed voice wavering. You can see the sweat on his brow. He never dreamed he'd have to report something like this. 'What we are witnessing here appears to be first contact with an alien species. Nothing has emerged from what is believed to be a craft so far.

'The object appeared on Friday night during the European meteor shower. The craft – potential craft – landed at three o'clock in the morning, local time, at which point France cut off international communications, including access to social media.

'At least twenty people are dead, crushed by the craft as it landed. The Prime Minister has chaired an emergency COBRA meeting and has joined talks with leaders of other countries to work out what is to happen next. The world watches with bated breath.'

He stops talking, and I get the feeling that he should be carrying on, but there's a horror in his eyes that suggests he can't. The screen cuts back to the earlier footage, news helicopters circling the enormous *thing*. The five of us on our table stare at one another. Aside from the television, the café is silent.

'What do we do now?' says Art.

I suggest we go to my house. I live nearest, and I've got alcohol.

Six

Shell-and-Terry

There's a noise outside the cell door and it wakes me from my reverie. A slot opens up near the floor and something is slid in. It glides with the smoothness of a curling stone towards me and comes to rest against my boot. It looks like the kind of bag you'd usually see hanging from an IV drip, filled with a dark orange liquid.

I pick it up tentatively and hold it up to the light in the corner. It's thick like marmalade and there are tiny yellow flecks floating in it. I wonder if it's food or something designed to kill me. Is it some kind of alien bomb? I can't see anything technological on it, just a thin cap that I flick off. I put my nose to the hole and sniff. The smell is somewhere between pine needles and salt water, a forest next to the beach.

It might be poison. I decide that maybe that wouldn't be so bad and squirt a sample onto my tongue, braced for my hunger pangs to vanish, either because this is food or I won't be around soon to worry about it. The jelly-like substance hits my taste buds. It tastes like blackcurrants, or beetroot. It's hard to say.

I wish that Shell was here to share it with me.

Shell Timmins is a sous chef for a fashionable restaurant in Fairmill, working most evenings but making the most of the ones she has off by drinking cocktails and having – judging from the notes shoved through her letterbox by neighbours – extremely loud sex. She's the annoying sort of girl who has never stepped foot in a gym in her life but retains a perfect figure regardless. Most men love her. Most women hate her.

She and I struck up a friendship when we were six thanks to a chocolate bar. There was no better way to be reminded of your social standing at primary school than by what was in your lunchbox. Our school was never as fussed about healthy eating as others – it was one of the last, I'm told, to let go of the Turkey Twizzlers – so lunchboxes had few restrictions on them and, like six-year-olds the world over, we knew that everything important in life revolved around chocolate and sweets.

Oh sure, our parents were responsible enough to not load us down with sugar, but our parents weren't watching us in the dining hall. A bag of Wotsits was worth two Penguins; a Fruit and Nut was worth one and a half Dairy Milks and, when Easter rolled round, all bets were off when it came to Creme Eggs.

On this particular day, I was sitting opposite Shell, who I knew only in the sense that we were in the same class, where we sat on different tables about as far away from one another as it was possible to sit, meaning we met occasionally at the stationary pencil sharpener at the back of the room, or whenever we were called upon to stand in alphabetical order for whatever reason, Scithers coming directly before Timmins.

My lunchbox that day contained a Twix and, while few of us would balk at the prospect, my six-year-old self didn't feel like it. I opened up the bidding and asked who would trade me something for it.

Someone offered me strawberry yoghurt, but that's no kind of trade. Priti asked if I wanted her Wagon Wheel for it, but I didn't because it was a plain one rather than the jam kind. Shell was the one who saved the day, offering her Time Out. There isn't much between a Time Out and a Twix, but on that day the difference was enormous. We swapped and a tradition was born. Almost every lunchtime after that, Shell was one of the few people I would swap with. Sometimes she did better out of it, other times I did, but neither of us ever complained. Like so many early friendships, it was created because of something so tiny, but the future implications were enormous.

Shell, Priti and I became an almost inseparable threesome, spending lunchtimes and breaktimes together, but a precedent had been set, and it felt like the rest of my life would be spent swapping things with Shell.

On cinema visits with each other and a dragged-along parent, a handful of her salty popcorn would be swapped for a handful of my sweet popcorn. At birthday parties, bowls of different coloured jelly would exchange hands halfway through. Polos for Tic Tacs; Mars for Snickers; Monster Munch for Quavers. During a school trip to see a performance of *Macbeth*, we shared Wine Gums and Fruit Pastilles.

As we got older, the swaps continued but with a very different flavour. At teenage house parties, we'd arrive with different bottles of artificially coloured alcopops and chug half of each pack and think we were drunk. In actual bars, we'd get halfway through whatever cocktail we'd chosen and swap them. When she was training to be a chef, I'd give her bottles of wine in exchange for free practice dinners. At slightly more mature parties we'd swap Rennies tablets for condoms, hash brownies for cigarettes, and on one occasion we swapped our own saliva in a kiss we both regretted and never mentioned again.

It's impossible to say why it became such a tradition, but it was abandoned almost as soon as she started going out with Terry. If there was something to swap at that point, she was going to swap it with him.

But among the swapping of sweets and drugs, we swapped so much more. She swapped her patience with me when I was going through rough times for my push to get her to find a career she would enjoy. I gave her my sofa after she had a blazing row with her flatmate, and she gave me a new DVD player when mine got stolen. We gave each other time and space, love and friendship and she stood by me throughout everything, never once wavering in our loyalty to one another. We may not have always liked one another's decisions, but we stood by each other when they turned out to have been the wrong ones.

Everyone gets a friend like Shell, the kind of friend who will always be there for you, no matter what the odds. All of my friends are solid and wonderful people, don't get me wrong, but if it was three o'clock in the morning and I was in trouble and only had enough battery life for one more phone call, I'd already have dialled Shell's number.

Terry Grey became a primary part of our lives on the evening of Shell's twenty-third birthday, on a freezing cold November evening. Shell had convinced us to go out in town, but the eastern side of the

South Greenfield high street wasn't accessible due to a power cut. It had, however, left the western side of the high street up and running, so the pubs on that side of the long road, which were always subpar anyway, were crammed with both their regulars and some irregulars. Had there been no power cut, there's no way we would have entered Ye Old Lamplighter unless we were threatened at gunpoint, chloroformed or dead – ideally all three.

The single room of the pub was hot and sweaty and everyone had too many coats because of the outside chill, meaning that the birthday celebrations were shaping up to be pretty crap as it took us twenty minutes to get served and then there was nowhere to sit.

When you're eighteen, standing up in a pub isn't a problem, but only a few years later the idea is intolerable. You find yourself wanting to be able to sit at a table and hold a conversation over your drinks at a volume that doesn't tax your vocal cords.

Shell, Priti, the newly-introduced Art, a handful of Shell's work friends and I were clustered under a mirror and right next to a speaker that blared out some godawful music from a singer I couldn't name if given the option to ask the audience *and* phone a friend.

We were saved from a night standing next to our own reflections and struggling to be heard over the noise by a fight breaking out somewhere near the pub quiz machine. Although I don't think anyone was quite sure what caused it or how it began, it soon rippled through more and more of the pub as people came to the aid of the two fighters and began throwing punches of their own.

The solitary bouncer, who stood outside the door looking like André the Giant's body double, leapt into action and took it as his moment of glory, grabbing people by the collar indiscriminately and turfing them out into the street, which was soon awash with flashing blue lights. By the time he'd finished and quiet order had been restored to the pub, there were enough empty chairs and tables for us to get comfortable and feel that the night was not going to be a washout.

The drink flowed – quicker now that the queue at the bar had dissipated – and the evening continued getting better and slightly more raucous, although the bouncer kept popping his head in as if checking if he'd missed anyone. It was when there was another round of gin and tonics being imbibed that Terry made his appearance.

A nose broken from rugby was his only obvious physical flaw, after years of a strict gym routine, team sports and running. His opening line, however, left a lot to be desired, given that it was, 'Can I take a picture of you so I can show Santa what I want for Christmas?' It wasn't even aimed directly at Shell, more in the general area of the table, but she was the first one to reply to it, if only because she melts in the presence of muscular arms.

I can't remember what she said, but it was something quick about being on the naughty list or... I don't know, I wouldn't be able to do it justice. Whatever it was, it was effective and she spent the rest of the night curling him around her little finger and not speaking to us if she could help it. This left us to get into a very intense game of 'Never Have I Ever' that somehow ended in such a manner that that evening gained two names, alternatively 'The Night Shell Met Terry' and 'The Night Priti Lost Her Bra To A Seagull'.

Terry was folded into the group rather quickly and while he may have had difficulty in following the plot of one of the Mr Men books, he made up for his lack of imagination and intelligence with simple comradeship. He was in the military and through that had learnt the importance of sticking together, meaning that even before he had apparently worked out which one of us was which, he had our backs, supported us in every endeavour and through an unspoken agreement of loyalty became the person you called to pick you up when you were stuck somewhere thanks to a diverted train or one too many drinks. I liked him immediately, and always would.

Seven

Neither Bang nor Whimper

Catsby has curled himself up on Terry's lap, as if knowing that he's the only person in the room who doesn't care for animals. We're drinking beer and red wine, sitting on my sofas and on the floor, watching the news unfold on the television. Or rather, we're watching the news not unfold, as nothing is happening. As well as the five of us from the café, and Catsby, we've also been joined by Ruby-and-Alex – she seems bright and breezy next to Alex, who is clearly still hungover – as well as Pete, one half of Peregrina-and-Pete. Peregrina is on a train down from Gloucester but knows what's happened and will be along soon enough.

The Prime Minister has been on television with a message. Every country is having a briefing from their leader, I'd imagine. I have little faith in these men and women in expensive suits being the saviours of humankind in this situation. The plans I made in my teens on how to survive a zombie apocalypse begin to come back. Thankfully, during one particularly nerdy moment when I'd overdosed on end-of-the-world films during sixth form, I had tweaked the plans to also be able to deal with alien invasion, vampire infestation and werewolf plague. Sitting in my living room with a group of friends, drinking beer and being glued to the television wasn't ever part of the plan. Right now, we should be defending ourselves from inside the Natural History Museum, where I know of a place that, to my mind, is the safest and most unobtrusive spot in London. I have, at least, stuck my phone on charge, in case we have to make a dash for it.

Despite the unreality of what's going on, there is a frisson of excitement bouncing around the room, particularly between the boys. Men, from what I've noticed, all imagine that they're secret agents and no one's told them, or that one day the fate of the world will fall to them and them alone. I think we get it with the Y chromosome. If women feel like this, I've never personally known any admit to it, which is why I reckon we could sort out ninety per cent of the world's problems if men would accept they've all been involved in a dick-measuring contest for the last four thousand or so years and put women in charge.

The Prime Minister, sweating and stumbling over his words, begs the country to stay calm (as if we'd panic – we're British!) and says that more information will be given as soon as anyone is able to give it. He scurries back behind his black door and, no doubt, retires to some underground bunker. Art and I are scrolling through newsfeeds on our phones; Priti has my laptop up and running. We're seeking out further information because the television is playing the same footage over and over again, the same ticker tape message passing along the bottom of the screen.

'The Americans are *really* pissed off,' says Art, iPhone in hand.

'Because of the communication blackout?' says Pete.

'No, because they think the aliens should've chosen them for first contact,' Art says, then laughs. He actually laughs – there's an alien invasion happening and someone is laughing. Everyone is laughing. It's unreal.

'Typical sodding Americans,' says Pete. I like Pete. At forty-one, he's fifteen years older than us, which was a bit odd at first, but he's seamlessly slipped into a friendship with most of us via Peregrina. He's a huge bear of a man with an enormous brown beard and tiny glasses perched on a hooked nose. When standing next to him, Peregrina looks even thinner than she already is. Like her namesake, the peregrine falcon, she's sleek and attractive, but also gives the impression that she could cut you down with a single word.

I like strong women – that's why I've surrounded myself with them. Women who take no shit from anyone. I'll say this for them, too – they have picked well with their menfolk.

After another hour, the news looks much as it did when we started watching. It's like when a celebrity dies and there's not really anything to say about it, but the news feels obliged to keep mentioning it and cutting to a man standing outside the deceased's house.

After two hours, Peregrina has turned up and been filled in on the events. She is a journalist and by rights should be the sort of person we go to for information on this. Tragically, she writes for a fashion magazine, which has about as much interest in the real world as a lion does in a garden salad. They'd only write about the apocalypse if a Kardashian released a range of underwear to mark the occasion.

After three hours we have, to be honest, become bored with the whole thing, watching out of a sense of duty. Lara calls to say that she and Steve have just heard about it, but the ship has already left port and they're cruising out towards the Atlantic.

After four hours, Priti-and-Art make a move, followed not long after by Terry. Ruby-and-Alex depart with Shell, leaving me with Peregrina-and-Pete. We order Chinese takeaway and spend the evening eating, drinking and playing with Catsby. The television remains on in the background, but since nothing is progressing, we only give it the occasional cursory glance. I had always figured that an alien invasion would be more exciting than this. It becomes so mundane eventually that we play a game of Scrabble. Peregrina wins with 201 to my 186 and Pete's 177. Catsby spends most of the game trying to eat a C tile.

We can't be bothered to pack the game away, so it sits between us on the coffee table, tiles and symbols scattered like we've been divining with runes. Full of MSG and beer and out of conversation – I'm not telling them about Georgina because Peregrina won't approve and she'll ignore the more pressing events around us to give me a lecture – we turn our attention back to the television. The French President is on screen, his dulcet tones barely distinguishable under the English dubbed over him.

'The French people are taking no military action against the landed object,' he says. Or at least, the dub says he's saying that. It occurs to me that he could be saying *anything*. 'We are keeping an armed guard around it, however, to stop the public from approaching. We do not know enough about the object to allow people near to it.'

Footage is shown of Paris but it seems that even the French people's interest has waned, and the crowds are far smaller than they were earlier. The world ends not with a bang or a whimper, but a disinterested shrug.

'What do we do if it is aliens?' says Peregrina.

'Given humans don't have a great track record of treating their own species with decency, whatever happens won't be pretty,' I say, nuzzling Catsby's sleepy head with my knuckles.

'Do you think they'll not even bother coming out?' says Pete. 'Or they'll scan the planet, realise we're idiots and move off again?'

'Maybe it's some big marketing ploy by a film company,' I say. 'Paramount Pictures will reveal all tomorrow. I wonder –'

When I wake up, I'm sprawled on the floor, having fallen off the sofa. Catsby is pawing nervously at my arm, meowing, a hint of genuine concern in his tiny voice. I manage to get one eye open and see Peregrina and Pete in a similar state next to me, curled together but collapsed, like two victims of Pompeii.

The last thing I remember was a flash of mustard yellow attacking every single one of my synapses, invading my field of vision so blatantly I was sure I could smell and hear it as well as see it. I prise myself up from the carpet.

'Guys? Guys, you OK?' I say. My mouth is furry and dry. I look at the clock – it's five past midnight, meaning we've been out for the best part of three hours. That wasn't normal, and I can't think what caused it. I was talking and now I'm here. It's like someone has taken the film reel of my life and snipped out a few frames. Whatever happened in those few hours, they're on the darkroom floor. The television is on standby.

I lean over Peregrina-and-Pete and they grumble and wince, untangle themselves and sit up. Sure that they're in one piece, I turn the television on. The BBC One newsroom suggests the same sort of activity as in my house. The newsreader is leaning back in his seat, arms flopping to his sides. The camera is wonky and the words along the bottom have been replaced by a ceaseless HHHHHHHHHHHH, like someone passed out on the keyboard.

'What happened?' says Peregrina. 'I saw a flash and now... what time is it?'

'What flash did you see?' I ask.

'It was yellow,' she says. 'A dark yellow, unusual.'

'I had the same thing,' says Pete. He follows up with what I think is an inappropriate comment, 'The same colour, Peregrina! It's like we're made for each other!'

'Or something serious happened across the entire planet, as I had the same colour,' I say, having absolutely no time for their gooey conversations. I flip through the television stations and everything is the same. The channels that were on live news, which was most of them, are now showing people in chaos, waking up and having no idea what happened.

Sky News appears to have woken up quicker than everyone else, so we stick to them. They cut to reporters in the field and the reality of the situation begins to dawn. The entire world went down during the Yellow Burst, as the media has dubbed it.

Shots of Paris reappear, streets full of people picking themselves up in confusion, and then things get worse. There's no footage yet, but people are phoning in with reports of death and destruction. Every road in the world is gridlocked with crashes, as drivers passed out and their cars, vans and lorries careered into one another. Trains have collided and ships have hit beaches and each other, many sinking. Most planes kept going thanks to their autopilot systems, and many pilots are waking up either far off course, or just three hours nearer their destination, but not all have been so lucky. Any planes coming in to land or taking off have fared less well. In this country alone, none of the major airports are left functioning.

Disasters continue to pour in and we watch the news, fascinated again. At least five nuclear power plants have malfunctioned, people in intensive care wards the world over have died, and large parts of the Western world are without electricity or running water. Thankfully, we have those at least.

With literally nothing we can do to help any of the bigger situations in the world, we decide to call it a night. I direct Peregrina-and-Pete to the spare room with instructions to help themselves to breakfast in the morning, and I go to bed, Catsby curling up on the pillow next to me. For once, I allow it. On a night like this, I wouldn't want to be alone.

Despite everything, I sleep well.

Eight
Yellow

There's a text message from Lara when I wake up. The cruise ship is, as predicted, full of blue-haired widows and stiff old men who are blaming the Prime Minister for the Yellow Burst. They'd been in the bar the night before when it happened and woke up irritated more by the fact they'd both dropped and wasted their drinks. Peregrina-and-Pete stay for a cup of tea and toast, before heading home to shower and, presumably, try and get on with normality, or have sex.

A worldwide clean-up mission has begun, with millions of volunteers helping those suffering. Perhaps the arrival of aliens was the thing we needed to bring about peace. Governments are naturally concerned about what's going on, and the news indicates that every single war on the planet has ground to a halt, the world's militaries beginning to prepare for something else.

The media is trying to remain balanced, taking opinion from both sides. Brian Cox is on the BBC, talking about what this could mean for humanity, but on the other side Katie Hopkins is doing her bit for the brainless, saying that it's a hoax and that we should carry on as normal, and that her children would never be allowed to befriend alien children. Twitter's biggest global trending topics are 'Yellow Burst', '#alieninvasion', 'Paris' and 'Justin Bieber', because some things never change.

Japan, as a nation that has spent forever being destroyed in fiction – and more comprehensively than any other country in reality too – appears to have the most advanced survival plans for alien invasion. The Vatican City is deserted as the Pope and his cardinals have hidden away to discuss the implications for religion in a universe where we aren't at the centre. Hoax or not, the world is already irreparably changed.

I call or text colleagues and friends I've not seen and, yes, they expe-

45

rienced it too. A thought strikes me and I pick up the phone and call
Gavin, one of my most level-headed friends.

'Is it important?' he says. He's as sharp as a nail, but talks like the
hammer.

'I take it you and Frederik had the same mess as the rest of us last
night?' I say. It's a stupid question and he isn't afraid to let me know
that.

'No, we were the only two people in the world who didn't pass
out,' he snaps. 'We stormed Buckingham Palace while you were all
kipping and are enjoying the first day of our reign as joint kings of
England. You idiot, of course we felt it too.'

'Then here's a question,' I say, 'If we saw yellow, what did Frederik
see?' Gavin moves away from the phone and I can hear him talking to
Frederik. The latter comes on the phone, his Dutch accent softer than
Gavin's Scottish one.

'I saw what, I presume, is your yellow,' he says. 'I don't think much
of it. I thought it was supposed to be cheerful, but it put me in mind
of repression. It sort of appeared inside my head though, like someone
was projecting it into my brain, you know?' Frederik, like all blind
people, could become an enormous boon for the science community.
Maybe we'll begin to understand more about it, if studying blindness
ever becomes a pressing matter again. Right now, the world has much
bigger things on its plate. Colour perception is a pea compared to the
rump steak that is alien invasion.

'Whatever this is that's going on, it's bigger than our own stories,'
he continues. He's right about that. I always wanted to be the hero
in a story, but now something is going on and there's nothing any
of us little people can do. I don't have any superpowers. Gavin comes
back on the line and our conversation dances around any mention of
the craft, trying to pretend that everything is normal – Gavin has no
time for fantasy and things that don't fit into his logical world view –
before he hangs up and I'm left in silence again.

An hour or so later, when I'm keeping Catsby entertained by
swishing a piece of string around, my phone buzzes with a text message. It's Georgina.

Hey, hope you're alright… thought I'd better check in with what's happening. Are you OK? Xx

I think about what I want to say in reply – ideally I don't want to reply at all, but that would be rude – when my phone buzzes again, this time an incoming call from Kay.

'Hello?'

'Dexter, have you got the news on? Are you seeing this?' she half-screams down the phone at me. The television has been on standby. I turn it on and am treated to live footage alternating between Norway and Portugal. Two more craft have landed – and this time there's actually footage of them settling down, slowly steaming and smoking their way onto terra firma. I feel very protective of the planet all of a sudden.

News reporters are flustered again, most of the ones I see having lost pretty much any semblance of professionalism. On the BBC, the presenter has taken his tie and jacket off, the top button of his shirt open, revealing a hairy chest. He has sweat patches the size of the Falklands under his armpits. On Sky, the normally unflappable female presenter has half her make-up done and is still wearing a paper towel around her throat, caught off guard in the dressing room when the news broke.

'What the actual…' I start, but Kay is shouting again.

'It's like 9/11 again,' she shouts. As an American, Kay feels the vibrations of that incident stronger than I or any of my other friends do. A former New York City resident, she knows a thing or two about what it feels like to be invaded. Granted, an Iraqi or Native American probably knows even more, but I don't know any of them, so I'm using the subjects I have to hand.

'Has anything come out of these craft yet?'

'No,' she concedes. 'The Paris one is inert. They had one of those heat sensitive cameras on it earlier and it was cold throughout.'

'Well, none of this means it's an invasion,' I shrug. 'E.T. and his people didn't invade, they were botanists. Maybe these are scientists, or the galactic equivalent of teenagers out for a jolly in dad's car.'

'I'm glad you can be so fucking flippant!' she snaps. The line goes dead. I probably went too far, but I don't know what else to do in this situation. Humour is my default mechanism and I can't take things seriously very often. I ponder going to Heathrow, to see if volunteers are needed to help clear up the mess but I decide that, given my lack of practical skills, I'd be more of a hindrance, and the odds of even getting there are small. I saw pictures of it on the news earlier and it was a mess, planes crashed and askew like a hurriedly abandoned child's play set.

Defying belief and probability, London is almost entirely still in one piece. Only two planes out of what must be hundreds flying above it landed within the city border; one hit the Thames and the other came down in St James's Park. The rest maintained autopilot and the correct height long enough to either stay in flight and head out across Europe or the Atlantic, or instead crashed out in the countryside or suburbia. Ridiculous odds, but those are the odds.

People always assume they know what they'll do if a film scenario happened to them, such as finding a dinosaur walking towards them down a street or developing the ability to fly, but the truth is you can't know how you're going to react. Did I envision that the day after alien life was moved from a theoretical branch of science to a very practical one I would be calmly playing with my cat and wondering how to reply to my ex-girlfriend? No, probably not.

I try to think of a reason why we would all get the same burst of yellow. I guess the fact that we're in an almost apocalyptic condition with mass death the world over should take precedence, but I feel so blasé about the whole thing. We're a generation that is continually bombarded with films, TV shows and books about strange things happening, so when they happen for real, we go with it. The news stopped being a harmless distraction a few years ago, as technology and politics shifted and things that once felt only possible in the diseased mind of a science fiction author began happening for real.

The doorbell goes, I shout that the door is unlocked and Ruby-and-Alex let themselves in. She looks like she's barely slept, the cuffs of her pale pink jumper damp and chewed. He is much taller than her and always has the look of a man trying to make himself comfortable in a hobbit hole. His blonde hair is spiked up and adds another inch or two to his height, so he brushes against the door lintel.

'What are we meant to do?' says Ruby, giving me a kiss on the cheek in greeting and dropping down onto the sofa. Catsby likes Ruby, and immediately jumps into her lap to nuzzle.

'Wait to see if we're about to be attacked or if Tom Cruise will pop out and announce his new film,' I say, shrugging.

'Either way, it'll be bad news for the human race,' says Alex. I'll give him credit, that's kind of funny, even given the circumstances. 'I wonder how much longer we have to wait.' As if responding to his words, the television cuts to footage of the craft in Norway which was steaming again, pale blue lights blinking up and down the shaft. The panicked voice of the newsreader is almost unintelligible but there can be no doubt that first contact is about to be made.

Here we go.

Nine

Peregrina-and-Pete

Peregrina Christopher erupted into my life covered in blood, her personality and charm taking up as much space in whatever room she happens to be in as her full name (Peregrina Genevieve Anastasia Christopher) does on any application form. We were fourteen years old and I was sitting in the nurse's office at school with a burning stomach ache. I was begging to be sent home, but schools never seem keen on doing that, so the nurse was keeping me there to see how badly I was faking and fiddling about on her computer instead.

As I sat and suffered a battle of supremacy between two narwhals in my stomach, the door opened and in came a mass of tissues wearing the purple blazer of our school. Somewhere under the tissues was Peregrina, and my first sight of her face included a lot of blood when she took the tissues away.

'I've got a nosebleed,' she said, as if this wasn't clear. The nurse tutted and moved round from her desk, balling up the tissues and handing Peregrina some more. Blood ran from each nostril like someone had left a bath running. Peregrina had pushed her glasses up into her copper – never blonde, never ginger, always copper – hair to keep them free of blood and sat down next to me, her breaths burbling liquidly.

'Hi,' she gargled. The new tissues were already almost entirely sodden. Before or since, I've never seen anyone with blood so desperate to escape its confinement.

'Unf,' I replied, grasping at my stomach. 'Hey.'

'I don't believe we've ever met,' she said. Even at fourteen I knew that this was a posh voice, and the feeling was driven home when she said, 'I'm Peregrina.'

No one is called Peregrina, or at least no one that you'll ever be allowed to speak to as an equal. Despite the pain, I had to look up at her, her hazel eyes full of innocence peering over red tissues.

'Dexter,' I said, and resumed groaning and grunting.

'What's the matter?' she said. 'Was it something you ate?'

I grunt in the negative, wishing I was making a better impression, but there was very little I could do. The nurse got up from her desk again.

'I need to pop to the staff room; don't either of you do anything silly.' She left. Peregrina got up and helped herself to more tissues, dumping the used lot in the pedal bin. She then insisted on making conversation.

'I think I've seen you around before,' she said, voice once again muffled by tissues. 'You're in my year, right? What form are you in?'

'10D,' I wheezed.

'Ah, well that's it,' she said. 'I'm 10J – we don't have classes together. Oh look, you are in a lot of pain aren't you? Come on, get down.' She indicated the floor and I raised an eyebrow towards the ceiling which I hoped sent the message, *Are you out of your tiny, posh mind?*

'No, come on, lie flat and it'll help the pain,' she said. 'There's no point scrunching yourself up like that – you'll just feel worse.' Figuring I had nothing to lose, I gingerly manoeuvred myself off the hard plastic chair and sprawled out on my back.

Peregrina knelt down beside me, still clutching her nose with one hand, but these tissues were far less sodden, so it appeared her nosebleed was slowing down. She stretched out a large hand with piano player's fingers and began gently massaging the area that was in pain.

It was the most surreal moment of my life up until that point.

Moreover, it was working. A bit.

The pain subsided a little, but it was still there. Whoever was stabbing me had traded in the sword for a butter knife. When the nurse came back in, she kicked up one hell of a fuss about the situation, got me back on the chair (which brought back the pain) and, once satisfied that Peregrina had stopped bleeding, sent her off.

'Thanks for trying,' I groaned at her.

'That's quite all right,' she smiled. She looked very pretty now her face was bloodless. She could pass for a minor royal. 'See you around, Dexter.' She left, stumbling over her own foot as she did so.

I didn't know at the time that this very weird but innocuous meeting would lead to me noticing Peregrina everywhere, swapping phone numbers with her, joining forces on the school paper, sneaking off from the sixth form prom to drink cider and pontificate about what the future would hold, going to the same university, flying to New York together for a weekend to celebrate graduation, and being asked to give a toast at her upcoming wedding.

It's more likely I would've realised something brilliant was happening if it hadn't been for the rather more pressing matter of my burst appendix that eventually *did* get me sent home from school, indeed for a whole week.

On balance, Peregrina was a more than adequate replacement for my appendix.

Peregrina met Pete Dunn over a photocopier at work about eighteen months ago. She'd come down to the third floor because the one on the fifth had given up the ghost for the umpteenth time that month, and while fiddling about with it trying to stop it from copying in A5, she was offered a helping hand by a tall, bearded man with tiny glasses perched on the end of his nose. He was wearing a navy blue polo neck, scruffy jeans and his hair looked like it had been slept on funny. They'd never met before, despite both working at the same company for about three years, as she was a writer and he worked in HR, although they knew one another's names from emails.

He introduced himself, and she did likewise, sensing immediately the butterflies in her stomach that hatch (I'm told) the moment you meet The One. He revealed later that he felt the same, which was very awkward as he had moved in with the woman he'd been dating for six years nine days ago.

They both claim, of course, that their relationship didn't overlap with his and Raquel's, but I've done the maths and it almost certainly did. It began at around the same time that Raquel admitted that she'd been having doubts about the move and that she'd cheated on Pete a couple of times in the last month. They split up and Pete fell into a far healthier relationship with Peregrina within a matter of weeks.

It was originally strange, having someone so much older than the rest of us around, but despite being almost forty when they started dating, he never came across as that much older. A more polite, charming and intelligent man you couldn't meet, and he patently adored Peregrina in a serious way, meaning that after six months he proposed. Peregrina – until then a staunch advocate of a future that involved her raising seventeen cats and shouting at kids to get off her lawn – accepted, throwing herself at him with such ferocity that the pod on the London Eye wobbled a little more than the other passengers liked.

As far as I can tell, Pete had genuinely never encountered his betrothed before that day at the photocopier, but he's a shrewd old bugger and I wouldn't put it past him to have somehow engineered their meeting. They kept the relationship quiet from most of their colleagues as well – dating and day jobs often mix about as well as potassium and water – which meant it came as a shock to some of their office mates when their engagement was announced.

Maybe it is the age gap, or maybe that Peregrina has one of those jobs that looks glamorous to outsiders, even though it's a lot of chasing up phone calls and sitting in airports in foreign countries with spotty Internet access, but they are probably the most mature of us. I've always adored Peregrina, and Pete is totally the right man for her. There's someone for everyone, and sometimes all it takes to meet them is to use a different photocopier.

Ten

First Contact

The lounge is filled with the eerie silence that accompanies an early morning snowfall – it seems harmless but you're very aware of it and its potential to complicate your day – as Ruby-and-Alex, Catsby and myself stare open mouthed at the television screen.

What appears to be a door on the side of the craft slides open and two figures are present in the gap. They appear humanoid in shape, although very slender, but they are mere shadows due to the way the lighting falls. The cameras are too far away, but the BBC cameraman, hands apparently shaking like an aspen in a high wind, is trying to zoom in.

'What the actual…' begins Alex, but Ruby shushes him. The aliens – they have to be aliens – are still several feet from the ground, and it is clear that they are wearing some sort of spacesuits. As the figures step forward, something else becomes clear.

It isn't two figures – it's one. What I had taken to be the two large round heads of a pair of aliens belong to the same creature, one with two arms and two legs, but also two heads, each encased in its own helmet. The streets around these events – taking place in the coastal Norwegian town of Moss – are packed with people but as quiet as a graveyard at midnight. You could hear a photograph cough.

The world freezes and then there is a little flicker of something bottle green in the corner of my eyes.

'Did you just…'

'Yes,' say Ruby-and-Alex. The bottle green is replaced with the turquoise of Caribbean oceans, then slides into onyx. The figure steps from the door and floats down to terra firma, landing silently on asphalt. The heads don't look at one another, but nonetheless you get the sense they are communicating. Occasionally I see flashes of colour

– maroon and cream, chestnut and tangerine. The whole planet holds its breath.

The cameras have zoomed in as far as they can, but what the alien actually looks like under its suit remains a mystery. The helmets have small black visors in a position that suggests their eyes are located in the same place as ours. The alien reaches for a silvery pack on its chest and holds it up to one of the visors, looking at something I can't begin to imagine, a readout of some kind, perhaps. It thumbs at something on the pack and clips it back onto its chest.

'What's it doing?' whispers Ruby.

'Might be reading the atmosphere for breathability, or something,' I murmur back. There is another flash of colour, mint green this time, but with flickers throughout of the same dark yellow of the night before, although this time we don't pass out. Surely it would be easier for the invasion – if that's what this is – to occur if the entire population is rendered comatose? I mean, I'm grateful that we're not, but still. If you've got a Planet Buster Weapon, you use it, right?

The alien reaches up and grabs at one of the helmets, the left one, and, without much fanfare or notification, pulls it off. The world gasps as one.

The head beneath is human only in that there appear to be two eyes and a mouth. It has very little colour, slightly blue, almost a translucent sheen to the skin, behind which are thin veins and what I assume is the brain, a fleshy mound of mushroom in the top of the head. The eyes are thin but wide, barely open and very black. There is no nose, or external ears, but a wide mouth with no lips. The expression is impossible to read; it's the sort of face that doesn't move around too much.

The second helmet is removed and the second head looks out onto the world and the gathered Norwegians. This one is similar to the first, but not identical. The head shape is different, thinner and with a pointier chin. Behind the spot where the right ear would be, a thing that looks like a feather or a fern protrudes a few inches, the colour undulating between red and gold.

'So,' I say. 'That's an alien, then?'

'Better than Jar Jar Binks,' says Alex.

'And less terrifying than a Dalek,' says Ruby, her voice cracking.

It might not be a Dalek, but it's still pretty damn scary. Here is undeniable proof of alien life, and none of us know what we're supposed to do about it. I struggle to cope with the regular pitfalls of adulthood like rent and taxes – self-help books are famously silent on what to do in case of first contact. That's why I'd fashioned a plan of escaping to the Natural History Museum in case of an emergency, although it wasn't a plan I ever thought I'd have to use.

A couple more bodies appear at the open door of the spacecraft and in turn float down to join the first, removing their helmets and revealing more of the weird heads. On one of the pairs, both of them have the weird feather, again in red and gold. Six pairs of eyes look out, but don't appear to be able to focus on anything.

The first alien steps forward to approach the nearest humans, who back away slowly. The cameras can't show us their faces – we're looking at the wrong angle – but I'd put good money on the nearest faces being disgusted. There is still silence. A few of the Norwegians at the front of the crowd grab one another; husbands, wives, boyfriends, girlfriends, I imagine. Despite the events, I still take it as a personal affront and bitter reminder that I've no one here to grab.

There are a few more bursts of colour – green, gold, green, and then shades of blue slide around the edges of our vision.

What happens next happens quickly.

The first alien withdraws something small and silver from its belt and fires it above the crowd. A small grey cloud hovers and, as if sentient, descends on the nearest couple. In righteous fear, they cling to one another but the grey cloud surrounds them and slides up and down the bodies. It shrouds their heads for a moment, then their faces become visible again, although nicked with tiny bloodied cuts, and the cloud moves down to their torsos and legs. Seeming to multiply in size, the cloud envelops them entirely.

Everyone is screaming and some people have turned to run but many more stare on open mouthed. Ruby, Alex and I have leaned forward, intently staring at the screen; even Catsby has jumped off my lap and is sitting in front of the television in rapt concentration.

And then a leg falls out of the cloud. It's severed with a jagged cut and coated in blue denim, but it is undeniably a leg and whatever blood was left in the femoral artery is spreading across the ground. An arm flies out next, followed by scraps of clothing. Thirty seconds or so later, the cloud disperses and returns to the device held aloft by the alien. Where the couple stood previously, now stands something that brings bile up to the back of my throat. And yet, if this was on a film, I would laugh at how outlandish it is.

The couple have become one being, much like the two-headed alien, although with much less precision and cleanliness. Blood and other unthinkable fluids leak over the remaining clothes and the human has two heads, connected clumsily in the middle, the woman's eye stitched to the man's cheek. The torso is twice as wide, sandwiched together with three arms sticking out from odd angles – one appears to have been removed and reattached at the waist on the man's side. With the legs, too, there are three, although one is all but ripped open, just flesh clinging limply to bone, the meat scattered around the floor like a butcher's offcuts.

The faces try to look at each other, try to scream, but there is a traumatised expression on each face. The now-joined body falls, dead.

Panic.

The screen is momentarily filled with the sight of Norwegians fleeing in every direction, tripping over one another, then more grey clouds following some of them or honing in on those couples paralysed with fear. It's immediately noticeable, to me at least, that the clouds only gather on pairs. Taking us out of the moment, the screen restores the image of a news studio, although one with no newsreader and, behind the glass at the back of the studio, people in smart shirts and professional dresses running back and forth in panic clutching paper, phones and each other.

'Fuck!' says Alex, standing up abruptly, hitting his shin on the coffee table and releasing a second, 'Fuck!' This stuns Catsby who turns and leaps back up onto the top of my chair and looks at me with an expression that says, 'Well, what are you going to do about this?'

'Did you see that?' whispers Ruby, the words catching in her throat like wool snagging on barbed wire. 'They put them together. And they died. The blood... the leg...' She's lost, muttering, and a few seconds later screams in a tortured way that I never would have believed possible from her. She's usually so calm, but I guess everyone has their limit.

Someone appears on the screen. It isn't one of the regular newsreaders, rather it appears to be a cameraman wearing a bulky headset and a grey jumper with a prominent toothpaste stain on the chest. He doesn't sit down, just stares out of the screen with the look of a man in court awaiting his sentencing.

'If anyone is watching this,' he shouts, breathless and crying, 'more are landing, across the world. They... they must have been watching and waiting. The cameras from Norway and Portugal show more and more of... them... coming out. They've already landed in Scotland. They're taking over the world. We're dead! We're all fucking dead!' He rips the headset off and disappears.

Ruby has stopped screaming, Alex holding her tight to his chest. She burbles and sniffs wetly into his jacket. Alex looks at me helpless, and I stare back, unable to comprehend what has happened.

'It's the end of the world as we know it,' I say.

But I don't feel fine.

Eleven

Ruby-and-Alex

Ruby Miller and I had been in the same class for four years at primary school, but rarely spoke to one another until Mrs Marsden set up an after-school book club. It turned out we were both obsessive about a series that was popular at the time, although I can't remember for the life of me what it was called.

What I do remember was that it was a series about a badger (who I think was called Basil) who was a detective and would hunt down and find whatever the other residents of the forest had lost – usually a cake, or necklace, or fishing rod. Probably in this day and age he'd find a dead body and be led on some huge epic journey through the seedy forest underbrush to find that there was a fraternity of evil stoats running everything. (Actually, that's not a bad idea – if I was a writer, I'd do something with that.)

Anyway, Ruby and I were both really into this series and chose it to talk about in the first meeting. We'd chosen different books in the series, our preferred favourites, but it was enough to lay the foundations of a friendship. It would soon lead to us being asked to take to the stage together to talk more about the books.

In an effort to get more of the kids interested in reading, the head had organised an assembly which would involve two students from each year talking about their favourite books. Whether we volunteered or were nominated I no longer remember, but Ruby and I were the ones for our year.

Ruby was due to speak first, talking about the plot of this book which involved one of the characters – I believe Mrs Vole – being pregnant and how she was trying to keep it secret from her husband Mr Vole so she could surprise him on Father's Day, or something like that. It was quite forward thinking for the time. How many pregnant animals does one see in literature? Mine was about Rupert Rabbit, who was trying to find his friends but was unable to track any of them down, because they were off planning a surprise party for his birthday. I forget what the badger had to do with any of this.

Just before the assembly began, Mrs Marsden asked us if we'd fetch some poster paints from the art supply cupboard for the post-assembly lesson. To this day I'll still never understand why she asked us, given she had a whole class of other kids to do her bidding. The closest I've ever come to a theory is that she was trying to take our minds off the upcoming endeavour.

The art supplies cupboard was near the staffroom so, entrusted with the key, Ruby and I trotted off to find the poster paints required, unlocking the door and yanking it open by its heavy metal handle. I brushed my hand against the wall to find the interior light switch and flicked it, bathing the shelves in weak light. Ruby followed me inside and we were so distracted by the mountainous supplies of sugar paper, paintbrushes, oil paints, sticks of charcoal, boxes of dried pasta, tubs of glitter, safety scissors, glue pots, bottles of PVA, chalk, hidden bottles of gin, sketchbooks, fabric swatches, abandoned projects from previous classes and coloured pencils that we didn't properly register the door clicking locked behind us.

We became aware of our predicament once we'd selected a rainbow of colours in little lidded pots – Ruby realised that she still had hold of the key and we were on the wrong side of the door. The door was thick and designed so it could only be unlocked from one side, although why that was the case was lost to us.

'If we shout do you think they'll hear us?' said Ruby, biting her lip and shaking like she was suffering from a bad case of tectonic shift. I was thinking that the assembly would be starting any moment without us, and the panic had caused my brain to revert to a prehistoric form and demand that my bladder empty itself soon before I had to run. I put the paints down and tugged on the handle a few times, but the door didn't move.

'We can try it,' I said, so we both shouted, our mouths pressed up against the door, screaming for help. No one came. I wanted to cry, but fought back the urge. I bashed my fists against the door, but it was thick and they had no effect. Everyone else was in assembly, I guessed, but surely they'd notice that we were missing. After all, we were to be star performers.

Ruby slumped down on the floor and hugged her knees, her lip trembling. She looked at me with the look of a child who has just learnt that Santa doesn't exist and said, 'What if they never find us?'

'They will,' I said, bending down and stroking her shoulder. 'Mrs Marsden will notice in a minute and they'll come find us. She knows where we went.'

In a show of what was probably one of the most disorganised and shameful moments ever witnessed in a British primary school, we were locked in the cupboard for half an hour. In the end we had a piece of sugar paper with HELP charcoaled onto it ready to slip under the door when someone outside called our names. No one bothered explaining to us why it had taken so long – we were seven, so what did we matter? – but I presume our parents received explanations.

It was definitely an episode that wasn't going to be forgotten in a hurry, but in that half an hour Ruby and I grew closer. We chatted about nothing in particular, the way that small children do, riffing on television shows, books we liked and favourite toys, but the sensation of being trapped in a small cupboard surrounded by so much junk was something that only we could understand and share. If I ever saw a crack in Ruby's eternally bouncy demeanour again – before first contact, of course – I don't remember it, and so I later came to think she had shared something more with me than she had meant to. Even at seven, you know how and when it might be best to hide your feelings.

Because of the drama, we never did get to do our presentation in assembly, but it didn't matter. We'd each gained a new best friend instead, and friendship is the one thing that can top reading in its importance and excitement.

That and alcohol, but we were still a long way to go until we discovered that.

Tall, thin, quiet and erudite, Alex Playfair is the polar opposite of everyone that Ruby dated during her teenage and university years. They didn't get together until after they'd both graduated from their universities (her Reading, him Canterbury Christ Church) and since then the course of love has run smooth, but it took long enough to get there.

It transpired, in time, that Alex had fancied Ruby since they were eleven years old and he'd watched her playing netball when he should have been playing rugby. It actually turned out that there were a number of girls in the year he was obsessed with, but Ruby was the one he carried a candle for with a light the size of Betelgeuse. He was far too shy to do anything about it though, and instead looked on from the sidelines as from fourteen to twenty she dated a string of dark, loud, domineering boys. She and Alex had friends in common, so often ended up at parties together, sometimes talking to one another, with her oblivious throughout to the fact that he would have rearranged the constellations for her if she'd simply asked.

It was only post-bachelors-graduation and at the start of their PGCEs (both commuting to Brighton) that Ruby realised that maybe Alex wasn't such a bad catch. Annie was perhaps the only one who may have had any concerns as she'd dated Alex for a few months a couple of years before, but she and Ruby were friends through me and Lara, so it wasn't a case of stealing a friend's ex.

Within a year they had moved in together. He had dropped out of his PGCE to work for a small Internet start-up company that had since gone from strength to strength. They were also supported by generous parents on both sides who wanted to see their children succeed in their endeavours, meaning that nothing came across as a struggle and they could dedicate rather more time to cultivating their relationship than others may have done.

Their lives together are catalogue comfortable. Although they've been shacked up for such a long time, there are still no signs of wedding bells in the air, and we assume no hidden receipts from jewellers in Alex's desk drawers. In fact, on the outside everything looks so perfect in their little paradise that I've always wondered if it is.

While no evidence exists for them to have ever even shared one cross word with one another, I (and indeed Lara and Iris, too) have often contemplated the idea that it's a very clever front for two people who are apparently engaged in a relationship that is beyond the realms of normal pleasantness, but actually are always two minutes away from beheading one another.

I think, deep down, we're all a bit jealous.

Twelve

Convergence

Quarter of an hour or so later, during which time we've stood there dumbfounded and exchanging little more than repeated whispers of 'Oh my God', there is a swift rapping on the door and it opens with such ferocity that I think it might burst off its hinges. We scream and Catsby leaps up like he's been electrocuted and shoots off into the corner between the bookcase and the sofa. It isn't aliens. Kay bowls in like a tiny whirlwind, mascara-streaked tears running down her face. She runs at me and throws her arms around my waist and I'm stunned for a second, before returning the gesture, squeezing her tight.

'What's the matter?' I gasp, fearing the worst of Jay, but he follows in a moment later, phone clamped to his ear, talking in a low, sombre voice. Kay lets go of me and falls down on the sofa, crying into her palms. Ruby sits down next to her and slides a comforting arm over her quivering shoulders.

'No, it's fine, um, well, I'll be in touch,' Jay says into the phone. 'Yeah, I know. Yes. I love you too.' He gulps out a goodbye and hangs up. His hands are shaking. 'Hi guys, sorry to barge in like this.' Polite to a fault, as usual.

'Under the circumstances... I don't think... um... well... did you see it?'

'Yeah, we did,' Jay says, sitting the other side of Kay and taking over comforting duties from Ruby, who leaps back up to Alex's protective embrace. 'ITV announced that New York had been invaded.' A hand involuntarily leaps to my mouth. Kay's family. We, tough as it is, must fear the worst. I go to the kitchen and pour a large glass of whisky for Kay, which she glugs back, tears still streaming down her face. I ask Jay, 'What about you?'

'Mum and Dad are alright,' he shrugs. 'The Midlands are supposedly safe. Scotland isn't, though.' Alex picks up the remote control and skips through the channels, all of them showing empty news-rooms, panic in Norway, or the snowy fuzz of inactivity. Facebook and Twitter become our news source and we skip through updates.

'Not just Scotland,' I say, flicking through the statuses of people who haven't yet considered that there might be more important things to do at the moment. 'Brighton, Oxford, Cardiff, London...' I think briefly of Gavin-and-Frederik. Other statuses talk about other countries falling. Spain is inundated. I wonder if Lara-and-Steve are safe at sea. Are the oceans any safer than the land?

It becomes too much and I excuse myself, slipping out of the front door to sit on the low wall that separates the pavement from the grotty patch of brown grass that constitutes my front garden. I light up a cig-arette and let the nicotine calm down my brain, which is struggling with the idea that I'll never see Lara-and-Steve again. And Gavin too.

'Mind if I join you?' Jay says, sitting down next to me. I offer him a cigarette and we both sit there smoking for a few moments. I notice that, sweetly, despite the impending collapse of civilisation, he not only drove here but has parked his Mini neatly in front of the house.

'What are we going to do?' he says, lifting his sunglasses up onto his forehead, his brown eyes shot with red and worry.

'I don't know,' I say, adding, 'Why did you come to me?'

'Kay said that you shouldn't be alone,' he says, although he sounds embarrassed by it. It's one of the misconceptions about being alone. People assume that if you're alone, you're lonely, but I don't think that's always the case. It's nice to know, however, that my friends care enough to worry about me given everything else.

There's a cry and we look up to see Shell-and-Terry pelting down the road towards us. I think at first they might be rushing past to Terry's parents' house, but instead they stop and Shell throws her arms around me, knocking the cigarette from my hand. I don't remember the last time Shell hugged me – she's not especially tactile outside of the bedroom, and I'm not welcome there.

One may wonder why my friends seem so intent on surrounding me, but I don't know if I can answer that. I've always been lucky with my friends. They've been there for me through the difficult times and, in turn, as far as I know, I've been there through all of theirs.

There's a lot to be said for simple loyalty, and it's about to mean even more soon. I've always (whenever possible) done right by my friends and while they've always had other people besides me – we've never exactly lived in one another's pockets like friends in any sitcom you care to name – they think me worth keeping around, for whatever reason. I'm sounding a little maudlin, and more than a little vain, so I'll move on.

Terry bends over to catch his breath and I prise Shell off me. She smells of cigarettes and apricots.

'Are your families OK?' I ask.

'Mum and Dad are in Dubai and I can't get hold of them,' says Terry, speaking with little emotion. The army kicks some of that out of you, from what I've seen. 'Shell's dad is alright. He said there's nothing in Portsmouth yet.' The question of Shell's two younger brothers, both at Birmingham University, is left unanswered, and I don't probe further.

'Go inside, there's wine and whisky and… I dunno, help yourself,' I say. Shell squeezes my shoulder and vanishes into the house. Terry stays and folds his arms, his tight green shirt struggling to contain his ridiculous biceps.

'We need to come up with a plan,' he says. 'I don't know if we'll be able to survive forever, but we have to do what we can. The women need protecting.'

'Those girls don't need protection,' I say, jerking a thumb over my shoulder to indicate the gathered. 'Shell once punched her ex-boyfriend in the face and broke his nose when he cheated on her, Kay spends half her life in the gym, and no one can ruin Ruby's mood for long. If anything, it's us that need looking after.'

'Whatever,' says Terry. 'But we still need a plan. Do you have any weapons?'

'Yeah, under my bed is my weapons cache,' I say, with sarcastic enthusiasm. 'Fourteen machine guns, nine pistols and a tank! Help me get them out, will you?' Terry takes a moment to realise that I'm kidding. Jay is looking around at the other houses.

'Do you think anyone here has a gun?' he says. 'If this was America, it would be easy.'

'I'm not knocking the British laws against gun ownership,' I say, 'but this is one of those rare times when you sort of wish they weren't in place.' I think for a moment, then snap my fingers, remembering. 'Three doors up, Mr Grossman. He goes off and hunts pheasants and rabbits and whatnot every summer. He must have guns.'

'Right,' says Terry, looking happy. 'Let's go and ask him for them.'

'He's probably not there,' I say. 'I haven't seen him for days.'

'I don't reckon it's going to be as simple as just asking for them,' says Jay. 'Is that Pete?' I look up and Peregrina-and-Pete are thundering down the road at a considerable pace. They are followed by others, each with a face shaped by panic, terror. A couple of doors open across the road and neighbours dash for their cars.

'Everybody inside!' shouts Pete and, without giving it much thought, we bundle back into the house, Peregrina slamming the door shut behind her. We look at the two newcomers but, before they can speak, our attention is snatched away by activity in the street. People, neighbours, are running past the window at a fair speed. Some people jump into cars, in various states of half-dress. Some have bags, but most don't. Panic is on the streets of South Greenfield and we turn back to Pete, knowing exactly what he's going to say.

'There's a ship landed on the edge of town,' he reveals. 'The news is on the radio.' Almost as quickly as it filled, the road is almost empty again, a few abandoned dogs following loyally behind the vanished crowd, sniffing one another, hoping that one of them knows what's happening. A tremor of fear runs through the room as it becomes horrifyingly real.

'Guys, I'm going to get some guns,' I say. 'Who's coming with me?'

There's a brief moment of inactivity, and then eight hands shoot into the air.

Thirteen

Jay-and-Kay

I count the freckles on my hands for the umpteenth time. Seven on the left, ten on the right. The food bag sits empty next to me. I drank the whole thing, and my hunger pangs have lessened substantially, but I would've rather had a bacon sandwich or a KFC bucket.

Actually, I could really do with a drink. Something strong and unapologetic. On the rocks. My mind plays in some lyrics to a track by Burnt Fudge, an indie band we all loved, which in turn leads it wandering to what I remember of the drunkest night of my life – the night I met Jay-and-Kay.

Jay and Kay Booker-Hines have to be discussed together because when I met them they already came as a pair. I met Jay first, at a party at Lara's house five or so years ago. We were twenty-one, and Lara was partying for one final time before she moved back to Cardiff to do her master's degree in Social Work.

I was an absolute mess, having got stuck into some vile Turkish alcohol that tasted of aniseed and regret. I found myself in the garden retching behind the rhododendrons, Burnt Fudge's latest single blaring out the back door, when a soft voice rose up from behind me to ask if I was OK. I didn't recognise it, so turned round and straightened myself up.

Jay was a few inches taller than me, helped by a grey trilby perched far back on his head, in danger of slipping off at any minute. I'd seen him on the edge of the party throughout the night but we hadn't spoken, and I remember being struck by the kindness he displayed in that moment. Someone he didn't know was in a bad way, so he tried to help.

'I'm Jay, are you alright?'

'Dexter,' I choked out. 'Hang on.' I raised a finger and turned again, firing a stream of puke into the flowerbed. I wiped my mouth with the back of my hand and felt very shaky. Jay placed his hands on my shoulders.

'Come on, mate, let's get you some water, come on now,' he said, and with the care of a nurse led me into the house and up to the bathroom where he sat me on the edge of the bath. A glass of water was thrust into my hand and he said, 'I'll get you some food, don't move.'

By the time he came back, this time with Steve behind him, I had fallen backwards into the bath and the water from the glass had soaked my shirt. The boys hauled me back up again and sat me on the lid of the toilet instead. I was given a bread roll and, somewhat mournfully, I tore into it, supplementing each swallow with a gulp of water.

I'm not sure how long I sat there, and I might even have fallen asleep, but when I next looked up, Jay had gone but there was a small girl with sharp, foxy eyes sitting on the floor, a glass of red wine in hand.

'Are you watching me?' I asked, trying to smile. I think I thought I was flirting.

'I was told to keep an eye on you,' she said.

'You're not English,' I said, listening to her accent. 'Is that Welsh?'

She laughed and said, 'No, I'm American. Are you feeling any better?'

'I don't feel great,' I said. My glass was empty, so the girl stood, filled it up and handed it back to me.

'What the hell have you been drinking?' she asked. She clocked that I wasn't in a fit state to answer and continued. 'I'm Kay, by the way. You're Dexter, right?' I inclined my head in a weak nod a couple of times. I either asked or was told to go and lie down, so I found myself on the bed in the spare room, phasing in and out of the universe for a couple of hours. Sometimes when I opened my eyes, Jay was there. Other times, it was Kay. Once it was Lara, but she was even drunker than me and was trying to be quiet by hushing herself with the volume of a leaf blower, a finger pressed to her wine-stained lips. When she tiptoed out of the room, she fell over.

When I woke up again and my head had recovered enough to allow me to make a movement, I sat up carefully and realised that it was morning. Leaning against the wardrobe, her head on his shoulder, and his arm wrapped protectively around her, each of them half-covered in a blue blanket, were Jay-and-Kay. They looked sweet, and my brain thought how lovely it would be if they were to get together. Two of the nicest people in the world – my benefactors on the drunkest night of my life; it was only right that they should find each other.

The sun moved round to let a beam of light burst through the partially drawn curtains and it hit Jay right in the face, causing him to wake with a start. He looked up at me and smiled.

'Hi, mate, how are you doing?'

'Did you stay here all night?' I asked. I was aware that my other friends who had been at the party – Lara, Ruby, Steve – were not present.

'We were staying over anyway, and Lara was in no fit state to look after you herself,' he said. 'I volunteered to make sure you didn't swallow your own tongue or something. You weren't in a good way last night. Is everything OK? You don't have to tell me.'

'My granddad died a few weeks ago,' I said, bluntly. A sad moment in anyone's life, sure, but generally not one to get paralytic over. Jay intuited that there was more to it than that and nodded, not probing any further. Kay stirred, rubbing her eyes with delicate short-fingered hands.

'Oh, awake then?' she grinned. 'God, my back aches.'

'Thank you both so much for last night,' I said, standing up carefully. I felt wobbly but I needed to go to the toilet. 'And it looks like some other good came out of it. You two should really consider going on a date. You're both amazing.' The pair looked at each other as if having a silent conversation told through smiles. Kay held up her left hand, and a diamond glinted in the morning sun.

'We're married,' she grinned, wider than any Wonderland cat.

'Bloody hell, that was quick,' I said, scratching my head and walking off to the bathroom.

They've never let me live down that moment of utter stupidity.

Jay and Kay met seven years ago on a forum for *Discworld* fans. He had the username 'LeicesterLewton', she was 'Woman_at_arms9' and it was love at first keystroke. Their conversations dominated threads on the forum, to the point that other posters noticed and passed various comments on the situation. They didn't care. It would've been perfect except for the slight issue that he was in Cardiff and she was in Brooklyn.

Because this is the twenty-first century, and it's not possible to hold back true love regardless of how many border control officials stand in your way, within a matter of months Jay had flown into JFK International Airport to meet Kay in person for the first time. He didn't return for a month.

Once he did make it back, there was a gap of about five weeks before Kay returned the favour and touched down in Heathrow. She didn't return for two months. This kept up for a year or so, before they both conceded that living with almost perpetual jet lag wasn't conducive to their lifestyles or bank balances, and decided that they were going to take a massive leap, hurry the relationship along and move in together.

I'm told the debate was fierce as to where they would live but, in the end, they decided on the UK, as Jay still had his degree to finish up, and Kay had dropped out of hers to work and was stuck as a barely paid intern at a publishing house. The next issue was that, while they could indeed live together, it wasn't as simple as coming over and settling in. Kay needed to leap through a number of flaming hoops with immigration to get permission to stay in the country.

This was helped along by Jay proposing and the two rushing through a small wedding with the minimum amount of fuss. They still had to endure months of red tape and question-and-answer sessions in sterile government offices to prove they knew each other and that Kay, who is one of the tiniest and most inoffensive people in either the UK or the USA, wasn't here to cause trouble.

After marriage, they decided to settle in South Greenfield because there was a plethora of cheap, but nice, places to rent, and they could both commute to London, where they worked as editors for rival publishing houses. The fact that they worked in the same industry but under different logos was probably the only point of contention they had, but it did mean they spent an inordinate amount of time at book fairs and launches sneaking off to hotel rooms and public toilets to have sex. On their return, when people asked where they'd been, they were able to say they'd been schmoozing with the enemy for insider gossip. It wasn't strictly a lie, although their schmoozing actually occurred while they were making dinner or in bed.

Having never known them independently of one another, in my head I sometimes have difficulty prying apart their personalities. Because they are so similar in attitude and interests – if not in volume – as far as I can tell their relationship has been blissful from the moment they met. They bicker in that manner of middle-aged couples despite only being a year older than me, but I've always put it down to the fact that their whole relationship was rushed – they've got to the later stages of comfort and familiarity long before any of my other friends have.

They are so intrinsically linked as a unit it's rare to find them separated, meaning that many intimate details of their relationship have never leaked out. Maybe they do hate each other, but I doubt it. You can't fake it for that long.

Fourteen

Guns and Teeth

There is a short tussle and argument about who is coming. Peregrina explains that there is little point in everyone going as we'll just get in one another's way, which shuts everyone up, even if it doesn't necessarily appease them. Terry, being the only one in the room capable of actually using a gun, is a logical choice and might have more of an idea about what we're looking at. Since I have been designated host for doomsday, I insist on going too. Jay throws his hat into the ring and he's too polite for anyone to contradict him.

'I'll be your fourth,' says Ruby.

'No, I'll go,' Alex says, grabbing Ruby's wrist. 'It's not safe for you.'

'Don't you tell me what to do, Alex!' she snaps, wrenching free of his grip. Her wrist is white – he must've been grabbing her tighter than we realised. From the image they project of their relationship, it's very unlike them both. 'We're in danger here and if you think I'm going to play the little damsel in distress you've got another think coming. This isn't a fucking Disney film, this is real life, so shut up and let me go.' Without giving Alex time to get in a response, she storms from the room and Jay, Terry and I follow saying that we'll be back soon. The others wish us luck (except for Kay who is still, understandably, crying into her sleeves) and we slip out of the front door and go up to Mr Grossman's house.

Mr Grossman, Angus, was never the most pleasant of people to have living in your street – one of those wealthy eccentrics with the compromising problem that he no longer had any wealth. The story went that his family owned much of Berkshire or Buckinghamshire or Bedfordshire, but he'd been written out of a will so, while he was still invited up to the estate every summer to hunt game, he didn't have the money to indulge in his hobbies otherwise. And when you're eccentric without having the money to back it up, people just think you're mad.

I hope that the street's evacuation means that he won't be present. As we reach his front garden, the house looks quiet, but the front door remains closed.

'Don't think he's home,' says Jay. We pass through his creaky, paint-peeling gate and up the path. I knock twice, but there's not so much as a curtain twitch, so I figure that we're safe. We need to think of a way in.

'Ruby, you've got small hands, see if you can reach the inside door handle through the letterbox.' It's the best suggestion I've got but even then the house will likely still require a key rather than just a tug of the handle. Besides, Ruby's hands might be small, but her wrist would probably be required to be on backwards to do anything of use. Nevertheless, she gives it a shot and fails. Jay looks under the doormat, behind and inside a pair of mud-caked wellington boots, and runs his fingers through the topsoil of a wilting rose bush's stone pot.

'Nothing,' is his dejected conclusion. He's brushing his hands clean on his jeans when Terry shouts, 'DUCK!' We follow the order just in time and come within a hair's breadth of being hit in the face by a ceramic gnome he has hurled at the large window of the front door. The window doesn't break, but the gnome is no more, shattered into hundreds of tiny fragments peppering the doorstep.

'Little more warning next time, yeah?' I say, holding up my forefinger and thumb a tiny distance apart. I look at the shattered remains of the former garden resident. 'Well, that didn't work but we're definitely looking at the right idea. Find something heavy and we'll smash the window.' The house next door to Mr Grossman's, the one belonging to the Fisher family, has a rockery in its front garden, so Jay and Ruby run round and pick up a couple of large rocks. Jay hurls his at the window in the door but misses and it clatters against the wood and lands in one of the wellington boots. Ruby keeps hold of her rock and bashes it a few times against the glass until it shatters.

Carefully removing the sharp shards from around the edge, she reaches in and opens the door from the inside. It swings open silently against the thick carpeting and the smell of an abandoned house escapes. The end of the world has been under way for mere minutes and already everything is decomposing? I shake the thought from my head. It's ridiculous – Mr Grossman is clearly on holiday; the house has that fusty smell that holidaymakers leave behind.

'Grossman, emphasis on the gross,' says Ruby, sniffing the fetid air. 'How long do you think he's been away?'

'I'm not sure,' I say, moving forward to peering into the undisturbed living room. 'Let's hope it wasn't a hunting trip and he's left his guns. Otherwise we're screwed.'

'Aliens have landed, Dex,' says Jay, patting my shoulder. 'We're already screwed.'

'Where do you imagine you keep guns?' says Terry. I can only picture those gun cabinets that popular culture would have us believe exist in every house in the southern United States, but that would be a tad tacky for the English, so I suggest they're locked away upstairs somewhere. We make a cursory look around downstairs and head up to the next floor.

'Is it me, or is that smell getting worse?' says Ruby, grimacing.

'Maybe a bird got in and died,' I suggest, but already I know that the smell is too intense for a single bird, and an ugly thought pops into my head and sticks like Araldite. Terry has already reached the top of the stairs and pushes open a door. The intensity of the smell increases tenfold, and he scrunches up his shirt over his nose.

'It's not a bird,' he says, muffled. 'Keep her away.' He waves vaguely in Ruby's direction, although appears to have forgotten her name. I am not one to try and physically restrain any of my friends – it isn't worth the effort – so Ruby instead marches forward out of spite and promptly gags when she passes into the room. She runs back out again a moment later, disappears into the bathroom and we hear vomit hitting porcelain.

Jay goes into the room next, and I'm therefore the last of us to see Mr Grossman's fleshy, decomposing body propped up in bed, a paperback copy of *And Then There Were None*, saturated in leaked fluids, held loosely in his right hand. It's hard to say how long he's been like this, but maggots don't set up home in your mouth after one night. It's one of the most disgusting things I have ever seen in my life, and given that I've already seen two humans get turned into conjoined twins today, that's saying something.

'Not on holiday then,' says Jay. I try to tear my eyes from the body, its skin marbled in colours that no human should ever be. The bed-clothes look crispy, like liquids have soaked them and dried out several times. His face is bloated and almost unrecognisable. One of his eye-balls has been entirely removed – eaten by god knows what, or rotted away. I gag and have to leave the room. I move to a second bedroom and sit on the bed next to a pile of dusty hardbacks, breathing deeply through my mouth.

'Dex, you alright?' shouts Jay.

'I will be,' I reply. I look around the room, trying to replace the image of Mr Grossman's body with any other image, but can see no indication of any weaponry. 'Any sign of the guns?'

'Nothing in the wardrobe,' Ruby shouts back. Feeling weak, I get up and return to them, clutching my shirt in front of my mouth and nose. Jay is absent, although I see a shadow in the bathroom that suggests the smell has got too much for him as well. Ruby, either recovered or powering through the situation, is rummaging through drawers of shirts, ties and socks.

I kneel down and peek under the bed, finding a few suitcases. I drag one of them out, in burnished leather that would once have been con-sidered very fine but was battered by wear. Empty. I hook out a sec-ond and with an 'Ah, ha!' get the attention of the others.

Inside are three hunting rifles, a pistol and boxes of ammunition.

'Is that pistol legal, do you think?' I ask, pointing at it. 'Is any of it?'

'Hard to say,' says Terry, rubbing his stubbled chin. 'I don't really know the ins and outs of the laws. Anyway, they'll do.' I reach under for a third suitcase but, aside from a balled-up sock, there's nothing in that one either. I click the gun suitcase shut again and we make to leave, Jay meeting us on the landing, his skin a hue better suited to a stick of celery. It's not the sort of smell that you acclimatise to.

'What are we doing about Mr Grossman?' says Jay. We look at one another but no one says another word. None of us wants to be the one who says we're going to knowingly leave a body out to rot. Everyone deserves respect, even in death, but none of us are willing to touch the remains or spend time trying to dig a hole in the garden. Without a word, we go downstairs again and back onto the street, sucking in great lungfuls of clean air.

The dog comes from nowhere: a large Alsatian that I recognise as belonging to the scruffy-looking bloke who lives further up the road and keeps very strange hours. It's not a friendly dog and approaches us barking and baring wet, yellow teeth. There's a demonic look in its eyes, but also the hint of fear, of a creature that doesn't know what to do.

'Back to mine, run!' I shout and, losing traction for a moment in my desert boots, head off back down the road. The others race after me, but the dog is fast and leaps at Ruby. She screams as she's flung to the ground by the heavy dog. I turn around and swing the suitcase in its direction, but my aim is way off and I miss. It's enough of a distraction though and the dog turns to look at me, affronted. Terry takes the opportunity to scoop Ruby up and carry on running.

The dog barks furiously at me and Jay, confused and angry. I jerk the suitcase at it again, but this time it stands its ground. Jay picks up a smallish rock and flings it at the dog's head which turns out to be a big mistake, as the dog lunges for him and before he can leap out of the way, or I can get between them, it sinks its grotesque fangs into his leg, piercing the denim and causing Jay to scream in agony.

Our lives have descended into those of farcical distress quicker than you can say, 'Is it just me or could those lights in the sky be incoming aliens?' Jay falls but the dog makes no attempt to let go. Blood seeps into his jeans and I make the next aim count, swinging the suitcase a final time at the dog's head. Leather connects with bone and the Alsatian removes itself, although a tooth is left behind, embedded in Jay's leg. The dog barks at me like a demon possessed, and I'm aware of further screaming.

I turn around, not really wishing to take my eyes off the dog, but also curious as to what's making that noise, to find Kay running at us, clutching a wing mirror she appears to have ripped off a parked car. Before I can stop her, she's pounced at the dog and smacked it hard between the eyes with the plastic casing, blood squirting out onto the mirror and her black jumper.

'Leave. My. Husband. Alone!' she shouts, punctuating each word with another thwack of the wing mirror against the Alsatian's cranium. It takes another full minute or so of her screaming and shouting before she stops and stands up, the dog in front of us with a smashed-in head, blood leaking out onto the pavement. She drops the wing mirror, sweeps her brown fringe from her eyes and stoops over Jay, pulling her jumper off and winding it around his leg in a vain attempt at stemming the flow of blood.

'Help me get him up,' she says, and it takes me a moment to notice that she's talking to me. Terry has reappeared by this point too, takes one look at the dog and raises his eyebrows in appreciation and shock. He takes the suitcase from me and Kay and I help Jay up to his feet. With great care, we help him back to my place, where everyone else is gathered, watching the news-less television and trawling the Internet for information. There is a flurry of panic and action when they see what has happened to Jay. It's like no one wants to be seen doing nothing.

I direct Shell and Alex to where I keep my first-aid kit, while Terry, Peregrina and I take a look at our spoils.

Fifteen

Annie-and-Matt

Annie Dickens and I almost never met and, perhaps, if the parallel universe theory is correct, this is the only universe in which we did. She and Priti had known each other since way back when, having had martial arts classes together when they were very young, but I never met her in those days. And after a few years, Annie and her family moved to Leeds.

That could've been the end of it.

But years later, in that way that makes you wonder if there's a god of coincidence moving things around behind the scenes, Annie's parents moved back to South Greenfield and Priti and Annie ended up at the same university and became friends again, picking up where they'd left off (although with more booze and poor decision-making).

Annie remained an enigma to me though, glimpsed through photographs online but never seen in person. It never made any sense. When not at university we lived in the same town, we shared a best friend, and if Priti's tales were to be believed, we had a huge amount in common. Yet whenever Priti invited us both out with her, something always came up and one of us was unable to make it.

That was until one September evening when Priti invited both of us for a drink and the universe complied to let us both be free and not tugged out of the ring by a last-minute emergency or forgotten prior arrangement. I turned up at The Ship, a pub we were frequenting at that point, and did a couple of loops around the low-ceilinged rooms, searching out Priti. There was no sign of her or anyone who looked like the Facebook photos of Annie that I was trying to reconstruct in my mind.

I fired off a text to Priti and decided to get a drink in, catching the attention of the barman and ordering a glass of wine. Next to me at the bar, a girl sat playing with her phone, although how she managed to see the screen over her spectacularly large chest was a mystery. She was otherwise petite, with dark blonde hair dip-dyed lighter at the ends. When she looked up, her steely grey eyes met my green ones as she searched them for something, like she'd spotted a flash of gold at the bottom of an ornamental lake and wondered if it was koi or coin.

'This is going to sound cheesy,' I said, leaning towards her to be heard over the chatter of the guys on a nearby table. She flinched back a little. 'Sorry, but have we met?'

'No.' Her voice is quiet but firm. She thinks I'm hitting on her and this is an absolute shut down.

'No, sorry, I'm not hitting on you, I swear!' I said, raising my hands in surrender. 'I thought you looked familiar. Sorry, I'll leave you to your evening.' She softened slightly, but not much, like she was deciding whether to believe me or not.

'It's OK,' she said, reaching out and fingering the stem of her wine glass. 'I actually was thinking the same thing about you. It's like I've seen you before, but I can't place you.' She gives a half-smile. 'Are you local?'

'Always lived here,' I said, taking a sip of my wine. 'How about you?'

'On and off,' she shrugged, 'although on at the moment.'

'Dexter.'

'Annie.'

A groan of dawning realisation burst from both our mouths and we laughed politely.

'So, at last I meet the famous Annie?' I said, raising my glass. She raised hers too and we clinked them together.

She said, 'And I meet the infamous Dexter.'

'Infamous?' I laughed again. 'I don't think I'd go that far. I dread to think what Priti has told you. Don't believe a word of it.'

'No, actually, you come out of it fairly well,' she smiled. She had a very pretty smile when she didn't feel like she was defending herself from creepy pub patrons. 'What's she said about me?'

'Many things, all of them good,' I said. I pointed at a table that had become free and said, 'Shall we?' We moved and continued chatting over our wine and the river of conversation between us never clogged, meaning that by the time Priti arrived we'd moved on far from favourite films and books and were embedded in a conversation about whether or not we'd ever unforgivably betrayed anyone.

Priti at first seemed put out by the fact we'd managed to bond without her there, but she took it on the chin and joined in as the conversation slipped round to relationships.

From that moment, Annie and I became good friends, meeting every few weeks for a non-stop barrage of conversation over a bottle of wine. In some areas she was intensely private, but in others she was wonderfully, refreshingly open and I can't remember any cross words passing between us that had a lasting effect, although there was a certain fire about her that I had a feeling would spell bad news for me if I found myself burnt by it. She wore a mask of cynicism, constructed from the remains of a number of failed relationships, but it was clear to everyone that it would only take the right man to remove it.

That would happen a few months before the invasion.

The story of how Annie met Matt Sullivan changes on an almost daily basis. No one was present and the details change depending who is telling the story, who is hearing the story, how drunk anyone is and, hell, probably even things like the weather and the pollen count.

However, the general gist is something like this:

It was a Friday/Saturday/Tuesday afternoon/evening and they were both in a local pub/bar/bowling alley with their separate groups of friends, although who these friends were has yet to be established. Either immediately, after a while, or as they were leaving, he approached her or she approached him and they introduced themselves.

He offered to buy her a drink – a wine/vodka and Coke/lemonade – and they got talking about music/films/art. When Annie's friends were leaving, they either asked if she was coming with them or left without saying anything, and so Matt had to drive her home. It was on this short drive home to her house (or maybe his flat) that they discovered that, while she was twenty-six, he was actually five years her junior, despite having two/three/four inches on her height-wise and looking around her age. Originally daunted (or deciding immediately that she didn't care), she and Matt shared a kiss at some varying time and place.

The next day, he called or she texted asking the other one out on a date that night. They went for dinner, or a film, or to a bar and discovered that their views on music, politics and/or television overlapped considerably. Later that night (or the next day, or maybe even the night before), they discovered that they were also sexually compatible. That happened four months ago and Annie has since been wrapped up in her world with her new plaything, who she's already pinning her hopes on for an eventual wedding ring (or perhaps not).

Suffice to say, we believe that they actually met on Tinder and are, for whatever reason, too ashamed to tell us.

Sixteen

The Fellowship

The nine of us – ten if you count Catsby, and I do – are ready to leave. The street outside is silent. A few more people and stray dogs have run past, but we've seen no aliens. We have decided to make a move to Fairmill where we can hide in the school, given that it's bigger and easier to find somewhere to tuck ourselves away, as well as having more supplies. We're walking. None of us knows how to hotwire a car, so the only car close enough that we could definitely get into is Jay's Mini, which is far too small and, while it would be quicker if we could go that way, it's one more thing to go wrong.

We collect up non-perishable food from my cupboards (there's surprisingly little as I've a bad habit of too-regular takeaways), the remains of my first-aid kit, and some of my jumpers that we can use for warmth as and when. Peregrina has hold of Catsby and is stroking him gently. She says she's calming him down, but I think it's actually doing more to help her. Terry has divided up the weapons.

I've been given the pistol and have it tucked into my belt. Terry has shown me how to work the safety so I don't accidentally shoot my arse off. The three rifles have gone to Shell, Pete and Terry himself. Jay is in agony still, and everyone is wary of touching him in case they do more damage. Pete used his switchblade to extract the tooth, and a couple of tea towels tied around Jay's leg are doing their best to stop the flow of blood. They are already stained red. We've fashioned a crutch for him out of an old spade I found in the shed. Kay clings to Ruby, although her eyes don't dare leave Jay for more than a second at a time.

'Everybody ready?' I say, thinking how ridiculous we look. There is a quiet chorus of assent and we move for the front door, not going too fast because of Jay who is helped to his feet by his wife. His face is sullen and grey under the brim of his ever-present trilby, and he's clearly frustrated he might be considered a burden, but no one is going to give him a chance to be self-sacrificing and insist on staying behind. All for one, and all that jazz.

We step into the street and head north. Our plan is to follow the train tracks up through St Simon's, Blackpond, and into Fairmill.

It isn't long before Peregrina points out the alien ship on the horizon to the east. It appears even bigger than it did on the television. My heart beats like a cornered mouse, and I'm sure I can't be the only one. The streets are already pretty quiet, just the occasional person with panicked eyes running away from something. Two or three cars pass too, ignoring the speed limit and with terrified-looking adults in the front and screaming children in the back.

It may have been a short matter of time, but dogs are already the dominant life form here. They look slightly confused and we thankfully find none that are aggressive. Some of them approach us for a sniff and a pat, but they soon scarper again, hunting out the trails that their humans have left behind. There is no sign of any alien activity either, save for the towering ship which stares down like one of the monoliths in *2001: A Space Odyssey*.

Shell-and-Terry are leading the way, followed by Peregrina still clinging to the nervously quiet Catsby. He's not much of an outdoors cat, but he's not showing much concern for the time being. Alex and I come next, although we're not talking – no one's talking – and he keeps looking around with jerky, fearful movements, reminding me of a meerkat. Behind us are Jay-and-Kay and Ruby, the two girls acting as supports, which is somewhat awkward given the fact he's also trying to hold a spade-crutch and they're both a good few inches shorter than he is. Pete brings up the rear, his gun ready.

After twenty minutes or so, going slower to account for Jay's leg, we arrive at the train station and stand on the northbound platform, looking down at the tracks.

'Are we safe to walk on them?' asks Alex.

'Isn't there one that we're not supposed to touch?' I ask, aware that we didn't give any of this much thought. What *are* we doing?

'They might not even have power going to them any more,' Jay winces through gritted teeth. 'Throw something metal onto the tracks, see if they spark. If they do, we should stay off them.' We look around for something metal and I wonder foolishly how easy it would be to rip apart the black railings that line the platform. A degree in English Literature is proving to be useless in an end-of-the-world scenario. It's not like Jane Eyre had these troubles and I can learn from her.

Down the end of the ramp that the staff use to get onto the rails are a few unused bits of railway track. Terry and Pete pass their guns to Ruby-and-Alex and go to examine how easy they are to throw. The rest of us stand around and look for any signs of aliens, or indeed an unexpected flash of mauve or burgundy in the corner of our eyes. A signal.

'What do you think those colours are about?' says Peregrina. 'First the big yellow flash, followed by little ones. Global psychological trauma?'

'I think it's how they communicate,' says Jay. He points at a bench with his spade and Ruby and Kay ease him down onto the malformed wooden slats, soaked and warped by years of British summers and no shelter. 'Humans have always been too obsessed with the idea that aliens, if we ever met them, would communicate like we do, but obviously not. If you ask me, they're speaking to each other and, since we can see colour, we're picking up what they're saying.'

This sinks in.

'And the grey cloud they killed those people with?' asks Shell. Jay, despite the pain he's pretending he's not in, appears to be enjoying putting his years of reading science fiction novels to use.

'Nanobots,' he says. Aside from Kay, who nods along with him, the rest of us look at him with a distinct lack of understanding. 'Oh, come on, nanobots!' Ruby shakes her head, Alex shrugs, I rummage in my memory banks through old episodes of *Doctor Who* and Douglas Adams novels, and finally say, 'That's super-tiny robots isn't it?' Jay goes to answer, but obviously gets another burst of pain. Kay squeezes his hand and, once sure that he's not about to keel over, continues on his behalf.

'Yeah, nanobots are very tiny robots that scientists reckon we'll be able to use to do things like surgery from inside the body,' says Kay. 'There are other applications too, but that one gets talked about a lot.'

'But that's hugely distant tech, isn't it?' I say, and immediately feel stupid. If aliens are capable of crossing the vastness of space and arrive in one piece on another planet, they're clearly more advanced in the technology department than humans. As a species, we're still impressed with *Angry Birds*.

'My theory,' says Jay, sharing a look with Kay, 'well, our theory, is simply that those grey clouds are thousands and thousands of nanobots that are supposed to merge people. The aliens have two heads so it's not too big a leap to assume that they were once singular.'

'We wondered if it was a breeding thing,' Kay puts in. 'Maybe they merge and become one being to breed, like anglerfish and stuff. If that's the case, they're trying to use the same technology on us, but the nanobots can't deal with human biology and it's messing up and causing those grotesque things we saw on the TV.'

As I wonder what anglerfish have got to do with it, Terry and Pete return and are confident that we can throw one or two of the spare metal parts onto the tracks. Shell and Alex go down with them to help lift, while Jay, Kay, Peregrina, Ruby, Catsby and I remain seated, all lost in our own thoughts. If Jay and Kay are right and, given the amount of science fiction they consume, it's probable, then humanity is even more fucked than I had first realised.

At least, most of humanity is. I can see a glimmer, a faint light at the end of the tunnel, which suggests I could be alright, for now at least. But is it a light at the end of the tunnel, or an incoming locomotive?

My thoughts are interrupted by the clang of metal on metal.

'Tracks are dead,' Pete shouts up. We make our way down onto the tracks, Jay-and-Kay moving slowly, but with Shell and her gun behind them, ready to take out anything that tries to make an ambush attack. We walk in single file up the railway, Terry leading us. That doesn't fill me with masses of confidence as, even though all he needs to do is follow the tracks, he gives the impression of someone who could get lost walking up a spiral staircase. I can't even begin to work out how long it'll take us to get to St Simon's, the next stop, and no one is much in the mood to do mental arithmetic and provide an answer.

After about half an hour walking, Jay apologising the whole time for slowing us down, St Simon's station comes into view. There is no one there. A few pigeons strut about the platforms, bobbing their heads and pecking at the concrete, like it's another ordinary day on Planet Earth. We decide that we should rest here for a while.

Shell goes first up onto the platform, wielding her rifle and looking around for any evidence of non-pigeon life. As someone who always comes across as so well put together, even after a bottle of wine, it is strange to see her holding a gun, her brown hair windswept and out of control. She looks back down to us, her green eyes trying to hide their fear but failing, and nods that it's safe. Everyone follows her up, with me bringing up the rear this time, looking backwards along the deserted track, my pistol pointed ready, even when my muscles protest at being held aloft.

We move into the small café on the platform and rip open some food, eating crisps and chocolate bars, and slumping down onto the hard, plastic seating. I wipe my brow and it feels like it's been days since I last slept, but it's barely three o'clock and I know I woke up this morning with far fewer worries. Time gets skewed when the world goes to shit. I eat my Twix and wonder if this is an elaborate dream, like the one I had a few months ago where zombies were chasing me through a dockyard, and I ended up escaping to my parent's old house and destroying the stairs so they couldn't get me. That was about as vivid as this.

Peregrina has let Catsby down after he got fidgety in her arms, and he's curled up under a table, looking slightly perturbed by the whole situation. He keeps looking at me like this is my fault. I check my phone, but there's nothing to report. I've got 52% battery, so I turn off everything that might speed up the discharge, but whatever I do, it isn't going to last long.

Jay-and-Kay are snuggled up close on a pair of seats. His trouser leg is wet with blood, despite the tea towels wrapping the injury. His face still hasn't returned to a normal colour.

Colour.

A flash of mauve in my left eye, and a shot of pumpkin orange in the right. My heart stops and we freeze.

'What do we do?' whispers Peregrina. Everyone looks at someone else, as if one of us has the answer. We don't need to discuss what it means, but we do need a plan. However, it's very hard to make a plan when you don't know what you're up against. How many are there? Which direction are they coming from? Are they capable of sensing us? There are too many unknowns in this equation.

We sit quietly for a moment longer, as a line of colour – various shades of red and yellow – snakes across our pupils. I have the horrible feeling that we're surrounded. I raise the pistol and notice that my hand is shaking like a jellyfish with Parkinson's. This is a nightmare.

Pete stands up and creeps towards the door, his ursine figure blotting out the window and putting himself in direct line of potential fire. He's raised the rifle a little and his finger is on the trigger. He moves forward a couple of steps. Peregrina reaches out for him, feebly, but she doesn't dare speak, so he doesn't notice. Without turning around again, he speaks.

'Four of them,' he whispers, yet it still sounds like the clanging of Big Ben in the otherwise silent room. 'Move slowly out the way we came in, back onto the tracks, and we'll have to run.'

'Run?' whispers Kay, harshly. 'Jay isn't running anywhere!'

'I can if I have to,' he says, although I can't help but feel that it's false bravado. His leg is in a bad way – there was something wrong with that dog. He stands up, propping himself up with the spade and hobbles towards the door before anyone can stop him. Shell gets up and joins Pete, and they both stand there with guns aloft. I gesture that everyone without a gun needs to get a move on – Terry is to stay.

'We'll hold them back,' I mouth, not really believing it myself, but the others obey and move back out to the tracks. Catsby doesn't move; instead he sits under the table and licks himself, like none of this is his problem. He's changed his tune.

I get a sharp, stabbing pain behind my left eye and my field of vision fills with an orangey-mustard sort of colour which can only mean one thing. Bullets are flying and I can't tell if it's us or them. I click the trigger of the pistol a couple of times and feel the recoil down my arm, but I've got my eyes squeezed shut, so I don't know if I hit anything.

'Run, now! Follow the others!' shouts Pete and, without giving it much more thought, we turn on our heels and pile out of the door. I nearly run straight into the door frame, but dodge it in time.

'We got three of them,' says Terry as we haul ourselves down off the platform and onto the tracks, trying not to trip up and jog towards the others. We catch up to Jay-and-Kay, the others already considerably further ahead, although throwing looks over their shoulders every couple of steps. Jay is, as I predicted, struggling, and trying very hard to convince Kay to go on and save herself. She is refusing to do so. They're both crying, scared and clinging to one another, yet still moving forward one painful step at a time.

Terry tries to pick Jay up, but Jay refuses and lashes out. I've never seen him angry.

'Don't! Leave us!' he shouts. I look up and on the platform I see the remaining alien, even uglier in person than on the screen. Maybe it looks malevolent, but it doesn't have much of an expression. It's looking down at us though and presumably projecting something into our minds, as an ocean blue wisps through my field of vision. Terry has already turned and run; Shell and Pete are hovering. I don't want to go.

'Guys, you have to come on,' I plead. I risk a glance up and see the alien extracting its silver box. 'You need to come with us, please!' But Jay-and-Kay are ignoring me, instead staring into one another's eyes. Kay clasps her hands to Jay's face, whispering to him that she loves him.

'I will always love you,' she cries, 'Always. Remember that.'

'You too, angel,' warbles Jay. He sniffs and chuckles through his tears, 'Remember the cone of ham?' And she laughs too, despite herself. Some long-standing joke between the two of them, a joke that no one else will ever get, but had maybe solidified their relationship for some incalculable reason. Here stands proof that no matter how close I am to my friends, I will never have that intimacy with them. I feel a large hand grab my wrist and I'm pulled off, but not before I raise the pistol one final time and shoot a bullet at the alien.

Somehow it hits, and the alien's left head explodes into something that looks like stringy blue spaghetti bolognaise. It falls back, but it's still too late. A grey cloud is descending on the Englishman and the American, and I finally turn my head away when the first screams start.

When I do risk a look back, there is a bloody mess of flesh and ripped clothing on the tracks, with a perfectly undamaged trilby resting on top.

Seventeen

Iris-and-William

Iris Burke is the most recently acquired of my friends, the two of us having met three years ago in a staff meeting on the first day of term. The school, Fairmill Community College, was the same one that I had attended as a student from eleven to eighteen, which made the whole thing a little less scary and daunting than it could have been. I had, at least, a vague idea of where everything was, although it turned out that the administration offices had moved, the Geography and History departments had swapped around for some reason, and a new Drama block had been built.

A few of the staff were the same, although they looked much older than I remembered, and while a few recognised me, most of the ones who had taught me had left, being replaced by a new swathe of young men and women who looked like they were pretending to be adults in their parents' work clothes. This included me, in a pale pink shirt, grey trousers and leaf-green tie.

I had been collared in the corridor by the Head of English, Anita Joyce, and had thirty copies of *The War of the Worlds* thrust into my arms, which I was assured I would need for my first class. Before I could go and find my classroom, we were being shunted into the staff room for a pre-student encounter briefing.

Even at the time I thought it was a pointless endeavour, given that the last three days had been endless meetings, lesson plans and trying to remember everyone's names. Ruby was already deep in a conversation with her fellow history teachers, so I tried to manoeuvre myself to an empty seat, dropping several copies of the play as I did. The woman I sat next to picked them up for me and piled them at my feet with the others I put down. She was blonde with watery blue eyes and a large garnet embedded in a silver necklace. She was my age, I guessed, and we smiled politely at one another.

'Hello. New to the game?' she said.

'Yep, and bricking it,' I said with a nervous chuckle. The headmaster was faffing about with some papers at the front of the room and other teachers were still piling in. 'Sorry, I haven't seen you around yet. I don't know your name.'

'Oh, it's Iris.' She smiled and held out a small, soft hand for me to shake. 'You're English, I'm guessing? No wonder we haven't met yet; I teach Food Tech.'

'Ah, yes, other side of the school and curriculum,' I nodded. 'Dexter, by the way.'

'Nice name,' she said. 'I used to have a dog called Dexter.'

'Um,' I managed, but our conversation was cut short by the headmaster, David Tubby, a man whose name fitted his frame and who possessed a body odour problem to match, finally deciding he was ready to speak and clearing his throat with a noise like a bulldozer.

David was fond of his own voice and played with his wedding ring as he spoke, rambling on about – well, to be honest, I can't remember a single thing he spoke about in that meeting. After twenty minutes of unnecessary introduction, all of which was reiterated in an email later in the day, the teachers moved with the hive mind of one and began to file out of the door clutching coffees, books, bags and laptops. Iris picked up half of my book stack.

'You can't carry them by yourself,' she said, smiling again. 'I don't have a class until second period today, so it's no bother.'

'Thank you,' I said, grateful. 'There's honestly no need.'

'Oh, don't be daft.' She tucked a strand of blonde hair back behind her ear. 'Now, which room are you in?'

As we walked to E5, navigating around the students – they were so *small* – we found out a few things about one another. She was single, having moved from Bournemouth to escape a troublesome ex-girlfriend, and had been teaching at Fairmill for a year. She was originally from Newton Heath, a few towns over. She had never read *The War of the Worlds*, but was a huge fan of Marvel comics and said that if she were to go on *Mastermind*, the Avengers would be her specialist subject.

Once at my classroom, she deposited the books on my desk.

'I know it's always daunting at a new place,' she said, 'so if you need anything, even just to touch base with someone when the madness gets a bit much, let me know. Email, call, it's always fine. I'm in classroom FT2; you're welcome to drop in.' I thanked her and she parted with a small wave as the Year 10s filed noisily into the classroom chattering like baboons, using slang that may as well be a foreign language for all the sense it made to me.

From this tiny act of kindness, a charmed friendship arose. We ate lunch together a couple of times a week, traded comic books for poetry anthologies, and I sampled her cookies and cakes whenever possible. She hadn't really known Ruby beforehand, but it turned out that they got on well. She did however already know Annie and Lara, having met through mutual friends, so we often hung out in the evenings too.

Iris – a genuinely kind soul and the final piece to the puzzle that is my social network.

How Iris met William Beery, however, is of practically zero interest to anyone who isn't either of them. They had been at school together, on nodding acquaintance terms, not seen each other for many years, and met again in a bar a few weeks after I'd met Iris. They've been together ever since.

He's tall with shoulder-length black hair and an implied troubled past that I've never been curious enough to ask about, but the burn scars on his neck and barbed wire sleeve tattoo up his left arm speak volumes. I get the continued impression that he doesn't like me, or indeed any of the other seven billion people on the planet he is not related to or sleeping with.

That's all there is to that.

Over a period of many years, these friends that I've discussed became my family. I'm aware that in the story of my life the word 'family' has been conspicuously absent so far, and that's for the simple reason that I don't have one.

My parents had one child, me, after years of trying. When I was ten they were involved in a seventeen-car pile-up on the M40 on a freakishly wet day in July. Both died instantly and I went to live with my mother's father, Ernest (he always insisted on being called Ernest, as if embarrassed by the familial link), who had more important things on his mind than the care of his pre-teen grandson.

I'm not suggesting that I had an abusive or neglectful time with him. In fact, it was nothing of the sort. He was already retired and I wanted for nothing as he wouldn't question spending his money on me. My friends were always welcome, he paid my way through university and he did love me, although he would never have said the words, or given any physical indication of doing so. Men of his generation didn't, I suppose. Or maybe he just never had the time – there were horses to bet on and cricket games to watch.

Ernest died after two strokes when he was seventy-six. I was twenty-one and, just like that, all alone in the world. He had left me whatever money remained, but the accounts, while not insubstantial thanks in part to my parents' life insurance, had dwindled due to the fact he was a shockingly bad gambler. It later turned out he was still paying maintenance to a woman he had got pregnant in the fifties. I found that out at the funeral, when she introduced herself to me, as well as her son, who was sort of my uncle. I never saw either of them again.

Since then, my friends have been my family more than ever. Priti, Shell, Peregrina, Ruby and Lara came to the funeral with me, making sure I was OK. I wasn't, and I can't pretend otherwise, but it made me appreciate them all the more. I had a few relationships, but my friends always came first.

At the heart of it, this is why I get so sad about my friends all pairing up. If they go off, I am left by myself, and no one deserves that. Not even Hitler died alone.

Oh god, don't go down that avenue.

Enough back story; there's an alien invasion in progress.

Eighteen

Midnight Mass

The walk to Blackpond is done in almost complete silence. We veer off from the train tracks after a while and cut across a golf course. Ruby-and-Alex are at the front, Shell-and-Terry right behind. Peregrina-and-Pete are doing their best to console me, but I can't shake the image my brain has created of Jay and Kay becoming, far too literally, Jay-and-Kay. Catsby is still trailing us, but at some distance, as if we're cursed and getting too close will only cause him more issues than his little feline brain can deal with.

Ruby-and-Alex stop next to a bunker and they split, Ruby standing on the lip of the sand and Alex running down into it, aiming fruitless kicks at the sand, launching great clouds of yellow and white. He screams, a scream of futility, and no amount of shouting from us can stop him. Breathless, he collapses down into the sand, burying his face in his shirt and half-heartedly punching the bunker.

Death affects us in different ways.

Alex had, to the best of my knowledge, not been particularly close to Jay-and-Kay, but then again I don't know him as well as some of the other boyfriends. Ruby joins him in the sand and sits down next to him, although not daring to touch him. The rest of us move to a small copse of trees and make ourselves as comfortable as possible among fox shit, leafy mulch and lost golf balls.

No one has any idea what to say, because the obvious stuff doesn't need to be said, and it's tactless to mention anything else. If not for the faint roar of cars on an unseen road, and the occasional chirrup of a few birds, the world would be utterly silent here.

Eventually, someone speaks. It's Shell.

'We need to find somewhere to sleep tonight,' she says. 'I'm not sleeping out in a field, not with wild dogs and aliens about.'

'I estimate we're about an hour from Blackpond,' says Pete. 'Once

Alex is… well, we'll get moving in a minute. Dexter, what food have you got?' I dish out some supplies and we eat in silence, later joined by Ruby-and-Alex. After half an hour or so, we rally our moods and make a move. The sky is overcast; thick, grey, marshmallow clouds scud the skies and we feel the odd spot of rain.

'I can see the church,' I say. Pete was right; it's taken us about fifty minutes. 'We'll go there and get some shelter.' The others acquiesce and the notion of having a goal, no matter how short term, buoys us slightly.

Blackpond is a small village with very little of note going for it. There's a train station, a sixteenth-century pub – The Letters Inn – and the imposing church that we're heading for. I have very faint memories of coming to the village with my parents as a small child, as it boasts a farmer's market that is locally renowned. I've not been here in twenty years, only ever passing through it on the train on the way to work or London.

The sun is setting and the world has taken on a sepia tone. There are still signs of life here, some people still in their houses, a few in the streets, hurrying from one place to another. There doesn't appear to be any electricity, though. We see an elderly couple making their way to the church.

'Do you think that's the safest place to go?' I ask.

'Church'll do me fine,' says Ruby. 'Big stone walls, hopefully kind and welcoming people inside. Aliens won't understand, but we can give it a go.' We follow the old couple to the church and pass through the graveyard. Tall foxgloves line the walls, not flowering yet, but I imagine they're a beautiful sight in the summer. Inside the church we are greeted, as Ruby predicted, by a kind and welcoming figure, the vicar, dressed in his black robe and white dog collar.

'Welcome, my children,' he says, arms open wide. I'd guess at him being in his late sixties, with thinning grey hair and a face weathered like the cliffs at Dover. 'Please, come and shelter. We are safe here. *They* have not reached Blackpond.' The seven of us, very conscious of our lack of religiousness, nod at him, give quick smiles and pass through to a couple of pews at the side of the church that haven't yet been taken. A couple of people look at our guns, but no one comments on them. Maybe they don't dare. I feel uncomfortable and conspicuous holding a pistol in a church.

The church is full of people; some look scared, others merely look impatient. Children of all ages run around and are chastised weakly by parents too tired to do anything more. A flicker of disgust laps at my brain, as I realise that humanity has been doomed for less than a day, a matter of hours, really, and so many of these people already look like hope is lost and they're refugees of a civil war. Very well dressed and clean refugees, mind, but refugees all the same.

'Where did Catsby go?' says Peregrina, speaking aloud the question I was trying not to think about. If everyone else is paired up, he's my partner, as it were. Catsby was (no, *is*) an excellent cat, highly intelligent and about as gentle as it's possible for a cat to be, showing a sometimes dog-like level of devotion. I always preferred cats because of their independence, but short of having to take him for a walk, I might as well have bought a terrier.

'He'd been following us,' I say, trying not to let my face betray any emotion. It's not that I'm scared of showing emotion – most of my friends have seen me cry – but if I start I don't know if I'll be able to stop. 'He'll be OK. He'll probably be better without us to be honest.'

The vicar passes by, introduces himself as Reverend Fawkes, and we give our names in return, although I don't expect him to actually remember them. He moves on and I'm left with my thoughts again. The others have paired up, hugging together for security and safety.

My phone is at 47% battery, the screen as dark as it is possible for it to go and, with an idle thought, I decide to try and call Gavin. It cuts straight to voicemail, and I wish I hadn't bothered because my brain decides to construct an image of the remains of Gavin-and-Frederik mixed together, left bleeding and rotten in their flat.

Because I'm a glutton for punishment, I call Lara too. Her phone connects, but after a few rings moves to voicemail.

I shudder and hug my knees, looking sadly at the children in the church, for whom this may be the last time they get to experience happiness. I wonder what will happen to the children left without parents but decide not to pursue that line of thought for the time being.

Maybe the aliens will get infected with Earth bacteria, like in *The War of the Worlds*, or maybe they'll win. Assuming they're trying to win.

I think back to what Jay-and-Kay said about nanobots joining people together. I have no reason to doubt them; it makes good sense. But *why*? Aliens were always going to be so different from us, but what reason would there be for joining bodies? Maybe they were right about that too – perhaps it's a breeding thing. It would explain why the nanobots are only attracted to couples. It's like they know.

My phone vibrates once and a text message falls into the inbox.

I don't know if you'll get this, but before we die, I wanted you to know that I love you. X

It's Georgina. There isn't a suitable reply to that message. I don't love her, never did, so I can't lie and say that, but not replying may suggest that I'm already dead. I'm not being callous, but surely survival comes ahead of texting your ex to ensure they know how you feel, right? Maybe I should lie and give her that hope to hold on to – I'm never going to see her again, after all.

I feel overcome with exhaustion, and my eyes get heavier.

I wake up later on the stone floor of the church. It takes me a while to reorient myself. People are singing hymns. I look at my watch – it has gone eleven o'clock. Peregrina-and-Pete are awake on the pew above me.

'We didn't want to wake you,' says Peregrina, smiling down at me. 'The others are asleep too, but we thought someone should stay up.' I sit up and see the other four in the aisle. The rifles are under the pew, as is my pistol. I smile and stretch out – flagstones are not comfortable and my bones feel like a badly constructed jigsaw puzzle. I pull myself up onto the pew and notice that most people are asleep, but Reverend Fawkes has a small choir up by the altar and they're singing a hymn I don't recognise. It's been years since I've been in a church.

The hymn finishes and an echoey silence reverberates about the church's interior. I'm not religious but I do admire churches and cathedrals for their beauty and calm. Reverend Fawkes takes position in his pulpit and extends his arms. It's like a nervous tic, or maybe a gesture they teach you when you're training for the priesthood.

'Brothers and sisters,' he begins, in that melodious sing-song voice that all religious figures use when in public. 'We have strangers here on Earth. Although they have not reached our little community of Blackpond yet, I feel that soon they will.

'The media, foul and cluttered cesspit of shock and awe that it tries to be, will tell you that these visitors are beings from another world, come to take our lives. But there is only one who can take our lives without our consent, and that is Lord God, amen.'

'Amen,' mumbles the crowd. I don't join in – something feels wrong. Peregrina is looking at her hands in her lap, but Pete is staring at Fawkes. I nudge him and he looks at me instead.

'What's he talking about?' I say, barely louder than a breath.

'I don't know, but I don't like how this is going,' says Pete. 'Something's wrong.' Reverend Fawkes starts up again.

'Therefore, it is my belief, and the Lord has told me that I'm correct, that these visitors are angels. The Rapture is upon us, my children. And although we thought it would come in days of fiery torment, it has come with an unholy silence. These angels of death have come to turn the Earth into a place of torture for the sinners. We must ascend to a higher plane. Join me, now, in our final drink.'

'I don't remember this sermon,' says Alex. He and Ruby have woken up, and Shell-and-Terry are stirring too. Fawkes steps down from the pulpit and I notice for the first time that there is a line of communion goblets on a trestle table at the front of the church. He beckons the first people towards him, displaying a smile with the inviting warmth of a fireplace in mid-January and, as if hypnotised, they walk towards the altar.

It happens in slow motion. The first two, a couple by the look of things, take a goblet each and drink from them. Before the liquid can finish emptying down their throats, they drop the goblets, which clatter against the flagstones and roll away under a pew. Gripping each other, eyes bulging, they sink to their knees, gasping and grabbing at their chests before falling like the goblets and all movement ending.

'Come forward, my children,' says Fawkes, looking around at the congregation. My friends and I aside, everyone else is pretty nonplussed about what's just happened, or so exhausted they've stopped caring.

Trying to leave a place that's in almost dead silence without being noticed is like trying to reason with a tiger that you're too stringy to be worth the trouble, but we have to try. We wait until the next people have gone up to Reverend Fawkes and taken a cup of whatever the hell they're drinking and stand up, picking up the guns and shooting panicked glances between each other, the door and the vicar. Our standing up does not go unnoticed.

'Ah, our new friends have nominated themselves, come, please,' he says, arms wide again. When confronted by a mad preacher who seems to have no qualms about killing his flock, what is the right course of action? It's another one of those topics not covered by self-help books.

'No, sorry, we need to be going,' I squeak, my grip on the pistol tightening. I sound like I'm trying to excuse myself from an awkward dinner party rather than save seven lives.

'Yes, going to heaven,' says Fawkes, moving towards us. Three more people have drunk from goblets and are choking and falling to their knees. A small mousy man, a verger at a guess, is refilling goblets with a dark red juice that probably isn't Ribena. More people get up to drink, and we're too frozen in terror and possibly curiosity to move. I feel more scared of the vicar than I do of the aliens. They are a distant memory here.

Fawkes moves quicker than I'd like and stands between us and the exit. Pete and Terry move forward first, rifles slung over shoulders, but neither can apparently bring himself to push the priest out of the way.

'You will not leave,' says Fawkes, in a voice as hard as the stones of the building he stands in. 'Only sinners will have a future out there. I have always known this day would come, and I have been preparing for the eventuality.

'When the angels landed in their heavenly craft, I knew what was going on. I was destined to bring my children together and with them pass on to the Promised Land. I cannot in good faith let you leave here. You must come with us.' He moves forward again, threatening this time, as if trying to herd us back into the church.

The punch that saves us surprises Reverend Fawkes, myself and, probably more than anyone else, Peregrina. The vicar's nose explodes in a mess of bright red blood and he falls backwards onto the stones. Peregrina looks down at her handiwork and casts a nervous glance at her fist, as if seeing it for the first time and it acted of its own accord.

'I punched a vicar.' Her voice is quiet. Pete grabs her wrist and, needing no further cue, we make a break for it into the night. It's cold and drizzling, but we run and don't stop until the church is out of sight and we're tucked out of harm's way between a bike shop and a bakery. None of us knows what to say, except Peregrina, who keeps muttering about her crime over and over again.

'I punched a vicar. I punched a vicar. Punched a vicar. Oh my god, I'm going to hell.'

'Don't sweat it,' says Shell, pulling herself up onto a dustbin. 'We're already there.'

Nineteen

Back to School

I wake with a jolt. I didn't even realise I'd fallen asleep – I think I worried myself into a coma. It takes me a moment to recognise where I am. I'm still in the cell. Still eight feet square, still featureless save for the floating orb of light.

My back is sore. My joints feel like they've got sand in them and, when I stretch, several parts of me click and crack. The harsh noise reverberates off the metal walls. I've no way of knowing how long I've been unconscious. Maybe one of the aliens did something to me.

My thoughts must have invaded my dreams, as the images of going to sleep in an alley hover like dust motes in front of my eyes. Suddenly, sleeping al fresco during an invasion seems like a welcome exchange for this, but then I remember what happened next.

Terry jiggles a credit card between the door and its frame at the back of the bike shop. It is the following morning and, while we've slept in that dank, damp alley, it's not because we felt comfortable or safe, just maddeningly exhausted. A day on the run in a freshly post-apocalyptic scenario will do that to a person. Had we been thinking straight, we would've made our way into one of the many abandoned shops or houses around us, but none of us had even entertained the idea. Besides, we would have run the risk of trapping ourselves. Better to be somewhere we could escape at speed.

I scratch my chin, feeling new bristly hairs poking through the skin and wishing that I could have a shower. Modern humanity is not designed for this sort of activity – we're more of an indoor kind of race, liking the comforts of power showers, Internet connections and toasted bagels. Terry fails to get any sort of movement from the lock, so Shell elbows him out of the way, rifle still slung over her back, and has a go.

I become aware that this is the first time since she discovered make-up that I've seen Shell without any on. Notorious for always slipping to the toilets to pop a bit more lipstick or mascara on, she's now bare faced and, actually, still not in the least bit unattractive. Her eyes look a little more sunken, her lips less defined, but she's still Shell, even with a gun. Terry has stubble, and his designer jeans are covered in dirt from lying in the alley. Mine are too, but at least they were cheap. Terry is the sort to spend a couple of hundred quid on a pair of jeans, then complain he doesn't have enough to get a round in.

Ruby wears little make-up anyway, but her blonde hair has morphed from a style worn on the head of a Greek goddess to something that looks like it's trying to eat her. Her eyes are ringed red – which explains who it was crying all night – and Alex looks much the same, still clinging to her as if leaving her side for one second will be the death of him.

I actually think that, given what we've seen so far, sticking that close to her might be.

Pete already has a beard, so he doesn't look much different, but Peregrina is kneeling in the mud, her breathing jerky and uneven. I heard her get up and vomit a couple of times in the night and she now looks dehydrated and is shaking. Pete rubs her back and looks at me with a glum expression, not really knowing what to say.

I dread to think what I look like, but I feel like it's been another night of monkey sex with Georgina. I still haven't replied to her. There's nothing to say.

'No, get off, I'm doing it,' snaps Shell, pushing Terry away with the heel of her hand. A look I don't like passes like a storm cloud across his face, but he resigns himself to letting Shell take control. After a few more wiggles, the door pops open and she goes inside, Terry following and me bringing up the rear. The others aren't going anywhere.

The door opens right into the staffroom, which is cluttered with cycling magazines, abandoned coats and hats, half-empty drinks bottles, and a bin overflowing with food packaging and more magazines. I explore the fridge and find several cans of Coke. I shove them in a carrier bag and fill a few bottles with tap water. We had food left in our rucksacks, but they were abandoned at the church in our hurry to escape.

In the alley, Ruby-and-Alex have at last stood up, but Peregrina remains on her hands and knees.

'Make her drink this, get some sugar and stuff inside her,' I say, holding out a chilled red can to Pete. He takes it and I give the rest of them to Ruby. 'One of you needs to get into that bakery too; we can stock up on food from there. I'm going back in to help Shell get the bikes.' I return to the shop where Terry is trying on a helmet and Shell is pulling bikes off of racks, checking tyre pressures and seat heights.

Between the three of us, we select seven bikes that are capable of doing the job. They're all sturdy and look like they could cross open countryside with few problems, although I'm trusting Shell's advice as I've not ridden a bike in years. Mine's a sporty looking thing in red and gold.

Alex found a rucksack left in the staffroom of the bakery and has filled it with crisps and bread. Turns out it's impossible to maintain a no-carb diet in the event of an alien invasion. We are learning so much. There are some meat sandwiches in the chiller but no one wants to risk it. Shell advises that anything that should have been frozen should already be avoided, just in case. The last thing we need is anyone falling sick.

We set off on the bikes in the direction of Fairmill, still aiming for the school and hoping that in the media blackout we're enduring we haven't missed the news that the aliens have beaten us to it. As we pedal out of Blackpond, down deserted streets, I turn for one final look and see a spacecraft hoving into view, looking ready to land in the village. I open my mouth to tell the others, but decide they don't need to know. We pedal faster.

The journey takes longer than I envisioned, because while the train line would take us directly there, we're travelling via winding country roads that haven't been maintained for years and are pockmarked with potholes, making it feel a bit like traversing a teenager's acne-ridden face. We don't see a single other person or vehicle the entire way. After an hour or so and very little talking, my legs are burning up as I see the first houses of Fairmill come into view. The school is uphill, next to the train station, so I power through the pain for the last few minutes, arriving at the playing fields third behind Shell and Alex.

For some reason, my first instinct is to run to my classroom, as if there's nowhere else in the building that would be a good place to hole up. However, Ruby is the one smart enough to point out that if there are people in the building, they will have gone to where the food is. We make our way to the cafeteria.

As we get nearer to the rugby pitch and then the playground, signs of life become more prevalent. While there are no people visible, there are cars that have been abandoned rather than parked, piles of bicycles and roller skates, even a couple of skateboards, and litter swirling around in disgusting eddies. I hazard a silent guess that once you arrive, you don't leave, or not at any pace quicker than a run, anyway.

Flickers past the windows suggest that there are people inside, although I don't get a good look at anyone, instead catching blurs out of the corner of my eyes. I feel like I'm in a particularly creepy episode of *Doctor Who*.

The doors nearest to the cafeteria are wooden with a couple of glass panels in the top, and given that they're usually open during school hours, I assume they will be now and barrel into them, achieving nothing but a sore shoulder. They shake a bit, attracting attention from the inside, as a lock clicks and the left-hand door opens.

Out steps a very tall guy who I haven't met on many occasions, but his picture has flashed up on my Facebook often enough.

'Will!' I cry. 'You're alive! Is Iris here too?' The potential survival of Iris-and-William is a boon and I feel a surge of adrenaline force its way through every cell. William is well over six foot tall, much like Alex, but has long scraggly black hair, iron grey eyes and is altogether far less welcoming as a person. Iris must see something in him, but while I can tolerate his presence, I always get the feeling he thinks he's too cool to be seen with any of us. He appears to be a perpetual teenager, despite being in his early thirties.

'Yeah, she's here,' he says, deadpan. He doesn't move aside, nonplussed by the fact he's outnumbered seven to one and determined to stand his ground.

'Let us in then,' says Terry. I don't think he and William have ever met.

'Did you get followed?' he says, tucking his hair back behind his shoulders, revealing his neck and its messy hodgepodge of white and shrimp-pink scar tissue.

'No, there's nothing behind us. Come on Will, let us in,' I step forward again, but William is immovable. 'What the fuck, come on!'

'I don't know,' he says. 'There's quite a lot of us in here already, and food is running out. Do you have food?'

'We'll go to sodding Tesco and loot it!' snaps Terry. 'Let us in the bloody door!'

'Will? Who are you talking to?' There's a voice from somewhere behind him and Iris pops her head out under his armpit. 'Oh my god! Ruby! Dexter!' She launches herself at Ruby with such force that Alex has to keep them both upright. Iris pulls off her, now crying, and hugs me too. I squeeze back and breathe in her sweaty tang.

'How did you get here? Why did you come here?' she asks.

'I don't know,' I say. 'It felt a sensible, secure place to go. Is it?'

'Yes, there aren't any aliens here so far,' she says, elbowing William out the way and leading us into the chilly corridor. 'There's about fifty people here, I think. We run a rota of people on look-out duty, guarding the doors and windows. We've still got limited power too, thanks to some backup generators. Not that we'll be able to do much if we are attacked. But you...' She notices the guns. 'Where did you get those?'

'Neighbour of mine,' I say, glancing at the pistol and disliking how it looks in my hand. I should be holding a pen or a sandwich, not a gun. Iris turns to William. 'Stay here and watch the door. And let people in for god's sake!' William looks suitably chastised and turns away, sulking like a petulant teenager. Iris looks back at us, grinning and crying at the same time. 'You won't believe who else is here!'

After we've thrown our bicycles into the pile of abandoned transportation, we are led upstairs to the library, the door of which hangs open. A man in his thirties patrols the upstairs corridor, armed with a cricket bat. The library feels cool and being surrounded by books makes me feel a bit safer. There's something very comforting about them. Iris walks ahead, the rest of us trailing behind, and when she gets to the centre of the room, she speaks. 'Guys, have I got a surprise for you!'

From out of the stacks, four people emerge. Priti-and-Art, Annie-and-Matt, all four looking in good health, albeit rather tired and, in the case of the guys, unshaven. There is much yelling, hugging, crying and rejoicing at this small victory as we grab each other and talk at three thousand words a minute, wondering how all this was possible. After a few minutes, we sit down at the reading tables in the centre of the library and tell our stories, lit by the feeble emergency lighting overhead.

Pete, Shell and I share the duty of telling what happened to us, trying not to make a big deal of the deaths of Jay-and-Kay, or getting caught up in an evil cult. Priti tells the story of the others, although there's little to tell. Iris, Annie and Priti live in Fairmill, as do their other halves. It was actually Annie who had gathered them together, which came as a shock to me, as she's always been so passive, quite content to let others make decisions and go along with them.

'Annie figured that there was safety in numbers,' says Priti, 'and Iris suggested the school as a decently fortified location. Most of the town doesn't have electricity any more, but there are still functioning generators here. There's food, lots of space and we have patchy Internet connections.'

'Is it global?' asks Pete.

'Pretty much every country has been hit,' says Art. 'There's less online than you'd hope, but I suppose people are trying to survive rather than update their statuses. Still, there's always some.'

'The President is still threatening the use of nukes, but it's a lost cause,' says Matt, squeezing Annie's hand. 'The Prime Minister is dead, by the way.'

'London?' I ask.

'London has basically been emptied,' Iris interjects. 'There are pockets of survivors according to Twitter, people by themselves in abandoned homes and offices. The aliens have begun to leave, although no one can answer why with any more ease than they can explain their arrival. They obviously don't feel the need to continue.

It's the towns that are facing the next onslaught.' It's then that I tell them about Blackpond, seeing the ship land there, and the news is greeted with a moment of silence.

As we talk, night falls around us, and we do our best to make ourselves at home among the stacks, having taken rolls of fabric from the textiles department and towels from the swimming pool to wrap up in and construct makeshift beds. Everyone is paired off and, once again, I find myself alone, leaning against the hard wall in the biology stacks. My phone is down to 24% battery. I switch the mobile data on for a moment, and a few Facebook updates from people telling their families and partners how much they love them come through.

In the aisle next to me, physics and chemistry, I can hear Ruby-and-Alex talking, words so quiet they're barely speaking them. They sound so close to one another that they may be passing the words directly into one another's mouths. And then I hear a word that I know I wasn't supposed to hear, which removes any sense of sleepiness from me.

I get up, tuck my phone back into my pocket and whisper to Priti and Annie that I'm going for a walk.

'Art and Matt are on patrol,' whispers Annie. 'Art's down in the history department, and Matt is guarding the gym entrance. Go keep them company if you want.' I nod that I will, but I know I won't. I actually *want* to be alone right now. I decide to go to my classroom.

When I arrive at it, I find one of the lights on and am annoyed that someone has already taken it for their own. I run a finger across my name on the door, wondering if anyone will ever call me Mr Scithers again, and push it open. The tables have been pushed to the back of the room, away from the windows. There's a nest made of sheets, pillows and a sleeping bag tucked between my desk and the whiteboard. At the sound of my arrival, a face peers out from it, haloed by green hair.

It's Georgina.

Twenty

The Reason I'm Single

There are more tears, but once again not from me. If I start, I'll never stop. Georgina throws herself around my neck, burying her face into my collarbone. When Iris did this a few short hours ago, my natural reaction was to hug back. Now, I just feel awkward.

I broke up with Georgina eight months ago after she went mad because I was never free enough for her. She has (or is that 'had'?) a tedious office job doing something repetitive with accounts, and was never willing to accept or understand that I couldn't simply leave my work when I came home. Anyone who says that teaching is an easy job is lying or doesn't understand. Alright, the act of teaching takes up a surprisingly small amount of my time, but so much else is given over to training, lesson planning, marking, preparing tests, meetings and research into recent educational theory. Don't give me any crap about those 'long, languid six-week holidays'. They're still six weeks too short to get everything done.

I give a half-hug back, which makes her cling even tighter, like a barnacle in a rock pool, and I wonder if I'll get her off me without the use of a crowbar. I'm pleased I didn't reply to her text saying that I loved her. I decide to immediately introduce a topic that should make her see sense.

'Where's Marcus? Is he here with you?' Marcus is Georgina's boyfriend of six months, a tall, broad-shouldered rugby player who splashes his parents' cash like he's Brooklyn sodding Beckham. Any brains he had were in his balls and, if the rumours are true, they've shrunk to the size of peas thanks to years of steroid abuse.

Here's the thing though. People think it's weird that I'm so vehemently against the idea of someone dating my ex-girlfriend, even though I ended it with her, but I still like Georgina, even if not in the way she wants, and Marcus bullied me on and off throughout secondary school. I don't have anything against her being in a relation-ship, but I don't think it should be *him*. She can do so much better.

'He's gone,' she says, extracting herself from me and sitting back on the desk. 'He and his family vanished as soon as the aliens... I called him, and he said they were going. He didn't even say goodbye prop-erly.' Fresh wails and more tears. I can't help but feel sorry for her. Whatever the case, that's a shitty thing to happen.

'He didn't ask after you?'

'He was like, "Yeah, stay safe" and that was it,' she says, hugging herself. 'End of the world and I've been fucking dumped. Again. Didn't even ask me if I was OK. Didn't even call *me*.' Georgina, like me, is parentless, but her loss was much more recent. Four years ago, she lost her father to cancer, and three months after that her mother had a fatal heart attack. Stress induced, the doctors decided. More than anyone else, she knows what I'm going through, and I understand her. We've ended up alone together, and it feels weird.

'Have you heard from Lara?' I ask, anxious to change the topic.

'No, of course not,' she says. With a weak smile, she adds, 'That must be one of the shortest marriages in history.'

'If I knew anything about current popular culture and who was married to whom, I'd have a smart rejoinder to that,' I say. She giggles through tears, takes me by the hand and leads me to her sheet-and-pillow nest. It feels rude to resist. We sit down and she puts her hand on my knee. It doesn't feel untoward; I think she wants to have some human contact.

'Who are you here with?' she asks. I reel off the list of people I have; feel a stabbing guilt that she's alone. I don't see how I'm going to leave here without destroying her further. We talk into the night, our quiet words like mice scuttling over one another in a cage. We sleep together, in both senses of the phrase, although throughout I fear being discovered. I can't decide if I'm more worried of being found in this position by aliens or by my friends.

I'm woken the following morning by a loud, persistent mosquito buzzing next to my ear. I reach out a hand to swat it and hit my phone instead. It's ringing.

It's ringing!

I sit up, unwrapping myself from sheets and disentangling Georgina from my legs. She's clinging to me like a koala afraid of dropping out of its tree. I snatch up the phone.

'It's Lara!' I cry out.

'What?' says Georgina, half through incomprehension, half through sleepiness.

'Lara's calling!' I gape, swipe the screen to answer the call and…

Black.

The phone has died, the battery run down to nothing.

My whole body is plunged into Arctic waters and I can hear my heart beating in my ears. I feel sick. I turn it on again but it turns itself off before the loading screen even passes.

I stand up, still cold but sweating, wearing nothing but boxer shorts. I pick up a chair and throw it at the wall, shouting as I do. Arms appear around my waist and I feel the pressure of a smaller figure behind me, gripping me, whispering that it's OK.

I turn around, hug Georgina back, and let a few tears fall, before taking a deep breath and slapping myself hard a couple of times.

'Enough,' I say firmly. 'Enough of this. We have to be strong.' Georgina doesn't say anything. She grips me a little tighter. She's naked from the waist down, wearing nothing but her top. Her skirt is bundled up somewhere in our nest with my jeans and shirt.

'We have each other,' she says, and that's enough to bring me back to reality. She's right, we do have each other, but we can't have each other if we want to survive. Last night's sex – probably the last sex I will ever have – was a mistake, and a very dangerous one too.

'We're not a couple,' I say, the words thudding the air, dropping like stones into mud. 'We cannot be a couple, Gee – there's too much at stake.' She pulls away from me, looks hurt again.

'What do you mean?' she asks, as I get dressed again, getting ready to leave. I'll take her with me, certainly, but I don't know if she'll ever understand. She repeats her words.

'Look, didn't you notice on the television? Did you see those first deaths?' I say, pulling on my shirt and jumper. 'Those nanobots –' (I'd filled her in on Jay-and-Kay's theory the night before.) '– only went for people who were paired up. Maybe it's a genetic thing, or a hormone thing. I don't know, but I think that if you and I were to enter into something again, we'd end up dead too. The aliens will find us and I think that they specialise in pairs.'

'But...'

'No, I mean, look at the aliens themselves! Two heads! What if they originally had one each, and when they pair up, they *literally* pair up? The nanobots are trying to do the same to us. I don't know why the aliens would want that to happen, but it's what is happening. Very badly.'

'They might do any two people,' Georgina proposes as I buckle my belt. 'You might have to be standing near to someone else.'

'But I don't think that's the case,' I say, lacing up my boots. Georgina has made no effort to get dressed yet. 'When Jay-and-Kay got merged, there were more of us there right next to them. Shell, Pete, me... no couples. We were left unscathed. Had Terry stayed, maybe he and Shell would be no more by now, too. There's something the nanobots can detect. They know when people are already mentally joined. They come in to do the rest.'

Georgina looks at me blankly, eyes red raw. Without make-up on, her face looks innocent and confused. She's a child, trapped in an adult's body, unable and unwilling to grow up. She croaks, 'Are you going to leave me, too?'

'No, I'm not,' I say, picking up her pants and skirt. 'Get dressed, we'll go back to the others. We'll keep you safe.' *And at a safe distance*, I think. Without a word she dresses and we haul up the sheets and pillows she's been using, taking them with us to form another bed in the library.

Priti is guarding the door to the library when I arrive, and I'm greeted with a firm slap to my left cheek. I drop the armfuls of pillows I'm holding and clasp a hand to my face.

'Where the *hell* have you been?' she shouts. 'You absolute idiot, walking off like that and not coming back! We've had people out all night checking across the school! We thought you'd been taken or something.'

'I was with Georgina in my old classroom,' I say, picking up pillows again, my face stinging. 'Clearly no one looked very hard.' Priti pushes the door open, grumbling to herself, and lets Georgina and I pass in. More shouting and chastising. Terry, Shell and William are missing, out watching entrances somewhere. Nonetheless, they treat Georgina kindly, mock when I ask if anyone has a phone charger on them – mine was the last to die – and fill me in on the events of the evening, which mostly involved a small family arriving with two cats at around midnight and taking up their place in an empty classroom in the history corridor.

The mention of cats makes me think of Catsby again, which I can't bear right now, so I volunteer to go and get some rations from the canteen. Annie and Ruby insist on coming too. They're worried I'm going to wander off.

It's quite orderly, although there's the same sense of doom surrounding the school that was in the church. People have given up hope, and I suppose I can understand why. We're trapped – just redecorating our house in Pudding Lane the week before London goes up in flames. The day passes with all the speed of a sloth with lumbago. The Internet works for a couple of hours, and then connections die. No amount of turning things off and on again brings back a web page.

We collate the information we have, spend the day taking it in turns to patrol corridors and doorways. Annie and I keep an eye on the music department for a couple of hours after midday, and I spend another hour or two with Peregrina on the flat roof of the assembly hall, watching the skies for any activity.

There is nothing of any particular note about the day, unless you consider the apocalypse still worth mentioning, until I return from the toilets at around eight o'clock that night to find Georgina's bed empty.

'Where's she gone?' I ask the library as a whole, but no one has an answer for me. Priti thought she'd gone to the toilet; Art, the canteen. Someone notices that one of the rifles is missing, too. I rummage through her sheets to see if she's left anything and find a battered paperback of *Dr Jekyll and Mr Hyde*. Inside the front page are scrawled two words in a handwriting I recognise as Georgina's.

Her last words are *Goodbye, Dexter*.

She's decided that she'd rather be alone than with me.

Twenty-One

Evacuation

The first we know of the incoming danger is someone running past the library, screaming something incoherent. Annie-and-Matt are the first to react, jumping up, clutching one another and hobbling to the library door like participants in a three-legged-race. They've been together such a short time, it is unfair to potentially see them snuffed out before they get a chance to go through the motions of breaking up or finding out if this is the real thing.

The shouts and screams are translated and we are given the news that one of the aliens' ships has been spotted coming in to land on the north end of Fairmill. The school is in the southern end of the town but at this point that doesn't feel like it should matter. All that matters is that we get away. We gather up our bags, shoving in leftover food and supplies. Terry checks that the remaining guns have been reloaded. There are thirteen of us in the library, and while I'm not superstitious, the number still worries an irrational part of me.

It's stupid.

'We'll go and grab bicycles and move on,' I say, as everyone packs. There's nodding and cries of 'I was going to say that!' as everyone sorts their meagre possessions out. We leave our phones behind – they serve no use other than as expensive paperweights.

'Where are we going to go?' asks Peregrina.

'Back to South Greenfield?' suggests Terry. 'Aliens should be done there by now and moved on, right?'

'No, dangerous to go back on ourselves,' I say, stroking my chin. 'Plus, there's the nutters in Blackpond to deal with on the way, if they're not dead yet. No, we'll go to London.'

'London!' shouts Priti. 'Are you actually funny in the head? You want to go to the capital that's crawling with aliens and become even more of a sitting target?'

'Be fair, Priti,' says Art. 'We know that the aliens were abandoning London. And it's the perfect place to go and play hide and seek with a rival species. They won't be looking for us because they'll already think they wiped it out, and even if they do, we can best them.' Priti looks unimpressed with him.

'London it is,' says William. 'Let's go, I'm not sitting around here to be killed any longer.' Iris-and-William leave the library first and the rest of us follow on behind, filing like termites out into the playground and picking up bicycles that look in decent condition. My original one is gone. This one is a poisonous green.

The race begins and we pedal for our lives back out of town, but it's when we're near the edge of the furthest-out estate that we become aware that we're not alone. A gold and silver shimmer of colour attacks our eyes and distracts some of us enough that we fly off the bikes and crash. I power into the back of Art and the two of us go over, taking out Shell, Matt and Annie in the process. Everyone else stops before the same happens to them, and only then, ahead of us, do we see four aliens emerge from the side of a house. Their eight heads turn to look at us, wide eyes and mouths looking grotesque. Four of the heads have the red and gold feather-like thing.

'Everyone split up! Don't stand with your other half!' I shout, but that's easier said than done because the natural reaction when in danger is to cling like a barnacle to the thing that you love. The first cloud of nanobots is fired towards us and I duck down behind some shrubbery, not daring to look at who was too slow to move. Priti-and-Art are next to me, so they're OK. I can hear the footsteps of the aliens getting closer, running towards us. There are colours popping in front of my eyes at super speed. I risk a peek up over the shrubs.

It's Iris-and-William. The merged version of them has his height, three eyes and one arm, the others scattered around their feet. Iris's torso has been attached to the front of William's, their chests pressed together. Half of her head, the right half, hangs on William's shoulder. Her hair has been attached around William's neck, giving him a sort of blonde frill. The surprise in the three eyes – two of hers, one of his, and one of them embedded in his right cheek – is palpable. Worryingly, despite the disgusting mess, this is a cleaner fix than Jay-and-Kay was, or the first ones on the television were.

The nanobots are *learning*.

There's a gunshot, and another. Two of the aliens fall to the ground, clutching their chests. Terry has taken them out at great risk to himself and a second cloud of nanobots heads towards the shrubbery he and Shell have hidden behind. But as the Iris-and-William thing falls to its knees and keels over from blood loss, infection or simply shock, I realise that the nanobots are changing direction.

The grey cloud whips over their heads and instead shrouds and begins to devour a tearful Annie-and-Matt. Alex fires his gun – my hands are shaking too hard to hold the pistol properly – and takes out another one of the aliens.

A huge burst of cerise pink attacks our eyeballs and one gets the feeling that no good can come of that. The colour feels too cheerful, and not for the right reasons. Those reasons become clear when I look over and catch sight of Annie-and-Matt.

With very little excess blood, they now stand as one. Matt's main body is complete, but has been adjusted to have Annie's arms and her head perches on his shoulder, looking otherwise completely normal. It still moves and blinks. As Annie-and-Matt spins around, trying to look at itself and work out what has happened, I note that their clothes have been ripped at the back and there are scars around their necks and down their spines, suggesting major surgery has taken place in a very short space of time.

Their spare legs and arms rest neatly in a pile, the cuts cauterised and therefore no longer bleeding. The whole endeavour is too precise to be welcome. The nanobots have obviously been busy with many people and have had time to reprogram their understanding of human biology.

Alex takes out the final alien, and does so by blasting it through the head, allowing blue blancmange to pepper the driveway. Given that he wasn't included in Terry's basic gun training, it's a terrifyingly impressive shot. I put it down to multiple paintball weekends for his friends' birthdays and stag parties.

Annie-and-Matt remains standing, looking at itself in shock, the heads turning to look one another in the eyes and, while they look like they want to say something, they don't know what it is. With one final look at us, Annie-and-Matt takes off at a run – on Matt's legs – back the way we came. If any of us thinks about trying to stop it, none of us makes an attempt to do so.

Once Annie-and-Matt is out of sight, we get up from our hiding places, taking in the moment of quiet to study the remains of the alien bodies, and pointedly ignore the bits that used to be attached to Annie, Matt, Iris and William. Speaking of, Iris-and-William sits in a bloody, crumpled heap on the driveway of a house that looks like it belongs to people who would rather die than be involved in anything like this. The house remains silent, but other doors creak open and a few people emerge. I want to shout at them, blame them for what happened and say they've been cowards, but thinking about it, I can't really begrudge them staying out of harm's way.

'We need to bury Iris-and-William,' I say, looking at the body out of the corner of my eye. 'I'm not leaving anyone else to the elements.' Terry shouts over at a middle-aged couple who have materialised from their front door.

'Can we bury them in your garden?'

It's blunt, and the looks on their faces suggest that it's not a welcome proposition. Fortunately, Priti and Shell have slightly more tact and approach them to ask in a more respectful manner. I see small children at a couple of windows, and regret that they have to see such a horrible mess.

As Priti says that the couple – Dennis and Josephine – have agreed to have their garden become a grave site, I catch sight of something small and orange by some bins. At first, I think it's a further sign of alien life and go to shout at the others, before I realise that it's something terrestrial.

'Catsby!'

Somehow, in the middle of this mess and mayhem, after seeing four more of my friends taken out by the alien menace, I manage to feel a moment of true euphoria. Catsby doesn't hesitate and runs for me, letting me scoop him up into my arms. He nuzzles his face against my neck. 'How did you find us, mister?' I ask him, but it's not like he's going to answer. After fussing over each other for a little while – providing a welcome distraction and brain-cleanse while Iris-and-William is taken round the side of Dennis and Josephine's house, and Pete, Peregrina and Art emerge from another house with large spades – Catsby gets restless and wriggles free of my grip. He meows a few times and, alright, it sounds weird, but I know what he's saying.

Like Georgina, he's going his own way. He arches his back and allows me to stroke him one final time, top to tail and, with a final lick of his rough tongue on my knuckle, he turns away and scampers off. Tears well up in my eyes and I gulp them back. Never try to tell me that animals aren't clever. They have emotions and personalities like humans and are intelligent in ways that we can't understand. He'll be fine. He's a smart cat.

A hand rests on my shoulder and I flinch.

'Where's Catsby gone?' says Ruby. I turn and don't answer, but instead pull her into a hug, wrapping her and her secret up, the secret she doesn't know I know. The word I heard in the library.

I let go and together we go to the back garden where Iris-and-William is to be buried, along with their remaining limbs and those of Annie-and-Matt, a decision that has been reached in my absence, but one I agree with.

Art, Shell and Dennis are digging, while everyone else looks on with paralysed looks on their faces, ignoring the packet of custard creams that Josephine has put down on the patio. We work in shifts to dig a big enough hole, each of us caked in mud and sweat a couple of hours later, but it feels right. Terry, Peregrina, Pete, Dennis and I put the body in the hole. We return to activity, filling the hole in again.

Once the hole has been covered and flattened as best we can, we stand around the impromptu grave, heads bowed. Everyone holds onto their significant other. I stand alone, as usual.

'Should someone say a few words?' asks Ruby. No one knows what to say. I wonder how far Annie-and-Matt got before shock and blood loss overcame them (them? it?) and did for them.

'You must stay tonight,' says Josephine, and there isn't anyone about to argue with her. The house has two spare rooms and two large sofas in the living room. Shell, Terry and myself draw the short straws and are put up in the dining room, wrapped in any remaining duvets and blankets Josephine finds. Dennis offers us a tent in the garden, but given the events of the afternoon and what we'd be sleeping on top of, no one fancies it.

Josephine does us a basic dinner, but none of us can remember the last time we ate, so it is wolfed down gratefully. I watch the older couple as we eat, looking sad at the head of their kitchen table. Dennis has the figure of a man once muscular, but it has gone to seed and he's deflated like a soufflé, his hair vanishing as quickly as his definition. Josephine is still mostly blonde, although grey at the roots and her eyes look like they've seen things that people shouldn't see. I'm not even talking about the recent events – there is great sadness in those eyes, but I don't know her well enough to pry.

Once everyone has retired to their quarters and Terry is using the loo, I find myself alone with Shell for the first time in a long time. She reaches into her pocket for her phone, but checks herself when she remembers we left them behind.

In silence, we lie down and wait for Terry to return.

'Did you know,' I say, words piercing the silence like a stalactite, 'that in Pakistan, children bury their baby teeth in the garden in the hope of a new sibling?' She doesn't reply and I wonder if she's asleep, but then she speaks.

'What does that have to do with anything?' she asks. I prop myself up on one elbow and look at her.

'I'm trying to prove that sort of trivia is absolutely useless,' I say. 'Always was, really, and it's not likely to be relevant ever again. Pakistan will be a wasteland pretty soon, if not already, or overrun with two-headed humans, and *Pointless* isn't about to be recommissioned.'

'I still don't understand,' Shell scrunches her face up and as if trying to read small print on my chin.

'*Catch-22* was originally called *Catch-18*. A billion seconds is over thirty-one years. Donald Duck's middle name is Fauntleroy. You can get out of pretty much any maze by keeping one hand on the hedge at all times. *That's* the sort of stuff I know. I don't know how to do first aid, or make a fire, or maintain a gun. Unless there's a pub quiz coming up, I'm useless. When it comes to the end of the world, doubly so.' Shell sits herself up too.

'Don't talk like that,' she says. 'We're working together here. None of us know what we're doing. Terry's in the army, but I know for a fact that he never shot anyone before all this happened. Look at the rest of us. Teacher, chef, journalist, graphic designer... humanity got creative and screwed itself over. The end of the world needs builders and doctors. We don't know any of them, but we'll do our best.'

'Remember Melissa?' I say, thinking of a girl we knew from way-back-when at school who one day upped and eloped with her boyfriend of three months and we never heard from again. 'We should have kept hold of her.'

'She was a dental nurse,' says Shell. 'That's hardly going to qualify her to deal with whatever injuries or illnesses we might get.' She pauses and sighs. 'We need to try and get some sleep if we intend to be in London by tomorrow evening.' Terry clatters back in at this point, stubbing his toe on a heavy doorstop and cursing, and slips under a duvet next to Shell.

Sleep is slow in coming, but deep and dreamless when it does.

Twenty-Two

Pub Brawl

The next morning, I wake up before Shell-and-Terry, who are enveloped in one another's arms on the other side of the floor. I shuffle out of the duvet, making as little noise as possible, slip into the kitchen and open the back door. I cast a quick glance at Iris-and-William's impromptu grave and decide it's best to pretend it isn't there.

A chill dances through the air, but I tug my jacket tighter around me and sit down on the patio, stretching my legs out and watching the birds at the feeder dangling from the shed roof. They don't seem bothered by my presence, but when the door opens again, they flit away.

'Oh, I wasn't expecting...' says Josephine as I turn to look at who's joining me.

'Sorry, I didn't know if I was allowed out here,' I say, scrabbling up.

'Sit down, sit down.' Josephine gives a weak smile, and after a moment's pause, I resume my seat. Her hair sticks up at the back and she's wearing a dark blue dressing gown, thin legs sticking out the bottom finished off with men's checked slippers. She brushes some soil off a metal chair and perches herself down.

'We can't thank you enough for letting us stay, Mrs Saltmarsh,' I say, using my politest voice. She doesn't say anything for a moment, just blinks and looks at a fearless sparrow who has decided it's safe to return.

'Josephine, please,' she says, rather stiffly. 'And it's alright.' I wonder if I've offended her and she looks like she's considering saying something else. We watch the birds for a few moments more before she offers, 'Not that it matters, but I'm not Mrs Saltmarsh.'

'I'm sorry,' I say, shielding my eyes from the rising sun as I look up at her again. 'I saw Mr... Dennis's university diploma on the wall. I assumed that was your surname.'

'It's his,' she nods. She isn't looking at me. 'I don't suppose any of this is relevant any more. My name is Turner. Until this week, I lived next door.'

'Oh,' I say. Is she about to embark on an excerpt from her unwritten memoirs? I get the feeling that she's been bottling something up and the cork is struggling to maintain its hold in the neck.

'Dennis has always been very kind to me,' she says. 'We've both lived in the cul-de-sac for about thirty years. My husband left me last year for a younger woman. Some bit of stuff at his office. I don't know exactly who she was. He upped and went one day.' My mind drifts back to Georgina. She puts a finger to her lips as if considering whether she wants to go on, or perhaps steadying herself to do so.

'Dennis was never married,' she continues, 'but he was sweet. He took care of me, but I suppose I'm old fashioned. I didn't know what the neighbours would say if we courted. But now, it doesn't matter. We've decided to grip the bull by the horns and spend our last few days together.'

'That's lovely,' I say, and decide that she's not someone who needs to hear the theories regarding the nanobots.

'The thing is, Dexter,' she says, at last turning to look at me, 'there's no shame in being single, and nothing wrong with it, as long as you aren't lonely. Surround yourself with people you care about and who care about you. That's all that matters, I think.' I don't know how to respond to that, but I'm saved from having to do so by Shell opening the back door and appearing for a breath of fresh air. Whatever passed between Josephine and myself dissipates, and she says she'll do a round of tea and coffee for everyone.

As we pack up our stuff, my brain alternates between singing 'Life on Mars' by David Bowie and replaying my conversation with Josephine, and neither helps me concentrate. It's weird to me that normal things like earworms and croissants (Josephine provides a very filling breakfast) still exist.

Guns at the ready, with vague protests from Dennis and Josephine who feel they're obliged to stop us but obviously don't want us sticking around to use up their supplies any further, we set off towards the train station. We have decided to follow the tracks into London.

Bicycles are abandoned again to save further accidents and Shell-and-Terry are leading the way armed with the rifles. Priti has the pistol. With my hands now free, I shove them deep into the pockets of my jeans. I feel caked with filth and I noticed a small blister on my toe this morning. I had a quick wash in the bathroom sink when I got up, but it's not enough. The girls' faces are devoid of make-up, and the guys are revealing which of them grows facial hair the quickest (it isn't me).

There are no big shapes in the distance, suggesting that the aliens have left Fairmill. We'd probably be safe here, for a while at least, but I still think I've done the right thing by suggesting we go to London. More supplies, more space, more chance of survival. Maybe.

The nine of us move with slow determination, not speaking much. The couples mutter to each other now and again, but I walk in silence, consumed by my thoughts. These keep repeating the same images, each of them as unpleasant as the last.

I think about Jay-and-Kay, and then Iris-and-William, and then Mr Grossman's rotting body swims into view, followed by the caved-in cranium of the dog Kay killed, then the abandoned legs and arms of Annie-and-Matt, which in turn morphs into an image of the people falling down dead in the church. I think briefly of Georgina and my heart skips a little, but it's replaced by imagined fates of Lara-and-Steve and Gavin-and-Frederik, as gory and foul as those I've witnessed. So much death in such a short space of time. My life has been one death after another, I notice. Maybe everyone's is. Things keep changing and the universe doesn't wait for anyone to keep up. At the moment, it appears to be working overtime.

I wonder how my students are faring. The thought of abandoned children flares up in my mind again. I've hardly seen any children since the aliens arrived, except those who have stayed with their parents. What's happening to those who have been orphaned? Given the aliens seem to be merging couples, children are exempt from that, so either we've misunderstood what the aliens are doing, or we've simply not encountered any children yet. I'm not sure that I want to.

'We're here,' says Art, feeling obliged to break the silence as we arrive at the train station and hop down onto the tracks. We don't even bother to check them this time – we haven't seen a single functional light all morning. We set off along the tracks, in single file, aware of every chirp, crack and chatter from the low shrubs, wondering if one of them bodes something more dangerous than a sparrow.

Humans, as a species, at first glance seem to have few decent survival traits, aside from our intelligence. We can't climb trees very well, we're poor swimmers, we have no natural defence against the cold, we don't move very fast and most of us can't hunt with our bare hands. However, humans do have one trait that not everyone may realise, but it's one that is about to make the day slightly less painful. Humans have greater stamina than practically anything else on the planet.

Hell, given enough time and distance, we can outrun a horse.

Fuelled by adrenaline, we plough on. Outside of Fairmill we spot a lone alien, two heads looking in different directions but neither at us. Terry takes it out with a bullet to the chest. As it dies, we see a vivid flash of violet.

'Do you think they recognise the train tracks as a path?' asks Ruby. 'If we're following a prescribed route, it wouldn't take much for them to follow us down.' The thought is enough to spook us, and at the next station we climb back onto the platform and continue the journey cross country. We're exposed, but so are any aliens.

We press on, across golf courses and fields of cows, past isolated farmhouses with no sign of human activity and cars abandoned on the sides of country roads. We see the occasional alien, but they are either unarmed or don't notice us until one of us has stuck them with a bullet or two.

In yet another unidentifiable field, after clambering over another splintery fence and spooking a rabbit, Priti hands the pistol to Art and drops back to keep pace with me.

'You need to stop it,' she says, looking ahead to the others rather than at me.

'Stop what?' I ask.

'Stop thinking about how you intend to save the human race.' She gives me a patronising look. 'This isn't *Doctor Who* or something, and you're neither responsible for the planet nor capable of saving it.

We're all in this together, and we're all screwed.' Priti speaks less than Gavin, but shares his bluntness.

'I'm not planning on saving the human race,' I retort, although I was wondering how I would react if selected to be the ambassador of mankind. 'I would like to stay alive and see what happens next.'

'What happens next is that we die anyway,' says Priti, shrugging her small shoulders. 'It would be nice to survive, obviously, but survival is only going to be short term, let's be honest.' If nothing else, she's a realist. There's no sugar-coating anything with Priti.

'I'm annoyed that I'm going to die and not find out how my book ends,' I say, thinking of the copy of Philip K. Dick's *Ubik* that's sitting on my bedside table. 'Still, if we find a bookshop, I might help myself to a copy and finish it up one night.' I feel a spot of rain on my cheek. Priti has felt something too and pulls her leather jacket tighter around her frame. There are a few more spots, then nothing.

'Do you remember that rabbit?' I ask, trying to pull up some happier thoughts from my memory banks.

'What rabbit?' Priti says.

'That rabbit we had at the school that time, when we met,' I say, thinking back to it. 'We were about five and we got to stroke a really cute rabbit. It's the first time we spoke.'

'I thought the first time we spoke was when I took your scarf?'

'No, it was definitely the rabbit,' I assert. Priti looks like she's processing that information, then shrugs again.

'To be honest, Dex, I don't remember much that happened before I graduated from university,' she says. 'It's easier to block out the past, don't you think? Surely you must try that more than most.' She pauses and clears her throat. 'Sorry.'

'It's OK. I like the past,' I say, half-smiling. 'I like it a damn sight more than I do this present.'

'That's fair,' she says. Art drops back at this point to speak to her. His facial hair has taken on the appearance of an unmaintained garden. His moustache is outpacing his beard, and rather a lot of hair is beginning to encroach on his neck. His once-neat goatee is lost among the sprawling foliage. Sensing that a couple always prefer being by themselves than with a third wheel – a feeling I know is always there somewhere, despite somewhat obligatory protests – I slink forwards, taking the pistol from Art and letting them discuss whatever they need to discuss.

Rural changes to urban as we start making our way through little towns and villages that have tacked themselves onto the edge of the capital so that the residents can say, 'Yeah, I live in London.' Ruby and I are in the middle of a conversation about which of our colleagues would fare best in a battle with extraterrestrials (the PE teachers tend to come off very well, armed with cricket bats and hockey sticks) when we meet the next band of aliens.

There are five of them – ten heads – and they're standing in the middle of the street around a burning car and several mangled human bodies that haven't survived the merging process. Terry is the first to see them, doing a cartoonish double take and ushering us into a front garden with a large box hedge to keep us out of sight. The lawn is spongy beneath my feet. I wonder if anyone still lives here, but the door looks locked and the curtains are drawn.

'If we take out one, it will alert the rest,' whispers Terry. 'Do we have enough ammunition?'

'I think so,' I say, shrugging off my rucksack and pulling out what remains. There's a lot less than we first thought, and I realise that we've lost more than we've fired. William had some in his bag, and I remember Kay putting some in hers too.

'Fill everything as much as we can,' I say, and we load the guns to full capacity under Terry's instructions.

'Maybe we should hide,' says Art, pointing at a pub in the next street called The Goose and Gander. Skulking low to the ground, we creep gibbon-like into the pub – the door opens with a single push – and settle down in the booths. There's no electricity, so while Peregrina-and-Pete go to find torches or candles, Shell and I set about pouring out warm wine and vodka. There's a pervading smell of something rotting somewhere nearby – I assume the owners and the pub's last clientele didn't get far – but we pretend we can't smell it and carry on. Peregrina informs us, on their return, that there is some mangled flesh in one of the back rooms that may once have been the landlords.

We light a few candles, although it's not quite yet dark enough that we can't see one another, and the alcohol buoys us. For a moment, we forget about the terrible situation that we're in. Terry starts telling jokes, and we're laughing, which still feels an odd sound in this new environment. I'm standing by the door, peeking through the green frosted glass in case of movement, but the street is deserted.

None of us thinks to watch the back door, or even check if there is one.

In the small hours of the morning, the existence of an accessible back door becomes apparent when a solitary alien stumbles in. I leap from my curled sleeping position in one of the leatherette booths and it takes a moment for both my eyes to unglue themselves and for me to realise I'm holding the pistol the wrong way up.

It becomes clear, however, that the alien is in trouble. Indifferent to us and not an immediate threat, it collapses to the floor, leaning against the bar. It seems to be struggling to breathe and is gripping its torso tightly. Terry has his rifle up, ready to fire, but Peregrina has rushed forward and makes soothing noises at it.

'Out of the way!' shouts Terry, but she ignores him. Pete reaches out a large hand and presses the rifle down so that it's aiming at the floor.

'Are you OK?' says Peregrina to the alien, as if it was nothing more than an injured kitten. Ruby and Shell join her, the three of them kneeling before the two translucent heads of the intruder. Close up, despite the double head, it is far less scary. It looks more scared of us than we are of it, clutching at its side with both hands, something dark and sticky oozing from the suit. The four eyes dart between our faces, not focusing on anything. If I could ascribe an emotion to it, and it's not easy, I'd suggest it was overwhelmed.

'Is there anything we can do?' Peregrina continues, stretching out her palm to pat the alien's arm in comfort. It looks at her in horror and flinches back, causing her to do the same. 'It's OK, we don't want to harm you. Are you hurt?'

The alien clearly has no idea what is being said, but it is too weak to do anything. It loses the strength to hold itself up and slides sideways down. We get three flashes of colour – cyan, magenta and cyan again. It's dead.

'Saved a bullet,' says Art, grinning. The smile vanishes from his face when everyone glares at him and he realises it was an inappropriate comment. I look back at Peregrina, open mouthed at her behaviour. She is just about the only person I know who would try to care for an enemy that wants her dead.

But, I realise, this particular alien was not an enemy. War is futile, as has been said before, because it trains people who have nothing against one another to kill. You can't generalise. This alien may have been forced along, like so many were in the wars of our own planet.

My philosophising is abruptly ruined when several windows of the pub are smashed simultaneously. I leap up, the others coming round and staggering to their feet as well, trying to work out what's happening. Pale blue hands appear on the sill and an alien sticks its heads up to look in, signals in three short primary coloured bursts and clambers in the window. Other faces appear at other windows and within seconds there are at least half a dozen in the room, shepherding us together in a small group near the bar. Everyone clings to someone else, although no one clings to me.

No nanobots are released though.

The aliens blast colour at one another, some pastel, some neon, an apparent conversation that looks like one of the bigger boxes of Crayola crayons on the market. They look at us too, as two of them pick up their dead comrade and carry him out of the front door. The remaining aliens, three of them, stare at us and then charge. Apparently with no nanobots at their disposal, they have to make do with other means.

I punch and kick, trying to do any damage possible, my ideas of war being stupid flung aside as I try to save my own skin. There's screaming, but I can't tell who it is as we shove and lash out. I stumble back over the legs of a bar stool and catch myself on one of the booths, and an alien follows me. It's unarmed and has been hurt; a deep cut in one of its necks is matted with a dried blue liquid. One of the heads watches me, but the other is turned to look at Priti, who is coming for one of the others with a smashed wine bottle, gouging a chunk from clothes and skin. A few of my blows hit alien skin, and it feels tacky and unpleasant, sort of like freshly chewed bubblegum. The alien lashes back, hitting with thick, three-fingered hands, gnarled nails on the tip of each.

I shove it back and into the booth, but it rights itself in one quick movement and clambers onto the table, aiming kicks at my chest and face. I can't reach to hit back, so pick up a pint glass nearby and throw it hard. It misses. The alien jumps off the table and onto Terry, who drops his rifle in surprise and knocks his head hard against the metal rail around the bar.

We don't manage to kill any of them, and with a peppering of blue and red words, they make a run for it, one of them carrying a screaming Art over its shoulder, and the other dragging an unconscious Priti along by her hair at speed.

'Hey!' I shout and run after them, but the third, who is not burdened by the weight of one of my friends, turns, raises a rifle – one of our rifles – and jabs it into my face, hard.

I hear my nose crack, and everything goes dark.

Twenty-Three

Recalibration

I look at myself in the cracked mirror over the sink the following morning. My hair is flat on one side and sticking up with sweat and blood on the other. Purple bruises cover my arms and neck, alongside further smears of plummy alien blood. My eyes are red and ringed black. My nose is definitely broken, casting a weird shadow over my cut lip. I reach up and touch it, wincing as my fingers graze it.

When the alien jabbed me in the face with the butt of the rifle, the shock knocked me out and it took half an hour for me to wake up. While I was out, Shell wanted to head out into the night and find Priti-and-Art, or what was left of them at least, but given that the aliens took our guns, she was talked out of it, or perhaps shouted down. I don't know, and I don't want to. Since then I managed to have about another half hour's sleep, but no one was able to doze off for long, fearful that something else was coming. Much as we had originally delighted in having free rein of the pub's alcohol, we realise that it's probably not the best thing to be wandering the streets of the apocalypse half cut, so limit ourselves to water and bottles of Coke.

We estimate that the Tube should start about half an hour's limp away, and from there we'll follow it into the centre of the city. After a breakfast of warm orange juice and smoky bacon crisps, we pack up what remains and sneak out into the streets, bidding farewell to The Goose and Gander, wishing it had kept us a bit safer than it did. With two more of our party given over to our invaders, there are seven of us left, all in various states of sleeplessness, anxiety and pain.

The hole left by the absence of a friend I've had for over two decades is both instantaneous and enormous. Priti and I could go weeks without speaking to one another and know that we'd pick up wherever we left off once our schedules cleared again, but it's only been a matter of hours and loss pervades every atom in my body in a way nothing else has quite yet. I feel homesick.

Now unarmed, we are moving slowly, which suits us fine given that in the fight with the aliens we got pretty bruised. Ruby's left eye is sporting a purple shiner, and there are mottled blue and green patches up Peregrina's forearms.

Ruby-and-Alex are spending more and more time whispering to one another, and I do my best not to listen. No one else is paying them a lick of attention, so it is only the three of us who know what they're talking about. I wish I didn't.

The Tube line comes into sight and we figure that we deserve a rest, choosing a nearby town house at random. A plaque next to the door announces that it's not a house, but rather the offices of Satterthwaite & Quin, a firm of lawyers. Pete and Terry shoulder the door and, after a few charges, it breaks open and they fall onto an oatmeal carpet. I have to stifle an inappropriate laugh at the sight of them sprawled over one another.

We move through the converted house and settle in what must have been a waiting room, with big plush sofas and a water cooler. Desperate, I dive forward and fill a paper cup of water and gulp it down, splashing it down my shirt. I suck in air and water and pour a second cup, then a third. Despite alcohol last night and juice before we set off, it feels like an age since I drank.

Throwing my bag with food supplies we'd taken from the pub down on the floor, I flop onto the sofa and close my eyes. The others navigate the small space, drinking water and settling into comfortable positions to rest, cuddle and check on their injuries. I'm tired in a way that comes when your body has already escalated past exhaustion, pure adrenaline coursing through my veins, keeping me awake. It reminds me of the first couple of weeks of university, when you're away from home for the first time; everything is new and shiny and you don't eat because all your energy comes from hormones and snakebite.

With nothing else to look at, I pick up a small stack of envelopes from a side table and flick through them. Red stamps adorn each corner but I find it weird to think that these people – E. Highsmith, J.

Orchard, M. Burke, G. McKenna – will never receive the legal letters that had been written for them. The contents don't even matter any more. They are further evidence of human existence that is, very probably, about to be snuffed out.

Ruby is recumbent on a sofa, her head in Alex's lap and her small hands folded across her belly. She stares blankly at the ceiling and says, with the manner of one discussing the weather, 'What's the one thing you're going to be saddest about not being able to do now that the world has ended?' There's a contemplative silence from the seven of us. I think again about *Ubik*. Is the loss of literature the biggest blow?

'Our wedding,' says Peregrina, looking at Pete. 'That'll never happen.'

'Booking that DJ was a waste of a deposit wasn't it?' he says, with a wink. 'Obviously, the wedding too, but I'm also sad I never got to see Australia. I wish I'd gone.'

'I'm going to miss food,' says Shell, fiddling with her rings. 'I would've liked a bit more preparation for the end of the world to gorge on chocolate, cake and champagne for a few days.'

'I'll miss the books I never got to read,' says Ruby, commandeering my thoughts for her own. 'All those ones that I should've read but never got round to: *Nineteen Eighty-Four*, *Brave New World*, *The Handmaid's Tale*, *Shopaholic Ties the Knot*...'

'I'm going to miss little things,' says Alex. 'I'll never go to a football match again, or win a pub quiz. And children...' He stops himself and Ruby squeezes his hand.

'I'm going to miss roast dinners,' says Terry, biting at his fingernails. 'Roast pork, especially, with lots of crackling, the saltier the better.' There's a momentary pause before he adds, 'And, if we're honest, I'm pissed off that I never got to go to Disneyland.'

'What about you, Dex?' says Ruby, turning her head to look at me. I chew my lip, still thinking of an answer.

'I think that I'm annoyed most about the fact that I'll never know what happens next,' I say. 'If we are among the few who survive the invasion and happen to still be alive when the aliens fuck off, maybe we'll see something, but I don't think we will be. Even if I'm dead, not knowing if humans survive this and rebuild is something that's rather unbearable.'

More silence.

'Thanks for killing the mood,' says Shell, but with a small chuckle. 'OK, I've got one. What *won't* you miss about the world?'

'The Smiths,' I say, without hesitation.

'I'm gonna go with the Kardashians,' says Pete.

'I won't miss writing Christmas cards,' says Alex, a strange sort of look on his face. 'Isn't that one of the most tedious tasks in the world?'

'You don't even write them, I do,' says Ruby, chucking him under the chin with her fist. 'You come along afterwards and add your name.'

'Yeah, well,' he says with indifference. 'I also won't miss those work trips to Llanfairfechan or some other Welsh hellhole to attend focus groups and do awkward team building exercises.' I've always managed to avoid going away with my colleagues – former colleagues – but even birthday drinks with some of them can be painful. Anita always had too much gin, and old David Tubby insisted on talking at length whenever possible about cars he'd known and loved, all the while wafting his un-deodoranted armpits around the pub.

'Right, we need a bit more of a plan,' I say, realising that we can't sit around undefended forever, quashing the ideas that are fermenting in my head saying that might be an easier option. 'I still vote we hole up in the Natural History Museum, which is plenty big enough for us to hide in. However, we first need some new weaponry, and there isn't any there unless we intend to fight with stuffed eagles and fossil casts.'

'There must be gun shops dotted around London?' says Shell. 'I mean, they aren't illegal with the right licences so someone must sell them.'

'Yeah, but I've no idea where any of them are, and I'd imagine people have already looted them,' I say. 'I reckon we should divert to the British Museum to restock our arsenal before we head for our final – or temporarily final – destination. The Science Museum won't be much use from what I remember, and the Grant Museum is taxidermy and bones. Unless the Tate Modern has an exhibition on about weaponry in sculpture, I don't think we'll have much luck taking out any aliens with a Rothko. There's the Petrie Museum near the British Museum, but it's all Egyptian stuff and I don't think it has any weapons from memory. I don't think the V&A has any weapons, either. Can anyone remember?'

'Art mostly, isn't it?' says Peregrina. 'We had a cocktail party there a few months ago with work. I remember a lot of clothes and sculpture.'

'Right, so are we in agreement?' I say. We wait a couple of hours yet, dozing and willing feeling back into our aching bodies. Finally, I stand up, feeling unsteady on my feet, my body having forgotten how bad the pain was while I was sat down. There's a murmur of assent and we make a move back out of the lawyer's offices, somewhat rested, and hit the streets again, where it has begun to rain.

Twenty-Four

The British Museum

We squelch our way to Russell Square as the rain pelts down on our heads and shoulders. My suede desert boots are ruined, and every so often there is a rumble of distant thunder over the deserted capital.

No aliens surprise us, but we are humbled and kept quiet anyway by the signs of destruction that pepper our route. There is occasional evidence of other survivors, but it is few and far between and exists mostly as shadows at windows. Once, close to Lincoln's Inn Fields, Ruby becomes convinced that we are being watched, and she and I both think we see a body in a thick army coat slink off around a corner. I wonder for the first time where the military are.

On Bloomsbury Way, we encounter one of the strangest things yet. There is a double-decker bus that has tipped over like a great elephant, unable to right itself. Most of the windows are smashed and, inside, the walls are blood-stained. Fingers, eyeballs, arms and other bits that might once have been livers and voiceboxes are scattered in and around the shell. Some nanobots clearly had a good time in there, but they've long gone and flies have begun to move in.

There are more flies than usual around the streets, presumably because of the sudden influx of openly rotting flesh for them to lay their quick-hatching eggs in. Rats, too, appear to have noticed that the streets are much emptier and along with the pigeons have not been slow in exhibiting their bravado by helping themselves to the last of the human litter, and indeed the last of the humans.

I see one rat carrying off a small ear in its sharp teeth and don't know whether to laugh or vomit.

By the time we reach the British Museum, we are soaked through, clothes sticking to our skin, although I actually feel a little cleaner at least. It's the first decent wash I've had in days.

Trotting up the steps, I notice that the front doors are already wide open, litter and pigeons gathering in the once-grand entrance. Inside, it's rather gloomy but we can see well enough thanks to the faint emergency lighting. Our footsteps echo in the silent atrium, although I can't believe we're the only people here. We may even be too late to find anything useful.

Ruby-and-Alex scan a floor plan of the museum, while the rest of us keep an eye out for any other movement. Ruby points out the weapons rooms and we follow them through different exhibits and staircases. I think of the millions of items stored here, now worthless. Would anyone ever need the Rosetta Stone again? Does the ongoing argument about who owns the Elgin Marbles seem futile? I can't even remember if they are still here or not.

The weapons are stored behind glass fronts, pinned, pegged and strapped to the green felt walls. They comprise three rooms and the white placards dotted about detail the history of human weaponry, from Stone Age to Space Age. We're not going to have much luck with a blunderbuss or musket, and there don't appear to be any unused bullets on display, so I suggest we focus our attentions on hand-to-hand combat weapons. They're very rusty and look pretty fragile, but they'll have to do.

Terry kicks at the glass of an Iron Age cabinet, but it resists. In a neighbouring room is a statue of Ares, which is commandeered, pulled from his plinth and charged into the glass like a battering ram. A security light flashes red above us, but no alarm goes off. We smash a few more and grab at swords, maces and daggers, arming ourselves with the ones that look to be in the best condition, although almost everything here is coated in a fine layer of rust after its extensive journey through time from creation to preservation. Ruby insists on a halberd, although looks ridiculous carrying it. She can barely hold it, so Christ knows how she intends to wield it against a cloud of nanobots or a two-headed alien.

'Stop!' a voice shouts and we swivel round to find ourselves facing two burly black men holding up rifles. My hands leap up over my head, but the others are behind me so I can't tell if they're doing the same. 'Drop your weapons!'

'We're not here to do any harm to you,' I say, my breathing becoming deep and panicked.

'This is our patch,' says the man on the left. He has a close-shaved head the shape of a pumpkin. The second man has matted black hair and glasses with large frames and no glass.

'We came here for weapons to use against the aliens,' says Peregrina, voice calm as a millpond. 'We were unarmed. We're not going to use them on you.' The two men lower their rifles, realising that unless Ruby makes a charge for them with her halberd, they aren't likely to come to any immediate harm. The man on the left moves forward and extends an oddly slender hand. I shake it – his skin is clammy.

'I'm Gary McQueen,' he says and, pointing at his companion, adds, 'Kevin Hawthorne.' Introductions are made, hands are shaken, weapons are not used. It turns out that they're a couple and should have been getting married a few days from now, although the slight interruption of an alien invasion and the fall of civilisation put paid to that. They lead, with us now feeling safer armed with tools not used in centuries or, in the case of the carved flints that Pete pocketed, millennia, down to the Egyptian rooms. In among the sarcophagi and sculptures there is a tiny shanty town of tents. They're constructed from sheets, towels and duvets like childhood pillow forts. There are about twenty-five people here, although we're informed there are more scattered throughout the museum; small pockets of resistance.

'Where are you trying to go?' asks Kevin. Despite his wide shoulders and rugby-playing figure, he's softly spoken, with an accent that suggests he comes from the dark blue Monopoly squares rather than brown or cyan.

'Natural History Museum,' I say. 'We intend to hide out there and then, well, we'll see what happens to us, I guess.'

'Have you eaten anything?' Gary says, and we reveal that our supplies are meagre. Displaying a friendliness that I don't remember from pre-apocalypse Londoners, Gary, Kevin and a couple of the others who are listening to us proffer food, some of it even fresh fruit and vegetables raided from nearby shops and houses. Although we're not shown where these are kept – we aren't going to be given that level of trust – they also have large supplies of canned goods. No one is risking anything that should've been frozen. We're also handed some spare towels to dry ourselves off.

Our group disperses and we join with the others already here, telling them the things we've seen and done, and the things we saw and did before the end. They tell us stories too, of the people and lives they've lost and the time passes in a pleasant blur. One man we speak to was an MP – he ran rather than staying at Westminster to help come up with a plan of action. He admits it was probably cowardice, but also that because of it, he's also most likely the most senior politician left alive. It's nice to talk to some new people for a change – I was starting to feel like we were the only ones left.

Towards the latter half of the afternoon, two more people arrive, a tall willowy woman and a man built like one of the museum's marble statues, arms full of more food from nearby pubs and restaurants. Small fires are built using books from the gift shop – for an English student who has been indoctrinated to believe that there is nothing more important than the written word, there are fewer signs more upsetting – and people set about opening cans and cooking food.

Kevin, I learn while our nostrils are attacked by the scent of an incoming meal, used to be a teacher too, working at a very well-to-do primary school in Chelsea. Gary, meanwhile, used to work in the perfume department of Harrods, another place that was, we're told, gutted by aliens in the first wave of invasions. Gary says he had been at work when the aliens first arrived, and when he left there were already dozens of mutilated bodies.

'That's odd,' I say, and I relay our theory about how it's only romantically attached couples that are getting merged by the nanobots. Gary gives me a look that suggests he's doing long division in his head, but then the fog in his expression clears and he says, 'You could be right, actually. There were – what? Five thousand employees at that place? It was the like the gods on Mount Olympus – everyone was sleeping with everyone else, so I guess they were the ones that were taken out.'

'Wasn't there a policy about dating within the company?' I ask. 'I mean, I worked at Starbucks for a bit and we had one there. Surely Harrods would?'

'The management turned a blind eye as long as everyone was doing their jobs,' shrugged Gary. 'I never gave the couple thing much thought, but now you say it... Does that mean it would be safer if I left Kevin?' I throw a glance towards Kevin who is chuckling at something Terry has said in between mouthfuls of stale pork pie.

'Probably,' I shrug. 'But, let's be honest, this whole thing is fruitless. We're going to die, aren't we?' Gary doesn't answer; instead he looks across at Kevin. Without looking at me, he abruptly asks, 'Have you ditched your partner to survive?' A flash of Georgina's worried face and green hair slides into view and I blink it away, choosing to eat another spoonful of my dinner instead of answering Gary's question. He takes my silence as an answer and nods a few times, that long-division look appearing in his eyes again.

Twenty-Five

The Unexpected Guest

It's dark by the time we've finished eating and everyone is sated with both food and conversation. The refugees of the British Museum insist that we don't go out again in the dark, but instead remain here with them overnight. However, there appears to be no offer of continued accommodation. They can't afford any more people in the place, potentially making their temporary home more obvious, crowded or short of food.

Although not actively unkind or unfriendly, aside from Gary-and-Kevin they're pretty guarded. We try to engage in small talk with some of them, but they hug themselves tighter as if we're the threat, and always seem to have one hand on whatever possessions they've managed to keep hold of. Many of them seem to have nothing to their name, but I suspect that it's because anything with worth has been sequestered away in their tents and will never be shown to us.

I doze in a sweaty sleep, dreaming of bodies ripped asunder, Annie-and-Matt running off as one through a burning housing estate, and Lara-and-Steve weeping, hiding in some forsaken corner of an unidentifiable room. The images feel almost real, but they are products of a hyperactive mind, struggling to cope with loss and worry.

I'm sleeping on the hard floor between Shell and Pete, when something nudges my foot. I ignore it, but it does it again, so I force my eyelids open a crack and see Gary looking down at me.

'What?' I mouth, but he beckons me up so, trying not to disturb my sleeping friends, I stand up, my legs aching and my back feeling like it's full of ball bearings, and go over to where he leads, in a corner underneath a strange Egyptian death mask.

'When are your lot leaving?' he whispers, his voice hoarse like he hasn't drunk anything in a long time. Perhaps he hasn't.

'Once it's light and we're fully awake,' I whisper back. 'It should take just over an hour to walk to the Natural History Museum.'

'I'm coming with you,' he says, and before he gives me a chance to protest, carries on. 'I was thinking about what you said last night, about how it's only couples that keep getting killed. I don't want to die. I mean, I guess I will, but not yet. I need to leave Kevin, so when you go, I want to come with you.'

'Are you sure?' I ask. 'I mean, I've got no proof. It's a theory.'

'I'm coming.' He is firm. I consider trying to argue a case that it's probably approaching a state some would say is heartless to abandon someone who you were supposed to be marrying to save your own skin, even if it does mean the survival of both parties. I'm still thinking of Georgina, I suppose. What's worse – dying together or living alone? I decide against saying anything as my bladder is alerting me to the fact that I need make a trip to the toilet.

I head out into the main atrium, which is draughty and dim, and not as pleasant or welcoming as it has been on the few occasions I've come here as an actual visitor. The pristine white walls and floor will never be cleaned again, I think, and it's a funny thought. The human race has been doomed for maybe a week – I've lost track of days and nights – but that week has been enough to ensure that so many things will never happen again.

I unzip at the urinal, letting loose a long, almost violent, stream of dark yellow, dehydrated pee. My mouth feels dry and when I'm done I stick my head under the cold tap and lap up the chilled water, most of it missing and soaking my face instead, although the wash is also well overdue again. I knock my broken nose against the tap and gasp at the pain that shoots through me. It thankfully doesn't start bleeding again.

I reach out for paper towels and dry my face off, throwing them in the bin after I'm done and realising what a ridiculous thing to do that is, akin to Jay still parking his car legally in front of my house. I wonder what's happened to my house, and if I'll ever see it again.

Absent-mindedly, I check my wrist only to remember that I'm not wearing a watch and have no idea what the time is. It's still dark outside, but indigo rather than black. I leave the toilets and cross the atrium to the front doors of the museum. The chilly air nibbles at my face like a small beaver working on a twig. There are a few lights around at windows but they're weak and presumably coming from candles and torches. It isn't raining any more, but the roads and pavements are shiny with puddles, reflecting the chalky, almost-full moon.

There's an untamed, unusual noise somewhere to my left and, heartbeat rising, I turn to look. There's nothing there, but it came from the direction of the gift shop.

I lift my feet up quietly, trying not to rustle the leaves and crisp packets that have gathered at the open doors and decide to investigate under the logic it's better to know what you're facing.

Creeping along to the open door of the gift shop, my heart thunders like a steam train in my chest and I hope that the noise was my imagination. Unfortunately, it turns out not to have been my imagination.

It's a lion.

She has her back to me and is sniffing at displays of carved globes as if plotting a holiday destination. At first my brain thinks of *Jumanji*, but then I think seriously about where a lion would have come from and realise that the only possible location around here is London Zoo. I guess with no one bothering to feed them any more and with the power off in the electric fences, instinct has kicked in and the animals have had to start looking for sustenance elsewhere, although this one is roaring up the wrong baobab if it thinks it can eat a souvenir key ring. She's a long way from home.

Stepping backwards carefully on the crepe soles of my ruined desert boots, I try and make as little noise as possible. I know that it's the lionesses that do the hunting, so we're in the shit in that respect, but I don't know if they work by smell or movement. I pray that it doesn't turn round, although at least when I'm mauled to death I won't have the added embarrassment of pissing myself due to my last act of life being to use the loo.

The lioness, however, is far too interested in tourist-tempting tchotchkes to pay any attention to what's going on behind her. I don't dare turn away so I back into the Egyptology wing and stumble into

Alex's prone figure, nudging him awake. He opens his mouth to speak but I hurriedly shush him and kneel down.

'There's a lion in the gift shop,' I breathe.

'An alien?' he whispers back.

'No, a lion!'

'That's what I said. Alien,' he repeats. I shake my head and mime the action of a growing lion displaying its claws.

'Oh, a *lion*,' he says, with a certain degree of nonchalance. The realisation hits him a second later and he jerks up, thwacking his skull against my own and causing us both to yelp in pain, in turn prompting Ruby and Shell-and-Terry to stir.

And suddenly everyone is awake because Simba's missus is standing in the doorway growling, crouched down on her haunches as if ready to pounce. Those of us with weapons grab them, the option of staying still ignored, and I catch sight of Kevin raising his rifle and, before anyone can speak, firing it at the furious feline.

The bullet embeds itself in her shoulder, making her even more furious. With surprising agility for such a large animal, she leaps into the middle of the room, sending us scattering to the walls. I do a quick headcount and, yes, Ruby-and-Alex, Peregrina-and-Pete and Shell-and-Terry are all fine and next to me, weapons held at various heights. Gary is trapped on the other side of the room, but gives me a look that says, 'Don't go without me.' It's my turn to be heartless, as I already intend on putting my efforts into saving myself and my friends, and not someone we picked up at random. They didn't want us to stay; why should we want them to come with us?

The lion takes an interest in one thin, pale woman standing beneath a solitary marble arm that once belonged to some great pharaoh's statue and, with little warning, makes another jump at her, drowning out her scream with the sound of tearing flesh and burbled final words.

I look at the others and, with little more than an expression of panic, somehow get across to them that this morbid distraction would be great cover for us to make a break for it. As if in silent agreement, we dive for the door and are mostly out of it before the lioness takes an interest. We would have escaped if it wasn't for the fact that Gary has chosen that moment to shout, 'Hey, hold up!' and Kevin responds, 'What the hell?' Gary ignores him and runs across the room towards us, but not quick enough, as the lioness tackles him from behind and he makes a garbled yelp as claws rip his shirt and flesh and her mighty jaws crush his skull like it was made of trifle.

The scream that follows from Kevin's throat has to heard to be believed. It is pained with the misery of a hundred lonely winter evenings, like sheet metal noisily twisted and moulded into a new shape by some ungodly machine. It is not a noise I imagined a human was capable of making. The rifle falls from his hands and clatters on the floor.

Kevin began to rush forward to where the lioness is crunching on bone, but a couple of quick thinkers behind him manage to grab his arms and stop him from running into danger.

'NO!' he shouts. His legs give way and he drops to his knees, unable to tear his eyes away from the horror in front of him. He shrugs off his minders and puts his head between his knees, bashing his fists futilely against the floor.

I'm frozen to the spot, and I can't hear the others moving behind me either. I can't help wishing we'd gone for it when we first could. I think we might still get away with Kevin not noticing that Gary was trying to come with us, but a moment later I realise that we're not going to. Kevin looks up, tears and snot mingling on his face. He's unrecognisable, his features contorted by grief, fury and futility.

'Where was he going?' he shouts, staring directly at us. I want to try and convey to Kevin that this isn't the time to be discussing it as his partner is being ripped into bite-sized chunks on the marble in front of us, but I'm too worried that he's going to pick up the gun and shoot one of us. He doesn't appear to remember it is still lying next to him.

'Why was he leaving me?' His voice is loud and angry, despite the sobs between every word. I cast a wary look at the lioness, but she's feeding. It's disgusting and I fight back a rising tide of bile.

'I don't know what he was doing,' I bluff, moving backwards, not wanting to be involved in this. Only Shell-and-Terry are still there, the others having made a dash for freedom. 'We need to get out of here, though. Now.'

'No,' says Kevin, a crazed look in his eyes that's highlighted by the empty frames. 'I'm coming with you.' Mad with grief, he jumps up and pounds across the marble towards us, but the lioness sees him coming. She turns to him and as she leaps at him, a blur flies past me in a grotty blue shirt and Terry bellows as he plunges his sword between the shoulder blades of the lioness.

The beast bellows in agony and Terry pulls the sword back out with a slurping kind of sound or, rather, pulls out the handle. The rusty blade has snapped off and is stuck in the beast's broad back. It's too late for Kevin – his face is not where it was before – but Terry is apparently determined to save the rest of us. The lioness turns to face him although looks ready to collapse. He helps it by snatching up Shell's sword and drilling it home up its right nostril. That one breaks too, leaving half the blade in the big cat's face. With a final noise that reminds me of the sound Catsby once made when I accidentally sat on his tail, the lioness collapses to the ground, sprawled out and dead.

In any other circumstance, a round of applause might have been appropriate, but everyone just stares agog at the four dead bodies and we take the opportunity to run outside.

Stood at the top of the front steps, we gasp for air, sucking in lungfuls of the crisp early morning.

'What happened?' asks Peregrina, her voice high and squeaky. 'Are we safe?'

'Comparatively,' I wheeze. 'We need to get out of here though. Lions rarely hunt alone.'

'I'll lead,' says Terry, standing up and wiping his half-bladed sword on his jeans.

'Do you know where you're going?' asks Shell. 'You always get bloody lost in London. Let Dexter show us the way.'

'I can do anything!' he hollers into the morning. I go to interrupt him but he carries on.

'Because I defeated the Lioness of London!' he shouts, then laughs somewhat maniacally at the sky, brandishing his sword. 'I am unbeatable! Let's show these fucking aliens that humans aren't going to be pushed around any –'

There's a whip crack sound, and a piece of Terry's brain lands on my cheek.

Twenty-Six

Ruby-and-Alex-and-

Shell screams.

Alex grabs Ruby and pulls her to his chest.

Peregrina-and-Pete look on in a shocked silence, fingers loosening on their weaponry.

I wipe the brain from my cheek and watch as Terry collapses to his knees, pitches forwards and tumbles like a man-sized Slinky down the grand steps of the British Museum.

A figure wrapped in a thick green coat runs across the road, hands raised high, one of them holding a sniper rifle. It falls to its knees beside Terry's body and reaches out to touch him.

'Don't you fucking dare!' Shell screeches. The person stands up again. It's impossible to tell if it's male or female, with a scarf wrapped around the lower half of its face, baggy jeans and old trainers, a thick coat and jumper and a stray wisp of blonde poking out from the bottom of the beanie on its head.

'I'm so sorry, he surprised me! His shouting! I... I didn't mean to shoot him!' The voice is husky and is followed by a few loud, racking coughs, so it remains impossible to attach to a gender. Shell is crouching beside Terry, lifting him up and hugging his body to her, tears streaming down her face. If I thought Kevin's noises were inhuman, they were nothing compared to this.

'He doesn't even look like a fucking alien,' shouts Pete, stepping forward and shoving the attacker in the shoulder. 'They don't make any noise!' He or she stumbles back and the rifle clatters to the ground. Peregrina steps forward and swoops it up before Terry's killer can grab it again.

'Hey, no, give that back,' he or she pleads, voice muffled by the scarf. Shell, however, doesn't need to hear that and stands up, launching herself at her nemesis with the same ferocity as the lion Terry killed moments before. The attack knocks the scarf and hat from the figure revealing it to be a woman, and the two of them fall to the floor, Shell straddling her, delivering slaps and punches to her face until her knuckles are bloodied and the woman looks like she's done a few rounds with Mike Tyson.

I know that women are as capable of violence as men, but in the last few days I have seen Kay bash a dog's head in, Peregrina punch a vicar and now Shell bludgeon the face of a total stranger into pâté. It's a bit much. When Shell finally returns to Terry to hug his lifeless body, I wonder if she's actually killed someone with her bare hands.

However, after a moment or two, the woman stands up and, eyelids half-open and her features resembling a Picasso painting, stumbles off into what can only be her last moments left alive in the city. If aliens and wild animals are both around and she's unarmed and can barely see where she's going, she doesn't stand a chance. I almost want to help her, but she's shot an innocent person. It's a difficult one to forgive.

We, however, are left with another difficult decision – do we try and bury Terry or not? There are plenty of gardens and green spaces around but... am I being heartless? Is this another Mr Grossman incident? We buried Iris-and-William, we *should* bury Terry, but I also feel we need to get moving. It can't be wise to spend any longer outside than is necessary. Trying to convince Shell of that, however, looks like it's going to be a something of a more difficult task.

Blood stains her top and hands as she grabs at Terry's head, his glassy eyes staring at nothing in the middle distance, a disinterested expression like he's watching a football match between two equally rubbish teams. She wails with a noise somewhere between a klaxon and a howler monkey.

'Shell, come on,' says Peregrina in her most soothing voice, but Shell grabs at the corpse tighter like it's a grotesque teddy bear. It might be as fresh as a Dunkin' Donuts coffee, but it still makes me feel weird – it's a dead body, after all. Peregrina tries again, 'Look, come on, we'll sort it out, please let go.'

'Guys, we have to get out of here now,' says Pete.

'We can't leave Terry's body out here,' says Ruby. 'Come on, Pete, don't be so callous.'

'I'm not being callous,' he growls. 'We've been found, so we have to go.' Ruby and I both turn to look where he's looking, our four eyes alighting on the eight eyes of two aliens. They're at the far end of the street, but they appear to be moving towards us, increasing their speed with each step. Any thought of burying Terry is abandoned as Ruby and Peregrina pull Shell off the body and we drag her into a run, which becomes easier when she notices the danger. Survival instinct kicks in.

My feet, aching more than I'd realised, pound the tarmac but every time I risk a glance behind us, the aliens are still in hot pursuit. I become aware of a hum in the air and turn once more. There's a grey cloud of nanobots headed right for us. I'm, presumably, safe, and so is Shell – Terry's death may yet save her – and it turns out that Peregrina-and-Pete have paid enough attention so far to stand either side of Shell, much as the look in their eyes suggests that to do so is killing them. However, given the choice between a metaphorical killing and a very real one, they have chosen the logical option.

Alex, however, still hasn't understood and leaps on Ruby to protect her, wrapping her up in his long limbs. With little choice, she presses her face close to his chest and I see a look of fear in her features as the cloud reaches the couple and gets down to its grisly surgery.

The two are engulfed for a few seconds but then, quite spectacularly, a gap opens up and Alex falls away, landing hard on the tarmac, although Ruby remains inside the swarm of tiny robots, screaming. The only sound worse than her screaming is the silence when she stops. The nanobots depart and, despite various lacerations to her head, limbs and back, she looks in fairly fine fettle.

Until, that is, she turns around to face us, revealing that her stomach has been slashed and clawed and ripped and various metal staples and pins struggle to hold her torso in place.

Ruby didn't need Alex to be merged with her because she already had something else to be merged with.

Her own unborn baby.

Back in the library, at a time in history that feels aeons ago yet is only a matter of days and hours, I heard her talking to Alex about when they might tell the rest of us that she was pregnant, or whether they shouldn't. I had, however, never considered that this would be the outcome if she ever encountered the aliens and nanobots at a range as close as this.

In shock more than anything, although the small river of blood pouring from her midriff down her jeans and onto her black pumps and the tarmac could be said to be at least partly responsible, Ruby falls forwards on her knees and twists sideways to land on her hip. Several streets from where Terry fell, she falls too.

To look at anything other than her mangled body, I glance up the street for the aliens, but they've gone. Perhaps the nanobots need constant charging and they only had one cloud. I look at Alex, his face milk white, eyes wider than Neptune's orbit. He stares at his girlfriend's body, unable to look anywhere else. Peregrina-and-Pete are still not daring to touch. Shell has stopped crying, and also stares open mouthed.

Alex turns and, with a speed I should have expected from his lanky frame, sprints off in a direction that I think is south. Realising that there's nothing I can do to help Ruby, I set off after him, sensing another person on my tail. His long legs make short work of the road, but we run for a long time before slowing to a jog and then more of an amble. I've no clue if he knows where he's going. I give up calling after him to conserve my energy, not knowing how far I'm going to have to go. Our pace has slowed, but he's still quite far ahead of me. As long as I keep him in view, I'll not lose him.

By the time I reach him, he's straddling the barrier on Waterloo Bridge, one leg dangling over the water, the other still safe.

We're a long way from either the British Museum or our intended destination. That is, intended before two of our party were suddenly and mercilessly wiped out. Life, as has been documented in any number of books, films and historical accounts, is not fair and neither does it make much sense.

'Alex, get down!' I approach him with caution, not wanting to scare him any further. It's a precarious seat, and if he slips...

Peregrina has joined me, red in the face and panting like an

Olympic hammer thrower. She puts her hand on my shoulder. Alex doesn't reply. He turns his neck further so he doesn't have to look at me.

'I mean it,' I plead. 'Look, come back down, it's going to be OK.'

'No, it isn't,' he says, his voice as bland as a dry cracker. 'She's dead.'

'But you're alive, and we need to keep you that way,' I say. I want to grieve for Ruby, one of my oldest friends, but in this moment, there is something more important at stake. Alex and I may not ever have been great friends, but I like him and, for the sake of Ruby, he needs to stay alive. I don't think it's sunk in that she's dead. 'We've been through a lot of loss, and I know this is worse for you than some, but it's horrible for me too. For all of us.'

'It's not just Ruby,' he says, his voice spooky when it's so emotionless. 'I still loved Annie too, in my own way.' Of course. I had forgotten they dated, although it had been very brief and many years ago. I couldn't believe he was still hung up on that. Then again, do we ever completely forget any of the people we love, or if not love, simply care for? We take what we learn from each relationship and channel that knowledge into the next one. He adds, barely any louder than the water hitting the bridge, 'And Kay, too.'

'What do you mean?' I ask, baffled.

'I was in love with Kay,' he says. Any last vestige of emotion has been sapped from his voice and face. He's beyond our help and beyond any normal human experience, unable to cope with the speed at which everything is happening.

His confession causes a few images and memories to click into place like a jigsaw puzzle I didn't know I was meant to be making, and I see how we missed the clues over the years about his feelings. I get flashes of him topping up her glass in the bar, or asking after her whenever she was mentioned, and one of our rare poker nights when he was far too happy at having bested Jay, like it proved he was a better person.

'Did you ever do anything about it?' I ask, wondering if it matters any more. She's dead, and so is Ruby. If I can't talk Alex off the side of the bridge, he will be shortly as well.

'No, of course not,' he spits. 'She's married and I was always with Ruby. But she was amazing, and I hate that she died not knowing.

She should at least have known. Everyone needs to know they are loved.' I think that Kay probably knew she was loved, by Jay at least, and didn't need to know about Alex. I decide not to mention that.

'We've all lost loved ones…' I begin, but I'm cut off.

'What do you know? Who have you lost that you loved?' he shouts, spittle flying from his lips. I realise that he has no clue what he's said or is thinking strictly in the sense of romantic partners – the only love that popular culture seems to consider worth talking about or living for. Anger erupts from my body, my chest and shoulders burning with the grief and pain and horror that I've been holding back for the last few days, weeks and years about the people I've loved and lost.

'Everyone!' I shout back. He stares at me. 'I have lost *everyone*! I have no family, so I resorted to being a fucking good friend, and then every single one of them paired up and forgot about me sitting by my fucking self every night until the end of the world, when they may have started to feel a little guilty! I might not fall in love with people, but how *blind* are you to imagine that I've lost no one in my life? I lost everyone before this happened, and I've lost everyone else one by one since then!'

He doesn't respond, but instead turns from me and looks out across the Thames. No boats sail up and down it, probably for the first time in two millennia. Gulls and seabirds scoot across its murky brown surface, attracted to something shimmering on the waves. I continue staring at him, furious, and I batter away the thought that I should push him and hurry things along.

'Well, you should be used to this,' he says, swinging his other leg over the bridge.

'No!' I shout.

'Alex, don't do this!' cries Peregrina through tears.

'I'm coming Ruby.' Alex's final words are swallowed up by a strong wind.

He leaps.

Twenty-Seven

Journey to the Natural History Museum

He didn't scream as he fell, I remember. He dropped like a stone. Silent. Accepting. If there was a splash, and I assume there was, my brain has decided not to add it to my memory files. As I sit in my room, I become aware of noises around me. There's still the gentle thrum beneath me, but occasionally there's a murine squeak somewhere behind one of the walls, or what sounds like footsteps near where my food bag came in. Was that hours ago? Days? Minutes?

Ruby's death is the one stamped on my retina most clearly. Of course I miss everyone, and I'm sorry I couldn't save any of them – though I've no idea how I would have even begun to try – but Ruby's is the one that brings me the most anguish, sadness and horror. They were all violent, yet hers felt a degree worse. More than a degree. It was unthinkable.

So was the thought that our numbers would have increased if we'd kept her alive. I shake my head, trying to get the thought to unglue itself from my brain. Of course, it doesn't work, so I try and focus on one of the few moments of hope and joy that made itself known during the worst week of our lives.

Then there were four.

Well, technically two, as Peregrina and I now have the unenviable task of navigating the dangerous streets of London back to where we think we left the others, who in turn had the even more unenviable task of disposing of Terry and Ruby.

The streets seem unfamiliar. London is not a city that was ever supposed to be empty. It should be full of people doing all manner of things on sliding scales of morality, illegality, usefulness and attractiveness.

Doors stand wide open; abandoned cars, taxis and buses clog up the streets, and there's the occasional skittering of a dog, cat or pigeon that makes us jump.

The grief hits me like a freight train out of nowhere and I find I'm unable to take a single step more, instead falling against a black taxi and bursting into noisy, unrestrained tears. Peregrina, somehow managing to keep her cool, steps forward and wraps her long, thin arms around me while I empty my body of its salt water. Faces blur across my wet eyes and I cry for Ruby and for Alex, for Terry, for Priti and for Art, for Annie and for Matt, for Iris and for William, for Catsby, for Georgina, for Kay and for Jay, for Lara and for Steve, and for Gavin and for Frederik. And then more tears for everyone else. The sheer emptiness of London highlights how quickly the aliens moved and how unprepared we were. There must have been thousands of them, perhaps many of them still kicking about, mopping us up like we're stubborn bacteria.

I've no idea how long we sit like that, me crying like a child and Peregrina sitting calmly holding me until I stop shaking and regain my composure. When I do raise my head again and think I'm ready to start moving, it's clear that she hasn't been quite so calm and has also been crying, her face streaked with shiny tear tracks. Her glasses look like they need a good clean.

We both stagger to our feet and make headway back into the city to where we think Pete and Shell are. There's still very little sound in the city.

'What's going to happen to us?' says Peregrina, her voice mournful and quiet.

'We're probably going to die.' My words thud like an anvil falling into mud.

'But then why don't we throw ourselves off the bridge like Alex?'

'Because we might not die.'

'That's optimistic of you,' she says. 'Don't see that colour on you very often.'

'I think I'm beyond pessimism.' I shrug, trying to reorient myself, reading street names that don't mean anything to me. A thought that's been niggling at me comes to the surface. 'What's worse is that we never get to properly say goodbye to anyone.'

'Well, we don't know when the attack is coming,' says Peregrina. 'I mean, we can watch for aliens, but Terry's killing is enough to tell us that there are plenty of other threats. Survivors are turning mad. And there's the zoo.'

'I thought that if there ever was a dystopian future it would take people a lot longer to fall to anarchy.'

'Me too.'

'But now we know it takes a matter of days.' I recognise a street and point down it, leading Peregrina to what I hope is the right place. 'Maybe humans are more fucked up than we thought.'

'Our brains are big, and adaptive to change, but not that quickly,' says Peregrina. 'Basic survival instincts kick in I suppose, don't they?'

'Must do.'

We walk on a little further in silence, double back on ourselves by mistake, take too many right turns but eventually appear back on another familiar street, this one littered with bodies, some single, but most of them merged, although not very well. The stench is unbelievable, and we hurry on through, trying not to step in any entrails that the rats haven't helped themselves to yet.

By luck more than judgement, we find Shell and Pete again, with lost looks in their eyes. Pete has our weapons poking out of a large rucksack on his back. Shell still looks dumbfounded, her face unable to hide the horrors she's seen.

'Where's Alex?' asks Pete, but a single look from me to him as I take a sword from his pack tells him all that he needs to know. He nods once, then kisses Peregrina on the cheek as she approaches to take her mace.

Peregrina-and-Pete walk ahead, while I fall back to walk with Shell, but what does one say in these sorts of situations? Gavin would know. I reach my non-sword-bearing arm out to her and waggle my fingers. She looks at my hand like it's something unusual, but clasps it tight with her own, interlocking her ring-drenched fingers with mine.

'How much further to the museum?' she asks.

'Not far, I think,' I say, looking around the streets, catching sight of the occasional shadow at a window: the last of London's survivors.

'I'm a bit discombobulated by the lack of people. Everything looks weird.'

'Everything is weird,' she says, her voice as bland as porridge. 'Why exactly this museum anyway?' I sigh.

'OK, well, it's pretty nerdy,' I say, 'but I'd always drawn up – mentally this is, I don't have spreadsheets or anything – a plan of where to hide should we get a zombie invasion. I never thought much of it through, like where to get weapons or food, but I read about somewhere I thought would be perfect to hide. You know the big blue whale model in the middle of the museum?'

'Yeah,' says Shell, stretching the word out and looking at me like I'm a bit mad which, given what else has happened to us lately, strikes me as somewhat unfair.

'Well, apparently there's a trap door in it,' I explain. 'Where better to hide than in the belly of the whale?' She looks at me, incredulous. 'Maybe it's an urban legend, but even if it is, there are enough places to hide in either there or the Science Museum.'

'I can't believe you,' says Shell, a half-smile creeping to her lips, almost despite herself. Death and destruction make you able to smile merely an hour or two after disposing of your boyfriend's body in this new world.

'Can't believe I'm quite that sad?' I say.

'No,' she says. 'I can't believe you thought that the Natural History Museum would be the best place to hide from zombies, when *obviously* you need a castle. The Tower of London would be great, due to the weaponry already in place and on display there, but the dream one is somewhere like Bodiam Castle, right? I mean, you'd need to get supplies in first as there's nothing there, but then you're set. High walls, functional moat. Safe as houses. We should've stayed down south.' It's my turn to look incredulous – Shell had never revealed a nerdy side to me before. Maybe it was the one thing we never shared. We change the topic and talk about the old days, trying to not talk about Terry, although he is present behind every word. Shell is holding it together by the flimsiest thread, and I don't want to risk a breakdown.

'We're here,' calls Peregrina from several yards ahead of us.

The great exterior of the Natural History Museum looms up before us, like a cathedral to science. The exhibits may well be something of wonder, but I've yet to meet anyone who isn't also enchanted by the architecture. Carvings of animals line the walls, staring down onto the desolate emptiness of London. There are lights on here and there throughout the building, suggesting that it still has a functional generator somewhere on the premises.

There aren't any aliens visible, and I feel emboldened and excited that we made it. I break into a run, holding my sword down so as not to slice my own head off, and hear the footsteps of the others behind me. There are an extra couple of pairs of footsteps, louder even, and I have to grind to a halt again to turn around. The other three stop beside me and we turn to see a lone zebra pound down Cromwell Road and veer up Exhibition Road. Hopefully there isn't a predator in pursuit, but we don't stop to find out and climb the stairs two or three at a time to the vast front doors of the museum.

I push on one and it gives under my weight. With joy at having arrived safely, the four of us fall into the main hall and catch our breath, trying not to laugh. The huge blue whale skeleton that dominates the entrance looks down on us graciously, as if bidding us welcome to her domain. I remember her installation. She's called Hope, and that fact provides a nugget of comfort, no matter how illogical.

I breathe in the slightly musty, sweaty air of the museum, revelling in being in one of my favourite buildings in the world once more, even if the situation isn't quite perfect for it.

'Do you think we're the only ones?' says Peregrina, but I shake my head.

'No way, it's too big,' I say. 'The lights were on, so there must be someone here. However, the place that we're going, I think we'll be OK.'

'I'm going to scout the upper floor here and have a look around,' says Pete, resting the flat edge of his sword over his shoulder. Peregrina nods that she's going with him and they cross the hall.

'Meet us in the Large Mammals Room,' I call after them, and they nod back. Shell and I watch them for a moment longer as they climb the steps and pass the statue of Darwin, still gazing down from his perch, before we move off to the mammals.

We pass through the long hall of mammals where stuffed tigers, bears and weasels stare blank eyed at us from behind their glass prisons, although my heart still does a nervous leap when we pass the lion. Shell and I move into the Large Mammals Room and there, surrounded by rhinos, hippos, deer, elephants and a giraffe hangs the blue whale, a monument to the biggest animal that has ever lived.

There are some dirty-looking clothes on a nearby bench, but no sign of any people. I nudge the clothes with the tip of my sword, and they drop to the floor, revealing underneath them a pastel paperback and a torch. Someone has been here, and may still be nearby. Nonetheless, we drop our weapons onto the bench and, grabbing the torch, clamber over the barrier and crawl under the whale to see if the urban legend is true, or whether we've been on a wild whale chase.

As I was always promised, a trap door exists, built into the stomach of the enormous model. Curiously, though, someone has already been here, and it's loose. Shell holds the torch in place as I work at the seams and push the door open. She passes me the torch and I shine it in and onto a bundle of clothes curled up in the darkness.

'That you back, then?' says the bundle. 'That didn't take long.' The voice is familiar and I go to comment on it but Shell is tugging my shirt and there's the sound of footsteps outside the whale, getting nearer.

'Step away from the whale.'

I duck back out of the trap door, hands held high and am absolutely floored by the sight of the person before me: a lanky, ginger figure with an uneven beard and damp patches across his plaid shirt.

'Gavin?'

He lowers his rifle.

Twenty-Eight
Belly of the Whale

For what I'm sure is only the second time in our friendship, Gavin initiates a hug with me. One moment he's standing there with his rifle aimed at my face and the next it has clattered to the ground and he's run at me, wrapping his thin arms around my shoulders and gulping back air and tears as his face is buried in my neck. It's the noise of a man who has been trying to be strong for a long, long time, but it has become a painful struggle.

'Gavin? What the hell?' I squeeze him back, dumbfounded that he's alive. We've come all this way and here he is. 'Is that Frederik in there?'

There's a noise from the trap door. 'Dexter? Is that you?' Frederik's legs appear from the bottom of the whale and he drops carefully onto the floor. Shell approaches him and introduces herself – they've only met on a couple of occasions – and guides him across to where Gavin continues to sob into my collar. I reach out and grasp Frederik's shaking hand. 'Good to see you.'

'Likewise,' he says, giving a half-smile. 'Of all the whales in all the world, eh?'

'Beyond ridiculous,' I say. 'How did you end up here?'

Gavin answers this, extracting himself from my grip and wiping his eyes with open palms. He's trying to restore the emotionless order that his body is used to.

'Do you remember when we came here one day, the two of us?' he says. 'You wanted to show me around and you said that there was a trap door in the whale and, should there ever be a zombie invasion, that was where you'd go to hide.' I don't remember telling him that, but I must have done. Gavin continues, 'And I guess, well, I hoped, that if you had survived it, maybe you'd still end up here.' It's an impossibly optimistic attitude to have, but I'm glad he has it anyway.

One could mistake his desire to see me one final time as a sign that he has feelings for me, but I know him better than that. It's simply that he doesn't have many friends. I adore him, but he rubs a lot of people up the wrong way, so people don't stick around very long. I think he wanted to see me again because he thought I might be the only person left, other than Frederik, who would care that he survived.

Besides, if he did like me as anything more than a friend, Frederik would've left him long ago.

The four of us sit down on the floor. I sit cross legged like in a school assembly; Shell hugs her knees and tries not to make eye contact with anyone.

'Is it just the two of you?' asks Frederik.

'No, there's two more of us kicking around,' I say. 'Peregrina-and-Pete. You've met her before a few times.'

'Oh yeah,' says Gavin, but it's clear he doesn't remember. 'What have you done with them?'

'They were exploring the primate section upstairs,' I jerk my head up in their supposed direction. 'I told them to meet us in here.' Gavin nods, chewing over an idea in his mind. He doesn't share it. There is an awkward pause, an end-of-the-world moment of rest.

'How did London empty so quickly?' I ask.

'Sheer numbers,' says Gavin, tapping on the butt of his rifle. 'There were loads of them, thousands, swarming from their ships like a wave of magma, destroying everyone in their path. A lot of people headed to the Underground system like during the wars, but that trapped them. The aliens wiped them out in days. You must've seen it – London is a ghost town.'

'Hold on,' I interrupt him. 'You say they're destroying everyone. Are you sure?' I relay our theory about the nanobots and aliens wanting to attack couples.

'That fits, actually,' says Gavin. 'Most of the dead bodies are merged to some degree, and those that aren't look like they suffered blunt force trauma of some kind.'

'And children?' asks Shell.

'We saw a few, huddled together,' says Gavin. 'I don't like to give that much thought.' Nor do I. I can't work out how to feel about the lack of children. Either they've already been killed by another means, or they're at home or in hiding, waiting for parents who will never return. Frankly, I don't know which is worse – it's the choice between a quick death and a slow one. I change the subject before the images become too concrete.

'Is there anyone else here?' I say, gesticulating to the museum around us.

'Yeah, there are others,' says Frederik. 'There are some people up in the earthquake exhibit, and a few more in the ecology section. There are also a couple of people in the cafeteria who were rationing the food between residents, but there's not much left. Some people have tried to eat exhibits but, well, you can imagine how well that went down.' We each grimace, wondering what makes anyone think that's a good idea.

Another thought occurs to me.

'Where's Oscar?' I wonder if their beautiful golden dog has vanished like Catsby.

'He's around,' says Gavin. 'We couldn't keep him with us in case he made too much noise and revealed our location, so we set him free. Obviously, he's not a wild animal, so he lives out in the gardens here and pops in now and then. The city belongs to the aliens and the dogs.'

With little else to say, we absorb the quiet of the museum. It isn't entirely silent. There's a dripping coming from somewhere, and I notice Gavin's breath is somewhat ragged and sharp. If there are any other noises, however, we are deaf to them. It's a big museum and we're deep into it.

'So if they took over the whole city,' says Shell, 'how did you survive? It can't be because you were hidden up in the whale.' I turn to look at Gavin, expecting him to give his story as to how he managed to convince the aliens that they were harmless – it's the sort of thing he'd have found a way to do – but instead Frederik speaks.

'That's my fault,' he says, smirking. 'I realised that I was experiencing these bursts of colour in a different way to Gavin and others we spoke to. These were the first colours I'd ever seen, and I was pretty amazed, but I think it was a definite advantage.'

'Fred had no preconceived notion as to what the colours meant,' Gavin says, taking up the story. 'We see red and we think fire or love or whatever, but he sees red and realises that it means 'turn left' or 'there's something in that room' and so on.'

'It completely depends on the shade,' says Frederik, 'and I don't think I'm exactly right on a lot of it, but it started to make a lot of sense. I could tell where they were and get us hidden accordingly. Without Gavin to steer me though, I would never have lasted.'

'That's pretty impressive,' I say, having to go for litotes instead of hyperbole, what with being English. 'So, you've been following their plans?'

'Such as they are,' says Frederik. 'I mean, I could be way off and it's luck, but if that's the case then celebratory cigars all round anyway. But what good is it doing us in the end? All we're doing is postponing the inevitable.'

'You haven't told them the best bit,' says Gavin, grasping Frederik's hand with a vice-like grip. 'Tell them what else you can do.' Frederik looks embarrassed and his eyes move unseeingly to a stuffed ibex in a glass case.

'It doesn't always work,' he mumbles. Gavin tells us instead.

'He can talk back,' he says, his mouth stretching into a wide grin. 'How cool is that? He can project certain colours back at them and they understand. There were several of them following us in here when we first got into this room. We snuck up into the whale and Fred thought out a message that said we'd gone or something, but did it as if he was one of them. They didn't notice the difference and left!'

'So we're safe?' says Shell. 'If they find us, you can redirect them?' Frederik sighs and runs a hand through his short black hair.

'But for how long?' he says. 'Even if they leave, the planet is in ruins. There aren't enough of us left to survive. We don't know how to grow crops or run power plants or anything useful.' His words mirror the conversation Shell and I had had while wrapped in blankets on Derek-and-Josephine's dining room floor. What good are we? If humanity had had some preparation, who would they have saved? The politicians and CEOs, or the farmers and scientists? The wealthy or the useful? I think I know.

There's a noise, much too close for comfort. We jump up and swivel our attention to the nearest doorway.

I raise my sword and Gavin brings up his gun as two heads appear around the corner.

Twenty-Nine

Gavin-and-Frederik

Oh, hang on, I just realised I never explained how I met Gavin, or how he met Frederik. Much as Gavin is one of my best friends and favourite people, because he's not local and I see much less of him than the others, I do sometimes forget to include him when telling people or thinking about my friends.

Gavin Napier came to my attention when we were working together at Starbucks for a brief while, although the exact moment that we met has been deleted from my internal hard drive – one day I didn't know him, and the next he was pivotal to my existence. I was twenty and had got a job alongside university and school place-ments simply because I needed a bit of extra money. I don't remember sleeping much that year, and I certainly don't remember pursuing any hobbies.

Gavin got his job around the same time as me. He was seventeen; a lanky redhead with so many freckles it wasn't unthinkable that Ron Weasley had found a way out of the *Harry Potter* books and joined us in the real world to make coffee. However, unlike Ron, Gavin had his head screwed on and wasn't distracted by such trivialities as being popular or even liked, especially. He had already locked in a sense of style and was the sort of person who would rather lose his job than be seen with a hair out of place.

One of the most shocking things to me about adulthood was that no one ever handed me a book on how to do it, which I know is a ridiculous thought but, when you're a child, you assume that your parents and everyone else knows exactly what they're doing. When you get there yourself, however, you realise that everyone has been making it up for the last ten thousand years of human history. I men-tion this because if there *was* a guidebook, the only person who might have owned one was Gavin. Hell, he might be the author.

Self-assured, never wrong (as far as he was concerned, anyway), and despite my seniority in time spent on the planet, Gavin always had an answer to and some advice for every scenario I or anyone else threw at him. And, frustratingly, he was right on every occasion, giving him an air of absolutely deserved cockiness.

There was something magnetic about him. Sure, his righteousness could grate a bit, but I still wanted to hang around with him, listen to his wisdom like he was some kind of ginger oracle, and after a while my feelings got conflated with something else. I'd been going through a questioning phase anyway, as I think pretty much everyone does at one time or another. It's part of growing up. We got closer, starting hanging out in some of my rare free hours, and one night did end with a kiss, but it was a kiss which told us both what we needed confirmed: that was never going to happen.

While I'm pretty sure in most cases that would've also spelt the end of the friendship, I still enjoyed spending time with him, and he was too mature to let something so petty get in the way of us being friends. When I left Starbucks, we stayed in touch and he left not long after. While he later moved to London for university (art history, of all things), we stayed in close contact and he is the youngest of any of my friends, never afraid to make a snide comment about me being ancient and decrepit, despite an age gap of only four years or so.

He's ridiculously perceptive, able to pick out any fault or flaw in someone's personality and hold it up under a spotlight, but at the same time knows exactly how to motivate people and tell them what they need to hear, even if they don't *want* to hear it. He speaks without a censor, never worrying too much if he's offending someone.

I was with Gavin when he met his boyfriend, the wonderfully named Frederik van Oorschot. Gavin was in his second year of university and I'd popped up to London to meet him after a morning lecture to take him out for lunch. He'd been struggling for a while with life – his father was terminally ill, his grades were slipping, he was missing shifts at work due to stress –so I'd been trying to be the best friend I could.

Unfortunately, Gavin is not someone who is especially receptive to acts of emotional generosity, running as he does on logic and reason rather than letting his feelings have control, so I couldn't be sure if I was helping or being a nuisance, and asking risked an answer like blunt trauma. Until today, I've seen him cry once, a month after his father's funeral. It was like watching Mount Everest crumble.

I met Gavin outside his lecture hall and, for the first time I could remember, he had initiated a hug with me. He always had trouble making friends who would stick around and put up with his, shall we say, insightful comments about their personalities and situations, and maybe he was grateful that I was willing to deal with it. I've always figured that, throughout everything, I've been a pretty good friend to everyone I consider worth my time.

A couple of corridors along, we found a figure on his hands and knees feeling around for his bag, apparently unable to see it despite it being just two feet in front of him. Then we noticed the white stick that lay a bit further away and realised that he *couldn't* see his bag. Gavin, far nicer than it sounds like I give him credit for, darted forward and crouched down next to the boy.

'Hi there,' he said, gently. 'Are you alright? My name's Gavin.' I stood back and watched the scene unfold. I've never been able to explain it, but I felt that something was going on that day, and I didn't want to interfere. I was an audience of one to the unfolding play, and I wasn't about to start heckling.

'Is my stick there?' said the boy, glum indifference in his voice. It was tinged with an accent, sort of American, sort of European. We found out later that it's Dutch.

'Yes, I've got it here, and I've got your bag too,' said Gavin. He slid an arm to the boy's elbow and helped him up. 'Come on, there we go.' Once standing, the boy was at least six foot tall and built like a rugby player, although his green bomber jacket may have been making him look bigger than he was. He didn't wear black glasses like some blind people, so we could see his glassy green eyes as they looked at a point a few inches to the left of Gavin's face.

'Thanks,' said the boy. 'Sorry.'

'What for?' said Gavin, and there was a genuinely puzzled hint in his voice.

'Holding you up, I'd imagine,' the blind boy said. He sounded like this sort of thing happened regularly and he was used to feeling like a burden. 'Someone shoved into me, knocked my bag off and then carried on. I was hoping someone was going to help me.'

'Well, of course I was,' said Gavin. 'What's your name?'

'Frederik,' said the boy, holding out a hand. Gavin moved his own to shake. Already, without knowing that Frederik was bisexual, I could tell that they made a good couple.

'Frederik, would you like to join me and my friend Dexter for lunch?'

'Oh, no, thanks, I'm not going to impose,' Frederik said quickly. His head turned a bit to face where he thought I might be. Despite me being silent so far, it wasn't a bad guess. 'I should be going. Thank you though, I can find my way back to my dormitory from here.'

'You're not imposing,' said Gavin, smiling. 'Is he, Dexter?'

'Not in the slightest,' I said. I'll admit, though, that I was a bit pissed off. I wanted to talk to Gavin about an issue I was having with my then girlfriend, Jess. However, you can't get annoyed with a disabled person without looking like an arsehole, and he was evidently quite sweet. Gavin had taken a shine to him.

After a little more cajoling from both of us, Frederik took us up on our offer. They chatted like they'd known each other for years and I was the one who'd been picked up off the floor. Frederik was going to be far more effective at taking Gavin's mind off his problems than I was. I made my excuses and left. Gavin tried to protest, but it was half-hearted. I didn't take offence; I've seen often enough how love envelops someone and the rest of the world becomes irrelevant to them. To Gavin's credit, he later called and apologised for abandoning me. Our own uninterrupted lunch took place a week later, and he didn't even hold me to my original promise of paying.

Three-and-a-half years later, they're still together, living in London with Frederik's guide dog Oscar. Rarely has there been a sweeter couple – one who sees nothing and one who sees enough for the both of them.

Thirty

They're Back

It's Peregrina-and-Pete. Still, thankfully, unconnected, save by one hand each.

'Jesus, don't do that to us!' I say, clutching at my chest. 'Did you find anyone?'

'There's a few people lurking, but they're human and for the most part unarmed,' says Pete. 'Who have you found?'

'These are my friends, Gavin, and that's Frederik,' I say, pointing at each, still unable to believe that the words are true. 'They… they were here.'

Gavin moves forward to shake Pete's hand and embraces Peregrina awkwardly, and then they're introduced to Frederik. Gavin has met Peregrina on a few occasions, but otherwise they're as good as strangers, connected though me.

Frederik suddenly acts like we've surprised him and Gavin at home and offers us something to eat. Gavin bounds over to the whale and hauls himself up into its cavernous stomach, reappearing a few moments later with a blue rucksack. He divides out food that must have been several days' worth of rations – bottles of lukewarm water, bananas, crisps and a packet of cheese biscuits. The last meal we ate feels days ago, but it was only the previous night. Still, nearly eighteen hours without food is more than enough. The six of us wolf down our food while I quiz Gavin-and-Frederik on their experience.

Have they been here since it started?

Where did they get the gun?

Has anyone else they know survived so far?

The boys answer my questions. The gun came from a specialist store somewhere in Kensington, and as far as they know, both of their entire address books have been rendered useless, present company excepted.

'After even the first day, most of London had been eclipsed by these things,' says Gavin. 'They used their little grey clouds to do that thing of whisking up people together and it caused a lot of mess. We decided to come here the next day. It's a miracle that we made it.'

'I'll say,' says Pete. 'It's desolate out there.'

'We're among the last survivors,' says Gavin, turning to Frederik and squeezing his hand. 'Not that I imagine two queer guys are really what the repopulation effort needs.' A small chuckle passes around the group. Gavin continues, 'Anyway, if everyone's eaten, how would you like a tour? It's very different here without the teeming crowds.'

'OK,' I say with relief, happy to have something to distract me before we formulate a plan to get more food and supplies. There's definitely room in the whale for us, as a temporary measure at least, but how long can we stay here? For the first time, I become aware of the short-sightedness of my plan. I was determined to get here, but I hadn't particularly given any thought to what happens next. It was only ever a thought exercise – I didn't expect to live through the apocalypse. I suppose I figured we'd wait until the aliens got bored and took off again, but there was no evidence that that was in their plans. Maybe they were acting as pest controllers, wiping out humanity for unfathomable reasons.

'OK, but I'm bringing my sword,' says Shell. We agree that weapons are worthwhile and set out from the Large Mammals Room on a bespoke tour of the museum.

Our footsteps echo throughout the cavernous chambers as we explore the magnificent, huge interior. The dinosaur wing is lit by emergency lighting, giving the fossils and casts an even creepier appearance than usual. The animatronic tyrannosaur has shut down mid-roar, staring vacantly at a point on the far wall, tiny arms reaching out at nothing.

In another long room, hundreds of species of birds stare out of their glass cases at us.. I look at forlorn eagles, grumpy dodos, irritated hummingbirds and pissed off parrots and wonder if there's any dignity in being the chosen member of your species to stand in a museum for the rest of time.

In the section of the museum dedicated to the physical sciences, we see remains from Pompeii, moon rocks and burnt-up meteorites and meet the families living in the earthquake exhibit. They have small children with them, who look far less terrified than one would imagine, but that might have something to do with the fact that they've been allowed free run of the gift shops and are surrounded by colouring books and oversized plush dinosaurs in lurid primary colours.

Whoever had been in the cafeteria has gone so we pass between the empty chairs and tables to see the fish, reptiles and invertebrates that were encased at the back of the museum. Crocodiles, lizards and fish stared back at us with their ancient eyes, and I realise that the whole planet is now a museum of a sort, as nothing is going to be improved on ever again. Even if there are survivors, they are never going to make the world as good as it was before, or at least not for centuries. Sure, it had its flaws, but on the whole, it was better than living in caves and in fear of bears.

As we look at corals and starfish, the day begins to feel like a regular day out, if a quiet one. We could be a group of untraumatised and freshly washed tourists out for a glance around the museum, with promises of a good dinner or a nice wine bar at the end of the day, provided we focus on the exhibits and don't breathe in too deeply. The calmness is ripped asunder, however, when a flash of pine needle green pervades our eyes, followed by a blood red.

'They can tell someone's here,' whispers Frederik. 'They're splitting up.' We're trapped – the only way out of this section is the way we came in.

'Convince them we're not here,' Shell whispers back, her voice raspy and fearful. Frederik turns his head in the vague direction of the exit and projects out a shimmery pattern that crosses through our eyes. It's a combination of browns and reds, and I take it at face value that Frederik knows what he's doing. At least, he's got more of an idea than any of us.

The colours subside and a reply comes moments later, more reds with some light purples interspersed. Frederik replies again, in orange this time, but his face suggests that something is wrong. There's a sharp burst of emerald green and Frederik says, 'They don't believe us.' Gavin steps in front of him and raises the rifle. The rest of us lift our weapons, moving back to the centre of the room.

They're in front of us again, two aliens, four heads, skin the same disgusting, unnatural shade of pale blue, faces that are impossible to read. The feather-like appendages on their heads quiver nervously, as if caught in a breeze we can't feel. The spacesuits of these two are ripped in places and the arm of one has been burnt by something. They hold no weapons, but each is gripping a small silver box on their belt, waiting to release a cloud of nanobots.

Four sets of narrow eyes glare at us, but before either alien can release their only weapon, Gavin fires and plants a bullet in the centre of the face of the left-most head. Its attached companion begins to project colour throughout the room; panicked shades of the rainbow that make me feel like I'm inside a kaleidoscope.

Seizing the opportunity, Peregrina rushes forward with her weapon, a dagger that once belonged to Henry VII, and stabs it deep into the chest plate of the already injured alien. The second alien shoves her aside with stubby fingers and kneels down beside its companion. The feathers on its heads have curled right up and are now merely red nubbins above where you'd expect to see an ear.

While one is distracted and the other lies dying, we take the opportunity to run, skirting around the side of the fallen pair. It's only once we're level with the fish again and have left the invertebrates room that I realise Frederik hasn't come with us. He's still standing before the aliens, his eyes turned to them but not seeing what is happening.

'Fred, come on!' shouts Gavin, throwing the rifle on a strap over his shoulder so it hangs diagonally across his back. 'Follow my voice! We've gone, you have to come too!' Frederik remains stationary. I become aware of flickers of colour dancing in the corner of my vision, orphaned colour swatches.

'The dying one,' says Frederik. 'It had children. Three of them.'

'Yes, but we did what we had to do,' Gavin says, stepping forward again. 'We can't help it.'

'They're like us,' Frederik is speaking barely louder than a whisper, but the aliens make no noise so there's no trouble hearing him. 'It was scared too. It didn't want to come here. It thought it should stay at home and… it joined the force to make its parents happy.' Tears sprung at his sightless eyes, but Gavin was close enough to him to grasp his wrist.

'It's done, and now is not the time to get emotional,' he says, sounding almost robotic. 'We have to go before we're next.' He tugs once and there's no give, but a second tug and Frederik finally moves, navigating around the aliens and coming with us back to the Large Mammals Room.

There's more waiting for us there, but this time they're not aliens.

It's Annie-and-Matt, still conjoined but nonetheless apparently content, despite the remains of their clothes being covered in stains that resemble dirt, ash and dried blood.

'You have to come with us,' they say, their voices in stereo. 'We can get you somewhere safe.'

Thirty-One
Hellos and Goodbyes

I could have fainted, but Pete was standing behind me and caught me as I fell, which shocked me back into full, if dazed, consciousness. My recovery is also aided by the appearance of the alien we'd abandoned rushing in, wielding nothing more than its fists. Catching us off guard, it springs forward and rips Gavin's gun from his hands, but it apparently has no idea how to use it, so begins to swing it around like a blunt instrument, hitting Pete in the face and smashing the lenses of his glasses, tiny jagged frames left around his bloodshot eyes.

We pile onto the alien who is the most tenacious one we've met so far, and is battered, bashed, stabbed and clobbered by us in turn, all the while reacting like Monty Python's Black Knight. My rusted sword is snapped in half, with the blade sticking out of its leg, and Shell gains a fresh shiner around her left eye.

After one flesh wound too many, it finally keels over in front of the large taxidermied giraffe and stops breathing.

I feel my sore nose and realise it suffered in the skirmish and is bleeding again, so I pull my shirt up to stem the flow. The blood feels warm on my skin and I run my fingers over my chin and cheeks to make sure the rest of me is in one piece. I'm very aware of the thick stubble coating my lower face, somewhat uneven and rough.

Now I have to focus on the next issue, which is that Annie-and-Matt is here, with his body, her arms and both of their heads looking down from his shoulders, smiling at me. No matter how benign the expression, it's weird. For people I never thought I'd see again, they seem to be coping very well.

'How did you survive?' I ask. 'I mean, let's not be rude here, but everyone else the nanobots have changed hasn't survived.' Neither head mentions the lack of Terry, Ruby or Alex.

'Their technology has learnt a thing or two from ongoing experimentation,' says Matt. As he speaks, Annie's lips move along with him, silently framing his words. It's disconcerting trying to look at them, and my eyes keep darting between each head, not sure which one I should be paying attention to.

'When we realised that we were in one piece, we ran,' says Annie, recapping on the last events of their lives we were present for. Now Matt's lips are going through the motions. 'We found some of the aliens and, well, whatever those robots did, we could understand them. They told us that we were safe and that they would look after us, and see no more harm came to us, provided we helped them. There were others there too, like us.'

'And so we thought about it,' both heads say at the same time. 'We stayed with them for two days. They're either deaf or don't understand our words as a language, so we could talk freely. They kept an eye on us though. We tried to convince some of the others to escape, but they'd either decided that this was the only way they could survive, or they simply didn't care enough to try.'

Annie's head alone takes up the story, Matt's mouth still forming the appropriate shapes.

'We made a break for it yesterday while they were fighting some more humans. Half a housing estate was on fire. Some residents had tried to trap and kill the aliens with fire but it had got out of hand. In the confusion, we fled. Being able to understand them, however, means that we've been able to hide from them and throw them off the scent. We followed some messages leading here and knew it had to be you. Don't ask us how.' I look at the others, wondering if they're having as hard a time processing this as I am. Frederik is sitting with his eyes closed and his head bowed, but the other four are indeed looking like someone has tried to explain quantum physics to them through the medium of semaphore.

'Have you learnt anything more about them?' I ask. 'What's with the body modification?'

'At one point one of them mentioned that they didn't understand why the nanobots hadn't worked on humans,' says Matt. 'It seems that they do all start with one head, and then when they reach sexual maturity I guess, they're blended and the single body can produce more offspring. None of them here look to be having kids any time soon, though. They were apparently shocked by our appearance and set about putting it right, as they saw it.'

It feels like the biological equivalent of forcing Christianity onto jungle tribes.

'And what's their purpose?' asks Peregrina.

'Materials,' says Annie. 'They're here to mine for stuff. Earth is rich in whatever they want. They mentioned things that we guessed were elements or some kind of material that we have that they need, but we've no idea what it is. They first needed to see if humanity could be roped into helping out, or needed to be wiped out. There appears to be a lot of dissent among them on that. The ones trying to get us to "breed" aren't actively trying to kill us. But even after two days with them, it appears that their attitude to humanity isn't improving. We keep fighting back and they think we're more trouble than we're worth. Death will outpace merging now.'

'Did you observe anything else about their biology?' asks Gavin. It's become a curious question-and-answer session, but it's interesting. We might be minutes from death, but we'd quite like to know what exactly it is killing us.

'Not directly,' Matt and Annie speak together again, and then Matt on his own. 'The feathers on their heads appear to be how they pick up their language. We saw one who had had his ripped off and he was clearly having difficulty communicating. It was basically shunned and the next morning it wasn't there at all.'

'So, what do we do now you've found us?' I ask, trying to keep the hopelessness out of my voice. It's been a fascinating conversation, but there are practicalities ahead.

'There's a safe space we've found,' says Annie's head. 'In the V&A.' The Victoria and Albert Museum sits across the road from the Natural History and Science Museums, dealing more with art and history. I'd been there once before on a school trip when I was about twelve, and my overriding memory of the experience was giggling at the naked statues of Greek gods and heroes.

I have matured a little since.

'There are other human survivors there,' says Matt's head. 'They've

taken to us alright, despite the occasional bit of gun-waving and general fear to begin with. You'll be safe there. It's protected by gunmen,
and they have good supplies.'

It doesn't take much to convince us. Gavin has returned to his emotionless self and, after introducing himself to Annie-and-Matt, begins
asking questions about how it feels being one and what happened to
them while the change was taking place. The heads answer as best
they can while we pick up the remains of our weapons, bags and food
supplies, as well as whatever else Gavin-and-Frederik had managed to
scrounge together and hide in the whale.

Pete-and-Peregrina head out first, muttering between themselves
in a manner that I don't much like. They have the air of people
secretly plotting something, and that's an uncomfortable feeling when
a plot has already been decided on. Annie-and-Matt leads the rest of
us out through the museum again. With one final look back at the
whales hanging from the room's vast ceiling, I contemplate clambering up to snap off the narwhal's tooth to use as a weapon, but decide
that I'm too far removed from my monkey-like ancestors to attempt
the climb. Besides, would it do me any good in the long term?

Outside, night is falling; I have no idea how long we were in the
museum. Time has stopped having any meaning. Time is a human
construct and, with humans fast dying out, so is everything they came
up with; time, electricity, religion, all slipping through the fingers of
the remains of our species as we struggle to seek out hope in this
hopeless world. Sure, we may find peace at the V&A but for how
long? From now on, everything we do is a temporary measure.

Annie-and-Matt leads us to the stairs that will provide us with
an underground entrance to the V&A, as the above-ground doors,
Annie's head informs us, have been locked and are heavily defended.

'Better breathe through your mouths down here,' says Matt's head.
'It doesn't smell so good.' Gavin pulls his shirt up over his mouth in
preparation, revealing a skinny torso beneath and wisps of ginger hair
around his navel.

'Sorry, but we're not going to come with you,' says a voice, and it
takes me a moment to realise that it's Pete. I stare at him, not quite

able to comprehend his words. 'We've decided that we have to go our own way.'

'What the fuck?' I say, moving towards them, wondering how Pete has convinced one of my best friends to abandon me – us – at this time, given that he's never shown any sense of domination over her before.

'We *have* to go,' says Peregrina, reaching out and grabbing my hands. 'We're not safe for you.' I stare at her, swapping my gaze between her and Pete, but they both look imploringly at me, eyes filled with sorrow and regret for endeavours not yet done. They can't be serious.

'You can't be serious.'

'We're the last couple standing,' says Pete. Evidently, he hasn't cottoned on to Gavin-and-Frederik and thinks they're friends. 'You know it makes sense. You have Annie-and-Matt to help you but, well, we're only going to cause problems for you. We'll go off and make it our own way.'

'There's no way we would have lasted as long as this without you,' says Peregrina. 'You were the one that kept us together; the one who thought of us as a whole, rather than focusing on one other person, as we've all been doing. Let's be honest, even Pete and I are just about each other, really.'

'That's not true,' I shout. 'You care!'

'Yes, we do,' says Peregrina. 'We do care, and that's why we need to go and save you. You don't need us. We're trouble as a twosome.'

'Our minds are made up,' says Pete. I look at Annie-and-Matt, Shell, and Gavin-and-Frederik, but they look back with tired eyes and don't say anything. Peregrina shakes her hands free of my grip and moves over to Shell, giving her a hug which she reciprocates numbly. Pete claps me on the shoulder, pushes his broken glasses up his nose and then takes Peregrina's hand as she reaches his side again.

'Good luck,' I say, my voice dry and hoarse.

'And you,' says Peregrina, with the same smile she gave me many years ago when we first met in the nurse's office at school. With nothing else to say, they turn and walk away down Cromwell Road to meet their fate. I hope they make it.

I shake the tears from my eyes and turn towards the stairs. As I reach the top of them, I feel a hand on my shoulder, put there for comfort, but I shrug it off and begin the descent, the smell of failed surgery already rising up to greet me.

Thirty-Two

Victoria-and-Albert

The tunnel, draughty and prone to echo but always somewhat grand in an understated way, is littered with bodies in various states of distress, decay and detachment. Most appear to have been merged to some degree or another, with varying levels of success, and the smell is almost intolerable, causing me to retch a few times.

Annie-and-Matt leads the way to the V&A's underground entrance, stepping over the bodies, and the rats, mice and rooks that are tucking in to an unexpected feast. Under a poster for a film that I'll never see, a husky is gorging on the remains of a man's stomach, ignoring us as we pass.

Frederik stops to throw up, his sense of smell heightened by his lack of vision. He's having a more difficult time of dealing with it than the rest of us.

'Nearly there,' promises the joint voice of our leader, navigating around an obese pair with bodies ripped asunder, clothes and flesh stained with dried blood and worse.

'How many aliens were there? Do you know?' I ask Annie-and-Matt, trying to take my mind off the walk. This used to be a quick walk, done in a minute or two, but now it requires stepping over (and in) the bodies of those who had retreated to one of the many underground parts of London in an attempt to save themselves.

'Thousands, hundreds of thousands,' says Matt's head, although he doesn't sound certain. 'The spaceships appeared all over the planet. Each one contained hundreds of aliens. Maybe there were millions of them. We've seen some take off, seen others talking about their comrades who were leaving. Some have stayed to finish clearing up and, well, finish us off.'

'They want our planet for their own,' chimes in Annie's head. 'But they don't want our stuff.'

'They'll take whatever metals they find precious,' adds Matt. 'But humans and our personal achievements? They don't mean anything to them.'

We reach the entrance tunnel to the V&A, and Annie-and-Matt leads us into the first corridor of the museum. Like in the Natural History Museum, emergency lighting is on in here, giving everything the pallid look of a man on life support. Although the room is devoid of dead bodies, some of the statues have been knocked over and smashed into fragments. A Persian rug that has seen better days is bunched up in a corner, as if someone had tried to steal it but thought better of it. Things take on a very different sense of worth when you're hanging onto civilisation by a knife edge. I realise that I haven't seen any money since we left my house.

The thought of my house brings with it an image of Catsby and then the random thought, 'Did I lock the front door?' I don't suppose it matters. I wonder if anyone thought it worth looting.

I feel at my lowest ebb as Annie-and-Matt leads us through the long hall to the room of Japanese artefacts at the far end, which they tell us is the safest room in the building.

Shell leads Frederik by the arm in front of me, and Gavin has dropped back to walk level with me, although there's nothing he can say. I can tell that he wants to speak, but I don't want to encourage him – while he's a good friend, he's occasionally inappropriate about when he chooses to dish out his words of wisdom.

However, it is he who notices what the rest of us have failed to.

'Where is everyone?'

'What do you mean?' says Shell, turning her head back to look at him.

'Annie-and-Matt said that the upper doors were locked and guarded, which I took to mean that there are people in here worth guarding.' He stops and raises his rifle again, pointing it at the entrance to the Japan room. The realisation hits Frederik first.

'It's a trap.'

'We're so sorry,' says Annie-and-Matt, not actually sounding all that sorry, before blasting a jet of lurid lime green from their minds into ours and, as it turns out, into the minds of the four or five aliens –

it's hard to tell with those heads – in the Japan room, armed not only with their belt boxes of nanobots, but also samurai swords. They've realised that humans can be fought hand to hand, which means we're in the shit, as there's just one gun left between the four of us.

I launch a punch at the nearest head, while Gavin fires his rifle indiscriminately, and by some rather large miracle he takes out two aliens in rapid succession, as well as a statue of some philanthropist or other, the remains of which topple down onto an enormous burial casket. Shell pilots Frederik back down to the entrance as quickly as she can, while Gavin and I launch our attacks. I grab the snapped-off marble arm of a Greek god and use it to club a couple more heads.

Half a dozen more appear. Screaming, either in rage or terror, I can't tell, Gavin charges at them, his slender frame somehow being enough to topple a few, one smashing a head open on a glass case, and he disappears off through the back of the exhibition hall. I elbow my way through the throng after him. Turning left, there's a small flight of stairs leading up to more exhibits, and that's where I spy Gavin. He's halfway up a roped-off wooden staircase, moving backwards and waving a sword around at the alien who's following him up.

The staircase looks old and the sort of thing that Do Not Touch signs were made for. With a final swipe, the alien is tipped back and falls hard, the step cracking in half thanks to years of weathering, neglect and woodworm. The alien crashes to the marble floor below, where it stops moving. Gavin's breathing is fast and heavy, as he realises he's trapped halfway up an old staircase.

'How did he get up there?' says a voice behind me, and I turn to see Annie-and-Matt, looking up at my trapped friend. Their presence infuriates me and, without giving it much thought, I swipe around and jab their joined body in the gut with the fist of my stone arm. Matt's head wheezes and Annie's head gasps, and the body falls to the ground.

'We're sorry,' they say in unison.

'Fuck off,' I snarl, whacking Matt's head with the arm. It connects with his skull with a loud crack, his head bouncing off Annie's. Unconscious, he tips forward and, unable to stop it, Annie screams as her head goes down too, smacking hard against the ground, blood spurting out from her nose and mouth. A tooth skips like a hockey puck across the floor and clatters against the wall.

I will be the most loyal, loving friend on the planet if it's reciprocated, but no matter how close you were to me or how many secrets we shared over the years and whatever depths of friendship we plumbed, if you hurt any of my other friends or betray my trust, my feelings about you can change in an instant.

Annie's still crying, but I can't deal with that now. I've got to get Gavin down and there are still two aliens in sight, coming at me armed with what look like table legs. I swing the statue's arm around again, but one of the aliens grabs it and yanks it from my grip. I punch out and the alien staggers back into his friend.

'Dexter! Catch!' Gavin shouts behind me, and I turn as he throws his sword in my direction. I yelp and decide not to try and catch it lest I slice my palm open on the blade, letting it clatter to the floor before picking it up and swiping it at my foes. It nicks one on the cheek and blue blood spurts out like a drinking fountain, but it's not enough to hold it back, and we engage in sword-to-statuary combat for a moment, until I finally manage to jab forward once more and pierce its body in the spot a human heart would be. Whether it has a similar organ there, I don't know, but it's enough to create a bigger bleed and the alien topples over. The second stares blankly at his fallen comrade, then at me, before running away.

'Gavin, try and jump down, I'll catch you,' I say, finally free for a moment to focus on the important things. Gavin sits down on the edge of his step and pushes himself forward. I drop the sword and stand beneath him, but the fall is higher than it looks, and so rather than landing in my arms, he instead lands boots-first on my chest, pushing me to the ground. We both roll and, aside from bruises, aren't hurt any further.

'Right, let's get out of here,' he says, helping me to my feet. I hand him back his sword and pick up my god's arm and we make our way back to the Japan room. Except we don't, because we've turned too soon and are in a room full of huge statues, with a large plaster replica of Michelangelo's David in front of us.

'Woah,' I breathe. 'That's enormous.'

'Not from this angle,' chuckles Gavin, pointing up at the plaster genitals. I roll my eyes but laugh anyway. Laughter still seems the most foreign noise of all in this new world.

Then we hear footsteps and, looking up, I see three aliens on the upper balcony. Two step up and over the wall, descending silently the way the first aliens disembarked from their ship a matter of days ago. It feels like years. The third, however, has no such patience and instead simply leaps awkwardly, but instead of landing on us, hits David hard and the whole statue wobbles.

While Gavin swipes at the two slow-descenders, I bash the third around the head as it slides down the statue's enormous body and lands with an ungraceful thud on the floor. More blue goo, and we're finally in the clear again. We run for the main entrance, more aliens appearing from who knows where. We sweep up Shell and Frederik, who are waiting in the atrium, and burst out of the front door and onto Cromwell Road.

A flash of pink in front of us spooks me, but I realise that it's not an alien message but a panicked flamingo, another escapee from the zoo. The aliens chase us out and we dive behind an abandoned car. A rainbow of colour pervades our vision again, lighting up the rapidly darkening sky.

'They know where we are,' says Frederik, 'and they're going to end us the easy way.' However, that's only Gavin-and-Frederik in trouble.

There's a bark and we turn to see a muddy dog, still golden furred beneath the crap, running towards us. It's Oscar, Frederik's guide dog, excited at seeing his masters again. We can't stop him and he bounds towards us, closing in on Gavin who's closest and leaping onto his lap, covering his face in rough licks. No one notices the grey cloud until it's too late.

I'd never given any thought to what would happen if a human got connected to an animal in this situation, but it turns out that the result – after forty or so seconds of tiny mechanical whirring, Shell and I looking on in horror and Frederik pretending that he can't hear anything – and scrunching his eyes up tight anyway – is not pleasant.

Oscar's body remains mostly intact, standing on the remains of his master, but his head is discarded, replaced instead with Gavin's. Patchy skin grafts show where the work was done. One of Gavin's arms sticks out of Oscar's flank like a special effect gone wrong, and we three remaining humans scramble up as Gavin-and-Oscar works out what has happened to it.

With good reason, he's not happy and indicates so with a furrowed brow. Gavin opens his mouth to speak but the words catch like a fish hook on the back of his throat, and instead he growls. He barks, and the effect is startling – humans should not make that noise.

More in fear than anger, he leaps for me, but I manage to turn in time and knock him sideways with my elbow, causing him to yelp. He rights himself while we break into a run, but he's fast behind us, blood trickling from his wounds that haven't been fixed quite as neatly as first appearances suggest.

Frederik seems to have an almost psychic ability to run without crashing into anything, but Shell is keeping a close pace behind him, leaving me to drag up the rear, now unarmed, being chased by one of my best friends and his dog. The intelligent spark in his eyes is gone, replaced by something animalistic and cruel. I don't know how to stop him from chasing us. Will the bodies reject one another and collapse of their own accord? I can't take that risk.

I jerk to a halt and raise my foot, kicking Gavin squarely in the face. His nose explodes in a mess of blood and snot – about time that happened to someone other than me – and he whimpers again, falling back. He slows to a meander, before collapsing on the tarmac. Sacrificing sensible behaviour for sentimentality, I approach him.

He lies still, looking shocked and dejected. His eyes aren't cruel, they're scared. I reach out a hand and stroke his fur. It's probably the weirdest thing that has happened to me thus far, and we're getting into some pretty stiff competition in those stakes already. Frederik joins me, having been led by Shell, and kneels beside his boyfriend-dog. Gavin looks at him and gently extends his tongue to lick Frederik's hand, the only affection he can give. He whines and looks at me with his wet eyes, as if asking why I did it.

'I'm so sorry,' I say, tears brimming at my eyes, shocked at having lost another friend. 'I really am, I'm so sorry. I don't know what to do any more.' It feels more real than ever. Gavin emits a weak little howl and closes his eyes. Frederik mutters words of love over and over again, holding himself back from reaching down and hugging the hybrid.

'I'll look after Frederik,' I say. I wipe my eyes with my palms. 'I'm pleased I got to see you one last time.' Gavin snuffles again, and a combination of shock and goodness knows what else takes its toll. He dies.

There is no time to grieve.

I stand up and realise one of the aliens has hold of Shell. Two more are coming for us, grabbing our hands and holding them behind our backs. I have no energy to resist.

'They know that we're incompatible for their machines,' says Frederik, his voice dulled by events that he couldn't see but didn't need explaining to him. I wonder if he forgives me. 'They're taking us away. We're prisoners.'

We are marched through the streets of London, the aliens not even bothering to restrain us – where would we run? Each of us is silent, alone with our thoughts, crying tears for the lost and the fallen.

Thirty-Three

The Tower

The Tower of London is lit up with artificial lighting; small orbs of pure brilliant light hover about twenty feet above us. There are four or five, and they light the courtyard up like the floodlights at Wembley. The three of us have been standing at the end of a line of people and, according to Frederik's translation – the aliens can't detect sound, or if they do, they don't mind him speaking – we are waiting for more prisoners to join us.

Frederik seems cold and detached, and selfishly I worry if it's because I, to all intents and purposes, just killed Gavin, but I imagine it's more to do with the fact that Gavin is dead, we are being held captive by a race from another world, and things are bleaker than the promise of another Hollywood remake.

The walk through London's streets was slow and depressing. We saw other humans though. The adults, I guess, were the few remaining singletons of the city, but each was being led by an alien or two in the same direction as us. Worse to see were the children. With no one left to combine, the planet is now awash with orphans and the aliens had managed to corral them into behaving by tying thick strands of a purple, rope-like material around a limb of each child and carting them off to who knows where. We see three groups like this, each of sixty or more children, wailing and crying, from little toddlers who keep tripping up to stony-faced young teenagers. If they do survive, at least puberty will be a cakewalk compared to this. They look like refugees fleeing a war zone, and in many respects that's exactly what they are, but it's one thing to see dirty, weeping children on the news and quite another to see them enchained in reality.

There are a hundred or so of us lined up in the castle's grounds, some sobbing openly, some looking stoic and one even looking like he's fed up and waiting for his train. Other small groups keep arriving, and, weirdly, I've never felt so much like I belonged. These are all the single people in London – for all that's going on, I don't feel like the only single person left any more. Not that any of that matters now – we can be but a short time away from death.

From the White Tower, more aliens lead more humans and among them I see a face that I had never expected to see again. Priti has survived, and is being led by an alien towards us in the small crowd. The left side of her face has been hit hard, plummy purple mixing into her dark skin, and she looks down at her feet. I call out her name, perhaps foolishly, but neither the aliens nor Priti react. I wonder what happened to Art.

And then I see him too, led by a different alien further back in the crowd. His hair and beard are out of control, having had no maintenance or product on them for a few days, and he looks scruffier than I've ever seen him. While Priti looks upset, his face is one of defiant anger, eyes staring forward as if seeing nothing. On top of everything else that already feels unreal, this feels even more so. How have they managed to survive?

Along with the other survivors, they are lined up with us until we form a rough rectangle, line after line representing the battered, worn-down remnants of humanity. Every few minutes an alien brings another two or three people over and they obey without complaint. If we're counting heads, the aliens outnumber us two to one. Occasional flashes of colour flicker across my eyes as I stand between Shell and Frederik.

A couple of people near the front shuffle and one reaches out to grab her neighbour, either for security, or to feel like she's not alone and dreaming this. The aliens are on her within seconds, bashing her hard around the head with a fist. They stand her straight again, a couple of feet from the man she'd reached out for. He doesn't move a muscle. The woman cries, louder than the other people here who are sniffing and sobbing.

We are powerless. No one is going to get out of this alive. The aliens keep us standing like privates on parade, some of them stationary around us, others circling the ranks, holding guns they've stolen from humans, spitting out coloured flecks of communication and casting their narrow eyes over us, as if daring another one of us to try and move. No one is apparently that stupid.

I, however, am stupid enough to try and speak to Frederik, given that the aliens haven't reacted to any other audio signals as of yet.

'What are they saying?' I mutter out the corner of my mouth, like a drunk in a betting shop giving a bad tip to a gullible novice. Frederik doesn't respond for a moment, his eyes fixated on the ground, and I wonder if he's heard me. I go to risk a second try, but he gets there first.

'They have deemed us incompatible with one another,' he says, the words almost imperceptible, like the final line of 'Bohemian Rhapsody' that everyone forgets on karaoke nights. 'I think they're waiting for instructions about what to do with us.'

'Kill us?' I breathe.

'Probably,' he says. The single word falls like a stone in dirt.

'I'm sorry about Gavin,' I say, adding after a pause, 'And Oscar too.'

'Me too,' he says. 'I'm sorry about everything.' I wonder if he wants to cry, although he currently looks like there's nothing further from his mind. He's too stunned to release such an emotion. He's almost turned into Gavin. He speaks again, 'We were going to get married, you know.'

'I had no idea,' I say. 'When?'

'I don't know, next summer maybe,' he sighs. 'None of it matters now.' I open my mouth a tiny bit to reply, but Shell hisses at me from the other side.

'They're looking agitated, stop talking,' she warns, and I look at the aliens at the front of our crowd. They do indeed look flustered. Sharp bursts of neon colour flash in front of my eyes and I want to ask for a translation again, but I can't. Maybe they could actually hear us. A group of them go off to a corner and discuss something in rapid-fire colour swatches, leaving a token few to stare at us with their expressionless faces.

I look around for Priti or Art, but they must be in a row behind me somewhere, as they're out of sight. While there's still time, I whisper what might be my final words to Shell.

'Shell, I'm sorry about Terry.'

'It's not your fault,' she hisses back, tears pricking in her eyes again. 'I'm just sorry I didn't kill the bitch that did it.'

'I don't imagine she survived much longer,' I say, finding myself in the position of telling my friend that she may have committed murder and, if she did, that that was a good thing.

'Too long,' says Shell, clenching her fists tight. She turns to look at me. 'Why are Priti and Art here? Why weren't they merged?'

'I was thinking the same thing,' I say. 'I can only think of one reason.'

'What's that?'

I don't get to reply because a burly man with huge shoulders and a tribal tattoo on his neck and cheek has roared out and leapt on the nearest alien, tackling it to the ground. Within seconds, there is pandemonium. Bright columns of red, the red of London buses, shoot up in front of my eyes and I stare through them at the clamouring of aliens and humans. The attack of the first man spurs others into action and in a blink there's a mound of writhing fighters ahead of us as indeterminate limbs of various species pile onto and into one another.

I grab Frederik's wrist and pull us back, snatching Shell around the waist as I do, making a break for the opposite direction to the fight. Art, not seeing us, races past and leaps onto the throng, grabbing a bluish alien head in his hands and twisting it hard like he's taking the lid off a stubborn bottle. With the others in my grasp, I make for Priti.

Her bruises look worse close up, and it takes her a moment to realise it's me. She flinches at first, before looking up, her face contorted like she's going to spit at her assailant, only for it to rearrange into something that looks painful but happy. She throws her slight frame around my neck.

'You're alive!' I shout.

'We need to get out of here,' she says. Our ears feel like they're being mashed as one of the blocky alien spaceships hoves into view, coming down to land in the grounds of the Tower. Reinforcements.

I try to remember from previous visits here if there is more than one exit, but instead my brain is recalling information about the zoo that used to be in the Tower, and a brief biography of Elizabeth I, none of which is useful at the present moment. Grabbing my friends, I make a break for the direction of the exit. I don't know where we're going to go, but my only thought is that we need to get away from there immediately.

The aliens, however, have begun to claim the upper hand. They're using weaponry both terrestrial and alien to take potshots at the humans. We're outnumbered and the plan of escape remains at the forefront of my mind, until three large aliens loom down on us from the side. I punch out indiscriminately, but my fists do nothing but pummel empty air.

A fist connects with my cheek and I stagger back. Falling onto my arse, I hear an unpleasant squelch and a blade of some kind bursts through the back of Priti's jacket. She falls onto her knees beside me and I see blood dripping from her lips as her body retreats into the foetal position, her small hands clasping the hilt of the weapon that felled her, as if attempting to pull it out.

There are several flashes of colour – blue, green, bluey-purple – and I'm pulled up again by my collar and, along with Shell and Frederik, frogmarched across the courtyard and towards one of the towering grey spaceships, not even taking in the piles of dead and dying bodies either side of us, but understanding that hope is lost. There is no escape now.

Thirty-Four

Uncertain Beginnings

My cheek throbs like there is a grumpy dwarf inside trying to prise a diamond from my flesh with his pickaxe as I am shoved in the back by a large gloved hand, not daring to look either side of me to check that Shell and Frederik are still there.

We are half-led, half-shoved up the ramp and into the spaceship, finding ourselves in a cramped, silver holding bay with three aliens and one other prisoner, a blonde woman in a red blouse and tight black jeans. Her feet are bare and filthy.

An alien presses a large, round, textured button on the wall and a door in front of us slides open. We are pushed inside and the doors close again. There is a small shudder and the room rises up with a slow whir. It's a lift.

Frederik is crying, large tears running down his face. Shell looks as blank as a sheet of printer paper. She reaches out and squeezes Frederik's hand. The other woman is shaking, dried blood crusting on her cut lip and scabbed chin. The doors slide open again and we're in a different room. A few aliens stand in front of us and sharp neon flashes of yellow and green pervade our senses.

'They want us to move forward,' Frederik burbles through his tears, so we follow our orders. Once the four of us are standing in the centre of the large, square room, one of the aliens comes to meet us and stands in front of me, both of its heads fixated on mine.

Turquoise, pink, brown.

I look on helplessly, and from my side, I get a flash of mauve and maroon. The aliens turn to look at Frederik, as do I. The leader projects back at him, but we all see the colours.

Cerise, chocolate, it says.

Maroon, mud, white, silver, Frederik replies.

'What are you saying?' I ask. The aliens either don't notice that

I've spoken, or don't care. Frederik doesn't turn in my direction, but replies anyway.

'They want to know how I can understand them,' he says. 'I'm telling them that I don't know.'

'Explain that you're blind,' I say.

'But is that the reason?' he asks. The head alien looks at the rest of us. The woman at the end is sobbing again, louder and louder. On the other side of him, Shell is also looking at Frederik, but choosing to keep quiet. Perhaps she's wondering why we haven't yet been killed. I'm trying not to give that any thought.

'What should I say to them?'

'Ask them why they're doing this,' I say. Annie-and-Matt told us one story, but given their betrayal, there's currently no reason to believe them. Frederik closes his eyes and points his head down. Has he heard me? He fires off a few colours: *grey, mustard, a greeny-blue.*

The reply is quick: *blood red, gunmetal blue, coal black.*

'They need our planet for mining,' Frederik translates.

'But we live here!' says Shell, sounding so like a child having a tantrum that it feels almost funny. In another situation, I might have laughed. 'They can't storm in and take the place, forcing their ways onto us and wiping out those who don't agree! Tell them that!'

Frederik looks concerned for a moment and then does indeed send a complicated message that may have been the template for Joseph's technicolour coat. When he's finished, the aliens share a thought, and we see a bright yellow with pale blue edges, a weirdly joyful colour. They're laughing. One of them speaks to Frederik again, and he translates back.

'They don't care. They want to know how we can say that what they're doing is wrong, when they've seen what humans have done to each other throughout history,' he says. 'It says that what they're doing is no different to what generations of humans have done to each other: stormed into lands that don't belong to them, forced their religions, technologies and diseases on the unsuspecting natives and killed anyone who stood up to them. It's hypocrisy.'

'But that wasn't *us*,' says Shell, and while I want to agree, it's a difficult one. It wasn't us specifically, but it was humanity, and we are part of that. Maybe we do deserve whatever happens to us. Sure, there were patches where we loved one another, developed friendships and considered kindness, compassion and companionship to be important, but more than anything we are a species that kills its own members and claims a greater good. These creatures are of the opinion that merging people is the only way that they can breed, so they're going to ignore our own biology and make it like their own. Maybe, despite what Annie-and-Matt said, they always knew it was going to fail. Perhaps it was just a quicker way of thinning out the population.

Shell is angry, far beyond upset. Frederik looks sad and hopeless. I am drained and so tired that, if I were to lay down, I would fall into an irresponsibly deep sleep. .

'We will take you as prisoners,' Frederik translates, toneless. 'You seem to think you know better, so you will come with us and speak to our... not sure on that word, but something like council or government.' Then what? Death? A museum exhibit?

'No!' barks the other woman behind us. I'd forgotten she was there. She rushes forward as if to attack the leading alien, but the head not watching Frederik was already looking at her and she doesn't last a second. The alien pulls out a short knife and the woman's throat is sliced open, a jet of blood squirting forward and landing on the alien's spacesuit. Another alien steps forward and drags her lifeless body out of the room, a trail of red in her wake.

The alien shoots a few more colours at Frederik – *cream, crimson, silver* – but he doesn't translate, instead shakes his head and closes his eyes. The alien turns and barks coloured orders at its crewmates, who move to a series of screens on the far wall. Each head looks into a small black screen and, after a few seconds, each one turns into a different colour. I sense that they've activated something, presumably the craft.

My mind reels as I realise that this could be the last time I'm anywhere near my home. Not just my house, but my planet. Faces and events pour through my head and the last few days replay like a sped-up DVD. Lara-and-Steve's wedding, Catsby, Peregrina punching the vicar in the face, Kevin-and-Gary's ugly deaths in the British Museum, Alex's suicide, Annie-and-Matt's betrayal, Pete, Art attacking an alien threat, Priti attacking a school bully in a hedge maze, serving coffee with Gavin, meeting Frederik, swapping chocolate bars with Shell, at a loud and sweaty Burnt Fudge concert with Jay-and-Kay, Georgina throwing my Kindle in a pond, Iris welcoming me on my first day at work, the moment we first saw aliens, hearing that my parents had died, coming round after my appendectomy, stealing bikes, breaking Georgina's heart, Jay's trilby on a pile of clothes, Ruby's mangled body.

Important moments mix with unimportant ones, and I realise that they were all important and maybe one day I'll realise I learnt something from one of them that may save my life again. I've survived this long, and I've got no idea what's going to happen next, but I'm not alone and maybe that's a better thing than I ever realised.

The floor beneath us shakes and everything rises.

THE END

Acknowledgements

Thank you to Unbound for taking a chance on the book and guiding me through the process of crowdfunding a novel. Thank you to Debi Alper and Andrew Chapman, my keen-eyed editors, for their patience, humour and understanding.

Thanks to my family, and to all my friends. I'm not going to name names for the fear of missing someone out, but thanks for believing in me, your ongoing support, and any drink you've ever bought me.

Thanks to the British Museum, Natural History Museum and Victoria & Albert Museum for being such wonderful institutions that I can wander round in for free in the name of research. Thanks to Frank Turner for providing me with a soundtrack that accompanied most of the writing of this book – as well as everything else I've done in the last ten years.

And thank you to everyone who pledged their support to make this book a reality. I really could not have done it without you.

Bonus material

Lara-and-Steve

Everything is relatively calm on the ship. Lara quickly notes that they are the youngest people on board by about thirty years, but also that there is an extensive wine list and cocktails available most of the day.

There had been some debate about whether the ship would be allowed to set sail given the news from Paris, but they'd finally been given the go-ahead as they were heading away from the incident. She was grateful, at least, that they hadn't been flying as, following on from the numerous crashes the night before, flights the world over had been grounded.

It does strike her as odd, however, that every time she sees a television that first day, it's tuned to adverts for the cruise they are on; an ever-repeating PowerPoint presentation highlighting the various shows, bars and swimming pools on offer. Even the one in their cabin picks up no reception, and when Steve asks a member of staff what's going on, she says there's a problem with the service that they hope will be resolved soon, and hands him some complimentary vouchers for one of the bars.

In fact, it isn't until late on the Monday night, while Dexter and his friends are dealing with a psychotic priest in a formerly quiet country church, that Lara-and-Steve realise things have gone to shit. Phone signal was patchy for the first bit of the journey, and then non-existent, until someone managed to connect to Twitter and learnt that they are one of the most concentrated collections of humans left on the planet.

Lara wakes up very early on the Wednesday morning, head pounding from the six or seven margaritas she drank the night before to blot out the thoughts of what was happening on land. Internet signals had died the previous day, and word had filtered down through worried staff and eager-to-panic passengers that the ship had begun to drift off course. With no ability to contact the mainland back in Britain, it was possible that no one knew where they were.

Lara slips out from under the covers and peers out of the porthole to the grey expanse of sea and sky. It is darker than she'd expected and she checks her watch – several minutes past seven o'clock. Where is the light?

The scream is her second hint that something has gone wrong. Steve wakes with a start and leaps to his feet, naked save for a single sock that he'd been unable to wrestle off in his drunken state the night before. He fumbles on a nearby hook for a dressing gown and wraps it around himself. Someone pounds past their door – lots of people. With a look at one another that conveys several emotions at once – not least panic, fear, surprise and adoration – Lara snatches up the key card to the room and they open the door, joining the crowd of silver-haired runners who aren't encumbered by false hips or crutches.

They pile into a central atrium and up the stairs onto the deck. If any of the staff present are meant to be keeping people away, they aren't doing a very good job as they stand, like everyone else, with their necks craned skywards. Directly above them hovers a large square. The base of one of these spaceships they'd heard about.

It's about thirty feet above the highest point of the ship, but it is so vast in size that it casts a shadow over the whole deck.

'What is it?' shouts an old lady, bent double and unable to tilt her head up to look. 'What's happening? Tell me what's going on!' She bangs her cane against the water-spotted wood in defiance, but it's to no avail. Everyone ignores her – Lara thinks it's probably better she doesn't know.

There isn't much screaming now. The odd blast, but generally people mutter and talk amongst themselves. A man, the captain judging by his uniform, stands on a higher deck with a megaphone and says, 'Attention, ladies and gentlemen!' Most people turn to him, save for a few old folks who either want to keep looking at the thing above them, or didn't have time to put their hearing aids in and don't know he's there.

'I think... I would ask you all to...' but he can't find the words and instead says, rather pathetically, 'Free drinks all round.' Despite the fact it's not even seven-thirty, this seems to be enough for some people, who immediately forget the aliens hovering above them and push their way back through the crowds to one of the bars.

Lara grabs for Steve's hand and squeezes tight.

'I have to call home,' she says. Steve nods, finally tears his eyes away from the shape and follows his wife back into the bowels of the ship.

An hour or so later, Lara dials numbers, trying to get hold of people. Her mum doesn't answer and her heart sinks. She tries another number and manages to get through to Kerry. They say a hurried goodbye before Kerry's phone dies. At least, Lara chooses to believe that it is the phone that has died. Georgina's phone doesn't connect either, nor Kay's. She presses the icon for Dexter and puts the phone to her ear. It rings for what feels like an aeon, before the noise stops and she hears a voice.

'– calling!' It's Dexter. But that's all she hears. His phone – it must have been his phone – dies too. Steve comes back in the room, a bottle of uncorked Malbec in each hand. He kicks the door shut and knocks the lock closed, passes one of the bottles to her and sits down on the bed, picking at the label. They both ignore the fact that they're already hungover and they've not had breakfast.

'Did you get through to your parents?' says Lara, panicked. 'I can't get through to anyone else now. Are your parents OK?' Steve looks up slowly, not quite meeting her eyes.

'Drink your wine,' he says, sombrely. 'It'll make things less painful.'

'What do you mean?' Lara says, eyes wide in fear. Then she hears the first screams. They can only mean one thing.

Dutifully, she slugs back a quarter of the bottle in one go, then wipes the cherry-red liquid from her lips. She gets unsteadily to her feet and heads towards the door.

'Where are you going?' Now it's Steve's turn to sound panicked. 'Lara, sit down! It's not safe!'

'I'm not going down without a fight,' she says. 'This is not how it ends.' She stops and looks at her new husband.

'You coming?'

Steve meets her defiant expression, glugs down a mouthful of red wine himself and stands the bottle on the bedside table.

'Anything for you,' he says. He grabs her hand and the door is open again. Lara-and-Steve head out into the corridor, the battlefield, and the unknown.

Gavin-and-Frederik

Gavin puts the phone down, eyes rolling like two errant lottery balls. Why did Dexter ask such inane questions? Of course he and Fred had suffered the same as everyone else. Gavin falls onto the sofa, landing on Oscar who yelps and extricates himself from beneath his occupant.

'Sorry fella,' says Gavin, scratching the dog behind the ears. The dog looks at him rather disdainfully and plods out of the room. Frederik appears with iPad in hand.

'Is he alright?' says Frederik.

'He'll be fine,' Gavin sighs. 'They'll find out it was something to do with a nuclear test or an equally barbaric practice.'

'Then what about this craft?' Frederik settles down in the armchair.

'Hoax of some kind,' Gavin says with a shrug. 'Just all a coincidence that it happened at the same time. It's weird though, I'm not denying that.' Gavin picks up the remote control and flips on the television to find that every channel is still broadcasting the same footage. He considers it something of an overreaction. There is only meant to be this level of coverage when the monarch dies, or the country goes to war.

'There's no point in panicking; there will be an explanation soon,' says Gavin, and it's at that moment that they hear the first window get smashed.

Their Hammersmith home looks down from the fifth floor into a street that has seen better days. It's only been twenty-four hours since he spoke to Dexter, and twelve since he last heard from his parents in Stirling – the phone doesn't even connect now – but the road looks as though it was abandoned weeks ago.

Frederik sits hunched over on the sofa, head in his hands. While Gavin deals with the occasional flashes of colour in his eyes as aliens pass down the street, kicking in doors and using their grey cloud technology on any people who happen to get in their way, Frederik is suffering much worse. The colours – the first rainbow he's ever seen

– are making him feel drunk. Each has meaning and he has realised, horrifically, that he can intuitively understand the language of these aliens.

He knows that they took so long to emerge from their first spaceships not because they were concerned about the air not being right for them, but because the overwhelming use of colour had confused them and they'd taken it to be a threat. Frederik, and Gavin once he'd been informed, had surmised from this that they came from a planet with very little colour, since it all had nuance and meaning that the majority of humans would never be able to understand.

Frederik also knows that they're attacking at random. This isn't a systematic eradication of humanity. They're just taking out the ones they see and assuming that anyone left will die off anyway. They're ruining the planet, making it ready for their own purposes, which are so foreign to Frederik that he can't make sense of those colours.

Gavin tries to tell him again about something Dexter said once upon a time about a place to hide in London, and that personally he would have preferred Edinburgh Castle, but Frederik doesn't want to hear it. He grips his head tighter and fights back tears.

On Wednesday, they make a plan. In an abandoned and raided corner shop that morning, while Gavin was helping himself to bottled water, toilet roll and dog biscuits, he picked up a London A-Z and hurried home to plot a route to the place he knew – hoped – would be safe. Frederik had pulled a collection of clothes out of the wardrobe and attempted to shove them into a couple of rucksacks, before becoming distracted by a phone call from his parents in Heerhugowaard. The city is besieged, but they've barricaded themselves in their home. Despite everyone involved still being alive, it's a goodbye phone call for sure.

The journey should take about an hour – Gavin had always been too reliant on the city's buses, tubes and trains to realise quite how close to the centre of London he lived – but they don't know what dangers they'll have to face, so they give themselves a whole day to work with, leaving under cover of darkness first thing in the morning.

They're up and out before the sun has risen. Oscar lags behind, rejecting the firm tugs Gavin gives to his lead, furious at the muzzle that's been put on him as a necessity to keep him quiet. Dog and owner mirror one another's snarls, while Frederik remains alert for a sound or colour that may indicate danger.

Unmolested and with a cooperative canine, they've amended the journey time to around an hour and a quarter, with a slight detour to a gun shop to pick up weaponry, even though Gavin has never fired a gun in his life. He knows that, logically, he's more likely to do damage to himself than an alien if armed, but the situation is now so bizarrely unreal that even his Vulcan logic circuitry has shorted out and he's stopped being rational.

The streets are empty of people or, at least, living people. Body parts, bloodstains, empty cars and abandoned belongings litter the roads. There are even a couple of alien bodies, suggesting that humanity had a go at fighting back, but ultimately was outnumbered and outgunned. As the sun comes up, they've managed to only travel a few streets because of Oscar. He alternates between being livid at his new muzzle and wanting to sniff everything that seems interesting. He takes his time, with no awareness of the desperation that Gavin and Frederik feel.

Every now and again they come across an alien or two and hide. Frederik projects colours that he's seen into the ether and the aliens seem to notice them but are unable to tell they're from a human source. Frederik then begins to worry that they do know and it's a double bluff, so every time they encounter something, they move slower with Gavin constantly checking behind him. It becomes a strain, with Gavin the only one able to both see and communicate any threat. By the time they reach the gun shop, they are hungry and drenched with sweat.

The shop has been partially looted, but there's enough still and no one else around. Gavin takes a rifle and, using a large hardback book under the counter, matches up the correct ammunition.

'You've never fired one of those,' Frederik reminds him.

'Do you think I should try a couple of rounds?' says Gavin, looking at the strange item in his hands. He feels like he's in a sniper film. 'It might attract a lot of attention.'

'From what you've said, the aliens don't seem to be able to hear anything,' says Frederik, stroking Oscar's head and gripping the lead tightly as the dog tries to pull away to sniff at a dismembered leg.

Gavin studies the gun for about quarter of an hour, using instructions gleaned from books behind the counter, before finally loading it and aiming a test shot at the building opposite. The rifle has more of a kick than he expects, and his thin frame is sent staggering backwards as the bullet crosses the road and embeds itself in a brick. He reloads and tries again. Another success. He finds more ammunition, shoves it into his rucksack, slings the gun over his shoulder and goes back to Frederik and Oscar.

When they do finally arrive at the Natural History Museum and Gavin gazes up at the enormous, beautiful edifice, he realises that he's been concentrating so hard on getting here that he hasn't taken any of the journey in. He's just grateful to be safe.

At least, he hopes he will be.

Gavin wakes up but can't actually be sure that he even slept. Say what you like about the architectural wonder of the Natural History Museum, or the awe-inspiring appearance of the blue whale, but none of it's terribly comfortable. Next to him, Frederick stirs too, grumbles something and stretches his hand out, the knuckles clicking grotesquely as he manoeuvres them.

'Anything around?' says Gavin.

Frederik doesn't reply for a couple of minutes, but Gavin doesn't ask again. Eventually, he says, 'No, can't see anything.'

Gavin hauls himself into a seated position, the large stuffed dinosaur he'd taken from the gift shop and was using as a pillow slipping down the whale's slight incline. It's their fourth day in the museum – possibly Sunday, if that even matters – but feels like the forty-fourth since any decent rest. A stray thought crosses Gavin's mind about why Oscar isn't sniffing around them, but then he remembers that they released him into the grounds on Friday. Frederik fumbles for a torch and flicks it on, for Gavin's benefit rather than his own. Being inside a perpetually dark exhibit doesn't affect his senses. Now able to see a little, Gavin fumbles in a bag for some food, and the two share a breakfast of slightly stale bread, Sprite and bananas.

At around midday, Gavin sets out on his daily reconnaissance. Frederik once again laments that he's sorry he can't be more use, and Gavin has to console him for a while. He doesn't begrudge Frederik anything for one second. He's happy and proud to defend him. As he walks through the Human Biology exhibits, Gavin contemplates how his life changed in that moment he met Frederik. Everyone's life changes when they meet their partner, sure, but in this case it seemed to be the discovery of someone who understood him, completely. Frederik and Gavin were both fearsomely smart, and extraordinarily kind, but each had had that aspect of them shafted in favour of one that didn't matter. In a society so obsessed with labels, Gavin was always 'the gay guy' and Frederik was eternally 'the blind guy'. Now, the epithets were hopefully a thing of the past. They were now Survivors.

Gavin climbs the stopped escalator that passes through the centre of the Earth into the rooms dedicated to the physical sciences, to see if any other people have arrived overnight. Sitting next to remains from Pompeii are a young couple, unwashed and tired. Their small children, two boys, were off running around, chasing each other with gift shop dinosaurs. They haven't seen anyone new come in. Gavin tries to be cheerful, but it all feels so forced.

He wanders through the museum, not meeting anyone new, and then arrives at the very top of Hintze Hall, with a view down over Hope, the blue whale skeleton, and the upper displays on either side that flank her enormous form. He crouches down and sits on the steps, his slim frame aching with the lack of decent food and sleep.

'Well done, Gavin,' says a voice, internal but loud. Gavin recognises it as his father's. Gavin isn't sure if he'd ever accepted his father's death or not. It had happened, and he had been heartbroken, but he chose never to dwell on it, and kept himself busy to distract from reality. Now, with no functioning iPod or biography to get stuck into, he was going to have to confront the truth.

'For what?' Gavin replies. He spoke aloud, but quietly. The answer comes to him in his mind, 'For being so strong.'

'What good is it going to do me?' he mutters. 'We're all going to die.'

'Yes, we are,' says his father's voice. That was like his dad – not telling Gavin that he'd see him again soon. Jack Napier didn't stand for any of that nonsense – there was what there was, and that was it. That's how Gavin knows that he's making up the voice in his head and coming to terms with things on his own – his father would never return like this. Another synapse fires the suggestion to Gavin that he's going mad. It's perfectly possible.

'I don't know what to do, Dad,' says Gavin, uttering the single truth that he'd kept hidden from everyone for all these years. People saw him as someone who always had a plan, and he liked that. It boosts his ego and, while he knows some people were annoyed by it, he always felt that having some semblance of authority and organisation made people think he could handle anything. He couldn't though, not really. It has all been an act – a great performance by any standards, but a performance nonetheless. He'd just been lucky a lot of the time. That's all life was – a series of lucky breaks. Although, perhaps now, they were all about to end.

'You'll know what to do when the time comes,' says the voice in his head. 'You've never failed yet.' Gavin knew he hadn't, but he's worked hard to make sure he never did. He could twist anything around to come out on top, but it was exhausting.

Something moves in the corner of Gavin's eye and he stands up abruptly. The voice and image of Jack disappears and he's back in the real world. Now is not the time for fiction – reality is pressing in all too desperately on every side. He's not sure what he saw, but he thinks it was people. They've gone now though, possibly into the room on the right that's full of gemstones and geological samples. Wherever they are, Gavin has a sudden sense that Frederik is in trouble.

Checking carefully for rivals, either from this planet or another, he skitters down the stairs again, his soft-soled shoes barely making a noise, and loops round and back down the staircase to beneath Hope.

There's no one.

He runs down the corridor to the Large Mammals Room, now cursing that he left Frederik alone. He should never have done that and, if it's not too late, he never will again. He'll finally move ahead with the wedding plans that have been idly discussed for months, without either of them officially proposing or coming to any decisions. If there's anyone left to officiate at a wedding.

There's a woman, late twenties perhaps, standing next to the whale's cavernous bulk. There's something oddly familiar about her, Gavin thinks, but she hasn't noticed him yet and he can't see her face properly. Then he notices the second figure, a pair of denimed legs sticking out of the infamous trapdoor. The woman notices him at last and begins tugging on the shirt of her companion as Gavin approaches.

'Step away from the whale.' Gavin holds his gun aloft, as the face of someone he never thought he'd see again appears from the whale's belly, a face that looks stunned, stained and exhausted, with black rings round the eyes and dried blood on the upper lip. He looks just as bemused.

'Gavin?'

Gavin lowers his rifle.

Peregrina-and-Pete

They walk, and if they choose to ignore the smells of offal and blood, the sights of dismembered carcasses and the traumatic memories of the last week, it's a lovely spring evening, although Peregrina could've done with a slightly thicker jumper and a shower. They see no living people, or indeed any aliens. These streets have been emptied, and apparently the aliens don't believe in keeping guard on places they've already ransacked. Occasionally something moves and makes them jump, but it is always a cat, a dog or, on one surreal occasion, a wallaby.

The streets are oddly silent, save for intermittent screams in the distance that they try not to think about, the snuffling of animals and the soft clump of their shoes on the road. Every few steps, Pete squeezes Peregrina's hand, a silent acknowledgment that he's still here, or perhaps a check that she is.

'Where are we going?' Peregrina asks eventually. They're deep down a residential street of Chelsea, large houses surrounding them, some with doors open, but many still locked as if the owners fled but insisted on protecting their lavish lifestyles. Maybe they're still locked in, starving or already dead. No faces appear at windows though, and only one in thirty, perhaps, has a light on inside.

'Where have you always wanted to go but never got around to?' asks Pete.

'Mauritius?' Peregrina says with a sad smile, thinking of the flight tickets in Pete's desk at home, their honeymoon destination that is never to be.

'OK, narrow it down to London,' he says, throwing a large arm around her shoulders. 'What London attraction did you never get to do?' Peregrina thought for a little as they walked.

'I never went to the aquarium,' she says, 'but if the power's been out for a couple of days, I don't imagine there's much left worth seeing.'

'Yeah, they won't have had the luxury of escaping,' Pete muses. He's still slightly unsure as to how the zoo animals managed to escape so fast. Everything about the apocalypse – and he was under no illusion this was anything else – seemed to happen so fast. He was determined to savour the remaining time they had, be it minutes or months. Pessimistically, he assumed the former.

'I never did the waxworks,' says Peregrina, suddenly.

'Madame Tussauds?'

'Yeah. I never got to go as a kid, and I guess it just never happened since,' she says. 'The queues were always miles long though, I don't know how anyone got in.' Pete pulls Peregrina across the road to a street map.

'Well, I reckon the queue won't be a problem any more,' he says. 'Now, which way is Baker Street on this map?' His cartographic attempts are halted however when a shade of mauve begins to dance in the corners of their eyes. Peregrina squeals and spins around in a panic, turning her heel over and gasping at the sharp pain that courses through her ankle.

'Where are they?' she says through teeth gritted in pain and fear.

'Better get ready to run,' says Pete, not looking up. He's staring at the map, trying to match it up to the rudimentary Tube map he has in his head so that it will result in them arriving at Baker Street. 'Can you see them?'

'Not yet,' whispers Peregrina. 'Pete, I think I've just twisted my ankle.'

'Can you walk on it? Can you run?'

'I wouldn't want to count on it.'

'OK, we're going.'

Peregrina shrieks as Pete whirls out, lifts her up and slings her across his broad shoulders. Her hand darts to her face to secure her glasses and suddenly she's being jostled as Pete breaks into a run with her tossed like a rug over his shoulder.

'I see one!' she shouts, and Pete seems to speed up, panting heavily but not responding. The alien heads turn and see them getting further away, but there's no colour and no grey cloud. It's alone and unarmed. It still decides that there's a chance though and breaks into a run, chasing them down. Peregrina screams, and Pete correctly interprets it to move quicker, but he's tired and underfed and begins to slow down.

The pale blue faces of the alien get nearer and Peregrina is suddenly jerked to the left as Pete disappears down a narrow alley. He drops her onto her feet, which she gingerly holds her weight on, before turning back to see if their pursuer approaches.

Silently, the alien arrives at the alley and stops. Its faces are unreadable, the feather-like fronds on its heads curling up and down quickly. Apparently undeterred by Pete's size and the lack of weaponry among them all, it moves in closer and Pete raises his fists.

The alien is quicker and lands a sticky fist on Pete's chin. It's not as solid as he feared, but it feels unnatural enough to confuse and disarm Pete for a moment. He staggers back into the wall, revealing Peregrina, who lunges out and aims a punch at one of the heads. She misses and catches it in the neck instead, but her engagement ring seems to have stung it, and it too steps back a little. She aims another punch, but as she steps forward, she lands hard on her twisted ankle and gasps in pain, missing entirely. The alien looks at the pair again, fists still raised, before sending out a stream of greens the colour of lawns, bottles and nauseous sailors. It departs, going back the way it had come.

Pete, still panting, looks at Peregrina and grins.

'So that's a vicar and an alien you've punched this week,' he says with a chuckle. 'Anything else you want to check off the bucket list while you're here?' Peregrina punches him in the arm too.

By the time they arrive at Madame Tussauds, it's very dark, with only the occasional street lamp still working. The exhibition's door sits open, and the lights inside are still on – another building running on a generator.

Peregrina limps over the threshold, with Pete just behind her, ensuring that no one is watching them enter. If they are, he can't see them. Inside appears to be deserted. There are a couple of waxworks in the entrance hall; Alfred Hitchcock is tipped back against the wall, and laying at his feet is one that was possibly a member of One Direction, but he's had his face stamped on.

'It's not quite what I imagined,' says Peregrina, easing herself down onto a velvet-topped bench, looking at a series of figures lined up like fallen dominoes against the wall. Several bodies seem to have already been damaged, and among the melted, crushed wax there are remains of very real figures.

'How's your foot?' asks Pete, kneeling in front of her to look at it. With care she tugs off her shoe and rotates her ankle a little.

'It'll be OK,' she says. 'Just feels a bit sore. Nothing broken – I'll live.' She realises what she's said, hiccups back an uncomfortable giggle and immediately changes the subject. 'Come on, let's have a look around.' Pete helps her get her shoe back on and helps her up, supporting her as they walk through the abandoned rooms, eking out the final joy of seeing those the world considered worthy once upon a time, now standing over drying pools of blood and congealing lumps of flesh.

'I wonder if any of this lot survived,' says Pete, waving generally over a vista of pop stars.

'Probably in bunkers set aside for the rich and famous that us plebs would never even imagine,' says Peregrina. 'Half of London is underground – what's a few more tunnels?'

A clatter from another room sets them both on edge, and the alien appears at the top of a flight of stairs just as they turn to look at it. Instinctively, they each reach out and grab the other's hand. There's no hiding. This is it.

The alien stares with its expressionless faces and pulls a silver box from the belt of its uniform. However, it can't seem to focus on them, and is looking around at the large number of figures in front of it – Peregrina wonders if it can't believe it's luck. A whole room full of people ready to be combined and not moving. It presses a button on the box and the grey cloud of nanobots encircles the waxworks of Posh and Becks, but after a couple of laps realises that there's nothing to work with and disperses, having a go at models of Colin Firth and Kate Winslet, who remain nonplussed about the whole situation.

'They'll run out of wax ones soon,' says Peregrina. 'We need to split up.' Pete instead grips her hand harder and pulls her towards him, wrapping her in his arms.

'It took me nearly forty years to find you – like hell I'm going to let go now.'

They're still holding one another tight when they feel the first nanobots begin their macabre surgery.